M000159585

Exit Ghost
By Jennifer R. Donohue

For Dad

Praise for Exit Ghost

S hakespeare as you've never seen it and witchcraft as he never imagined — this brilliant modern retelling is a distillation of everything I love in Donohue's short fiction. It is a wild cry of pain and love and revenge and grief, a quest for justice, and a paean to friendship, packed with intrigue and action. — Premee Mohamed, Nebula award winning author of *And What Can We Offer You Tonight*

Beautiful and brutal — Kel, bookseller extraordinaire

EXIT GHOST IS A NOVEL that stays with you. Jen Donohue's unbelievable writing skills are on full display here in this ghost story murder mystery tale of grief, healing, intrigue, and friendship. Donohue constructs a tale as thrilling as it is emotional and involving, finely weaving strands to a profound and gorgeous narrative until the splendid final page. — Zachary Rosenberg, author of *Hungers as Old as This Land*

I'VE BEEN WISHING FOR a longer read from Donohue, and here it is. A fabulous blend of witchcraft, ghosts, and the grief that never quite leaves you. —E. Catherine Tobler, author of *The Necessity of Stars*

A SUPERB MASH-UP OF Shakespearean tragedy and witchy magic. A highly-addictive read! —A.C. Wise, author of *The Ghost Sequences*

JENNIFER R. DONOHUE revisits the topographies of grief and of recovery through a witchy retelling of Hamlet that takes the reader into dark places. Rituals, ghosts and an adorable Doberman, this is a tale with heart and with power. — Anita Harris Satkunananthan, author of *Watermyth*

THE MODERN FANTASY retelling of Hamlet which I never knew I needed, set on the Jersey Shore with a snarky gender-flipped Hamlet and her dog named Yorick, a vivid cast of characters, and witches and dark magic galore. A deeply atmospheric, immersive story of grief, loss, love, mystery, doubt, and revenge. Slyly witty in its homage to Shakespeare but also very much its own thing, Exit Ghost is beautifully written, compelling, and moving. — Vanessa Fogg, writer and reviewer.

EXIT GHOST IS A WITCHY, queer, and riveting tale of family, vengeance, lust, the excellence of dogs, and a bit of ghost-induced madness. Donohue skillfully weaves magic (and Shakespeare) into the Jersey Shore landscape, delving deep into the complex and crucial bonds of friendship and love between the characters. It's a gripping read, full of heart, soul, and wicked witchcraft. — Maria Haskins, writer and reviewer

EXIT GHOST IS A "WONDROUS strange" tale that casts a spell on you. Donohue weaves this witchy yarn full of grief, love, and pluck as Juliet plumbs the depths of her self and her magical abilities. Endlessly delightful and thoroughly satisfying, Exit Ghost makes you want to reach for a tarot deck and cozy up with the familiar comfort of a furry friend. — Shelly Jones, author of *Of Weeds and Witches*

GRIEF, MAGIC, SECRETS, and vengeance collide beautifully—and explosively—in Jennifer Donohue's Exit Ghost. This is a dark, heartfelt tale that shows everything is possible, but it always comes at a price. —Gabino Iglesias, author of *The Devil Takes you Home*

EXIT GHOST CAPTURES the deep senses of grief and loss in Shakespeare's classic tragedy, and reimagines it into a modern story of strong friendship, powerful magic—and maybe even something like hope. Jennifer R. Donohue builds a strange and richly detailed version of the Jersey Shore, complete with ghostly visitations, mystical acid trips, a journey through the underworld, and a trip to Madame Marie's, and introduces a sharp but lovable cast of characters. You've never seen Hamlet quite like this before—Donohue does the Bard and the Boss proud. — Kay Allen, poet and editor of Sword & Kettle Press

EXIT GHOST IS A MASTERCLASS of a novel, awash in blood, and magic, and Jersey Shore sea salt. It's a tale of loss and the lengths one compelling mess of a woman will go through to right the wrongs she and her family have suffered. This heartfelt modern retelling of Hamlet elevates itself far past those humble roots to become something truly extraordinary in Donohue's capable hands. Exit Ghost is an absolutely terrific novel by an incredible wordsmith that will continue to haunt you even after you put it down.

~ Meghan Ball, writer, editor, and New Jersey goth

Exit Ghost © 2023 by Jennifer R. Donohue

Cover design Jennifer R. Donohue

ebook ISBN: 978-1-945548-21-5

hardcover ISBN: 978-1-945548-22-2

Author Note

This book contains depictions of a practice of witchcraft that is not intended to be a step-by-step guide or representation of what any real live practicing witches do. My witches here are largely self-taught, gleaning power from objects that might be considered as such by real live practitioners (salt, certain blessed Catholic items) and from rituals derived from real books such as the Keys of Solomon and really just pure instinctual vibes. My intent here is to entertain, and to represent a fictional, messy, society-that-isn't-really-a-cohesive-society, and I have written other short stories with these types of witches in them before, which I will list in the back of this book, along with where to find them.

Additionally, I've listed below the trigger warnings for this book:
Self harm
Suicide
Suicidal ideation
Disordered eating
Drug and alcohol abuse
Grief and grieving

~

ADIEU, ADIEU! HAMLET, remember me.
[Exit Ghost]

~

Chapter One

A rranging the ritual took time. The circle of sea salt, covering the hardwood bedroom floor. A folded t-shirt, one of the last ones he wore, softly prickled with black dog hairs and the rotary phone from his office resting on top. Music in these things was always optional, but for this circle, for her dad, it was necessary. Jules slipped a crackling record on the turntable, one of his Zeppelin albums. Sprawled on her bed, Yorick groaned and laid his head on his paws.

As the witching hour neared, she lit a scattering of balsam candles about the room, broke a razor free of its plastic moorings and made a small shallow cut above the tattoo on the inside of her bony left wrist. The music ended as she flicked her blood into the guttering flames, and she waited in the silence, the magic's tidal pull roiling around her.

The phone rang.

Yorick groaned again as Jules reached across the circle to pick it up, kneeling on the floor.

"Hi Dad," she said.

The line crackled, and the tips of her fingers began to sting. "Jules," a voice answered at long last. Her scalp prickled, tightening against her new scars.

"Yeah, Dad, it's me." Her voice crackled in her throat. Just hearing him again grabbed at her breath. "Tell me what happened to us. Tell me who did it."

"Murder," the voice said slowly, from great distance. "Murder in my orchard."

"I know, Dad. I was there." She started to cry, swallowed hard, struggled to talk around the burning in her throat. "What should I do?" Her tears were a steady drip-drop into the salt. Like her blood, they could only strengthen the connection. The phone cord shuddered, and she could feel resistance, static, confusion.

Silence, frustrating silence, but the connection was still there. That goddamn salt barrier; did she really have to protect herself against her dad? Jules felt her dad's spirit beyond the salt, beyond the phone, like when she was little and they played hide and seek and she just knew he was in the room but wasn't quite sure—

"*IT WAS HECTOR!*" the voice thundered, roared, filling her ears, her head, overwhelming in its sudden strength. Jules was knocked into from the side, receiver falling from her hand and onto the salt, vision bright with sparkles. Deep in the house, a clock struck four times, and when her vision cleared, she was curled on her side breathing hard, with Yorick standing over her, his big head slung low, hair standing all along his spine as he growled towards the circle. The turntable thumped a slow heartbeat.

"It's okay," Jules murmured through numb lips. "Good boy, it's okay. It's just Dad, it's okay." Yorick looked at her for a moment uncertainly, then settled on the floor next to her, sniffing. Her left hand felt like she'd pushed it into a snowy television screen, and she put her right arm across Yorick's warm velvet neck and breathed in his warm doggy scent. She needed to clean up, but couldn't make herself move just yet.

It hadn't been right. She couldn't find her dad's cell phone, that would've worked better. But something else was wrong, something else kept her communication scratchy and indistinct, put too many layers between them. She would have to research it. She would have to—

Chapter Two

She fell asleep, or passed out, and woke at a dawn with a train whistle slipping through her open window and Yorick licking her face in steady concentration. The room was as she'd left it, salt circle smeared into the tassels of the throw rugs, phone and shirt and records strewn about. She got up slowly, head pounding, especially over her left eye, starbursts of light in her vision. Yorick followed her back and forth as she picked things up and set the room to rights. The salt she just kind of pushed around with her foot until it was along the baseboards. Lazy protection, and the maids would vacuum in here soon enough, but she simply hadn't the energy to do more about it.

She stumbled into the bathroom and shook one of the orange bottles on the countertop. Not too many left; how many refills were they liable to give her? She'd have to talk to the doctor each time, okay fine, but she'd been out of the hospital like no time at all. They'd dug most of a bullet out of her skull and cobbled it back together, then waited a couple of months for her to wake up. They'd refill the damn prescription.

A knock at her bedroom door, the knob rattling. She'd remembered to lock it, at least. "Juliet?"

"I'm in the bathroom, Mom. I'm going to take a shower." Was her voice right? It was hard to tell.

"I don't like you having this locked."

"Yorick is with me. If anything goes wrong, you know he'll bark the house down."

"You know Mr. Poling has all the keys to this place. I can just get him." Not to her door. She changed the lock herself, three years ago, in the middle of the night. Not long after she met MaryAnne and started studying.

"I'll see you in the breakfast room in half an hour." Jules turned the shower on. She'd have to pay attention, though. It wouldn't do to have Mr. Poling, or anybody, interrupt once she was on the course. Could it really have been Hector?

She turned the shower as hot as she could stand it and stood under the spray, the cut on her wrist stinging. She thought maybe if she could get warm enough, she'd melt the cold place lodged in her chest since she woke up in the hospital and her all-too-clear perception of her father, slumped over shot in the ocean orchard, was all-too-true. She'd been robbed of the immediacy of her grief, of the ability to cry or even keen for him when she found him, stunned in those precious seconds before a second assassin's bullet ricocheted off the bench and, diminished, found her skull. Then blessed velvety darkness, for a very long time.

The warmth made her crawlingly dizzy after a while and she edged the water into cold. Her hair had only about grown back to pixie cut length, and shampooing it gave her a weird feeling, suds falling unhampered down her neck and onto her shoulders. Sometimes things didn't smell right, and she finished up when the normally coconut shampoo turned to lemon in her nostrils instead. "Brain injuries are fun," Jules muttered, toweling off and casting a baleful glance at the other triptych of prescription bottles lined up on the bathroom vanity. There was an antidepressant, antianxiety and an anti-inflammatory, because apparently they (the doctors "they") assumed she was depressed, on the verge of panic, and or her brain was going to swell beyond the confines of her skull at any given moment. The painkillers she appreciated, and took. The others, she did not.

At home, finally out from underneath the watchful eye of nurses and techs and doctors, she could dispose of those down the toilet at the expected reasonable rate and not have to worry about cheeking and palming and all that. At least she knew how. Every last one of those drugs hazed her out, cut her off, from the thrums of magic. What she'd used to contact her father. What she'd used other times, though with her teacher, and her friend. She'd been physically damaged, yes, emotionally as well, and preferred to feel both things. She'd even reap the benefit of the raw boost to power they might give her, call upon it and have her revenge. Yorick grunted from just outside the bathroom door. "You can just come in here," she said. He huffed, pawed a nylon toy over to gnaw on.

Jules reached for the painkiller bottle again, stopped herself, and instead hunted up the razor she'd used last night. She considered a moment, then cut a small shallow notch across her hip bone, maybe an inch or less. The blood beaded in a line, and she smeared it off with a thumb and washed her hands. The buzzing and lights in her head lessened with the scratchy-new scar. Jules stepped over Yorick out into her bedroom, threw on underwear and a bra, pulled a black sundress over her head. "Where are my shoes?" she asked. Yorick cocked his head and looked at her, processing, then climbed to his feet and went to nose aside the comforter which slithered off her bed at some point last night. A pair of plain black flip flops crouched there, curved to the shape of her feet. "Good boy. Let's go to break-fast." She passed a hand over her damp hair; she missed the weight of it, braided and pinned up to the back of her head. She didn't miss the weight of it, dragging at her temples, coming loose at inopportune times. She should do an undercut while it was this short.

When Jules walked into the breakfast room, Hector turned his head sharply at the snap of her flip flops and the jangle of Yorick's tags and from the thinly veiled look of patrician disgust on his face she knew she'd made the right decision. Gladys' parents always thought she should've married Hector; Jules' father was a dark horse, not even in the running when Gladys and Hector met him at their ivy league college and folded their new scholarship friend into the social circle.

The emerald on Gladys' finger was so big it looked fake, and Jules wondered where her other rings were, the ones from her dad.

"I'm not accustomed to sharing my breakfast table with animals," Hector said, setting aside the morning paper as Jules sat down and Yorick lay down behind her chair.

"Yes, I suppose your college years are long behind you," she said, looking at the big frat ring he still wore.

"Juliet!" Her mother snapped.

"As are yours, wouldn't you say?" Hector replied at the same time.

"My diploma is framed on the wall there so yeah, I guess. But I might just go on down to Asbury Park and apply at Madame Marie's! What do I need to study for ever again?" Hector, her father's best friend. Hector, Gladys' second choice. Hector, Jules' godfather. Was he always such a son of a bitch? Was being second choice enough to kill the first choice even after all this time?

The staff brought in breakfast then, eggs benedict, a favorite of the household, Hector included. He wasn't always awful. "Juliet, you are not going to work at a fortune telling booth," her mother said. "Or a tattoo parlor, despite your obvious interest in that field." From their angle, Jules' visible tattoos were brimstone on her right index finger and the occasional flash of the witch's knot nestled into the inside of her left wrist. The cut she made last night was obfuscated by her beaded bracelets, a rosary and an evil eye charm. She had to be careful, where she cut. But she'd known that all along.

"Oh, I'm sure I wouldn't have any talent at tattooing, Mother. You know I can't draw."

Some of your drawings might still be on the fridge, her father would've said, and Jules could almost hear his voice in her right ear. Behind her on the floor, Yorick growled very, very quietly.

Then her mother and Hector were looking at her expectantly. "I'm sorry, I didn't catch that," Jules said.

"I asked what your plans for today were," Gladys said.

"I hadn't really made any. It's beautiful out, though, I should get some fresh air."

"I don't like you doing that alone, take John with you." Like it was an option. John was probably already suiting up for his day's security work.

"I won't be alone, I'll have Yorick."

"Yorick doesn't count," Gladys said, pursing her lips.

"We've always used dobermans for protection." Security didn't help us in the fall, she thought.

"Fine, yes, Yorick counts, but take John or one of the other security staff with you. I want to know you're safe."

"Fine, Mother." Never mind the estate wasn't as impenetrable as they'd always thought, its piled black rock bulkhead in the inlet, witness to tides and ships passing. They'd never considered how much the passing tides and ships could witness them right back. Or perhaps they had. But it had never come up in polite conversation.

"We're just worried about your safety, Jules," Hector said, and certainty of guilt or no, Jules almost acted right then, plunging her breakfast knife into his throat. She managed to withhold the impulse, but still had the flash in her mind, the blade sinking into the soft flesh, the sudden gush of blood, hot and thick, running down her hand and wrist, dripping onto the white linen tablecloth.

"May I be excused?"

Chapter Three

Like it or not, Jules had been dealing with the family's security team her whole life. They hovered at the perimeter of her birthday parties, they did background checks on her prom dates. It didn't mean she needed to make it easy for them, especially not John. She was directly on her way after she was done pushing food around on her plate with murder in her heart.

The ocean orchard was not her father's folly, but he'd been the most recent one to foster it. The apple trees were twisted, salt-stunted things which occasionally, with much coaxing, bore funny palm-sized apples that were improbably sweet. Beach roses draped over the big black rocks that ringed the island, but split aside in places to let a small party down to the water, where they'd sometimes launch a canoe and go fishing, or walk down at low tide to poke at horseshoe crabs and clams. They had other, larger boats, docked elsewhere. They were much more of a production, and an entirely different kind of outing. Their little bridge 'to the mainland' was on the other side of the island, but a local highway bridge arched over the inlet not far from them. It used to be a drawbridge that went up on a schedule Jules never quite learned, backing up traffic for half an hour or more when the boats left in the morning and came back in the evening, for parties or fishing or both. Locals knew to just turn their engines off and chill out when the drawbridge was up; tourists did not. There were still drawbridges, but she remembered that as the worst one.

Amongst the trees in the ocean orchard were many marble benches, commissioned by whatever railroad baron forebear thought it was a good idea to plant apples on a sandy little island to begin with. At some point, somebody, maybe his wife, realized it would only bear fickle fruit and so made it a curiosity to lounge in and while away blue-skied summer hours, filled it with sculptures in unexpected places, planned out a human sized chess board.

Her dad's favorite bench was near to the rocks, sun and salt scoured like a pair of worn-in jeans, and like denim, it had soaked up spilled blood greedily and locked it away in its very being. Jules didn't doubt somebody'd tried to clean it, as soon as the crime scene crews pulled up their stakes and tore down their tape and didn't come back anymore. But the stain was there, and would be there, either forever or until blood was answered with blood. She wondered.

There was a jagged chip out of the edge of it, where the bullet that hit Jules ricocheted off, and the marble there was crystalline and damp in the morning air, shockingly white again like it had just been quarried in Italy, or wherever it was marble came from. It was dazzlingly bright, the sun flickering off the water, and maybe she wasn't thinking straight.

Yorick came as far as the nearest trees, about twenty feet away, no closer. Even when Jules tried sweetly to coax him, crouched and making kissy noises, he rolled his sad brown eyes at her, the corner of his mouth tightening, his ears folded back and his nub tucked tight. She didn't try to force him. It was enough for her that Yorick had appointed himself her guardian angel, and that he seemed to still be sniffing around for her dad even as he made himself her shadow. How can you explain to a dog that somebody is gone, when you feel like you don't really understand it yourself?

"You're going to make me lose my job," John said from right behind her. She was still staring at the deep red-purple stain on the bench. She wanted to touch it and didn't want to touch it. She should've come out here last night, to communicate with her dad. In her room was safer but it had been so hard. It wasn't what she wanted. She was going to have to try again.

"Oh were you officially hired?" Not long before her life had taken its odd skip, its plunge into darkness and loss, John had gone to the private security school the state police ran, and was a probationary hire. Of course they were going to hire him, he was Mr. Poling's son. It would not do, to not hire the son of your long time security head, who had grown up with your daughter.

"While you were...gone." He didn't know how to approach it either apparently. God, he was distracting. His tone was fairly neutral, not quite friendly. He was rarely friendly. John was in a good mood, then, or thought differently of her, or was under strict instructions to treat her with kid gloves. John was very good at following instructions. Distantly came the jangle of Yorick slumping onto his side under the tree and sighing mightily. His best, clearest way to express his disapproval of this human nonsense in this terrible place. "Why are you out here?" John asked after following Jules around in silence for a little while longer.

"Tell me what happened," she said. Looking out across the water dazzled her more with each passing moment.

"You know what happened."

"I know what Gladys told me. And I know you won't spare my feelings." She should've turned around to watch his face, to watch for the angry twist of his mouth. It was rare she missed an opportunity.

"They know it was a single gunman," he said after a long pause. He hadn't asked her for any kind of quid pro quo and probably already regretted it. "My dad said the rifling on the bullets they recovered was the same."

"And where do they think the gunman was when he fired?" Or gunwoman. How many women performed assassinations? Or was her father's death just a murder, and it's her mother's that would've been an assassination.

"They'd say the bridge, but there are traffic cameras on the bridge. No gunman there. So probably a boat in the inlet. It's probably why the second shot missed you, current and waves."

"But the first shot was perfect." Maybe they thought Jules was her mother and that's why they tried for two. Maybe they wanted Jules and her dad out of the way, to have Gladys all to themselves. It was Hector, her father said, firmly, angrily. The hair on the back of her neck stood up. Jules never knew anybody who died before, not really. She was too little to remember Mrs. Poling, John and Una's mom. She'd never tried to speak to the dead before. What she'd done, what they'd done was...different.

"Perfect enough. Through your father's ear." Jules kept a grip on herself, though the ground seemed to sway like she was standing up in a boat. It sometimes did anyway, now. Like the smells thing. Like the tingling in her arm thing. "Silenced. Suppressed, I mean. The second shot wasn't, though."

"So that's why everybody knew."

"Between that and Yorick. We heard the shot, which was still kind of muffled, but if you know gunshots you know gunshots. And then he started howling, but it wasn't normal, he was just wailing like a banshee."

"Who was supposed to be on my father's security detail?" she asked, as though that would make a difference whether he was bulletproof or not.

"I don't remember. But he was like you, you know, he just did what he was going to do. Difficult to keep a line on."

"I know, I know. I'm not looking for blame. Just reconstructing the morning in my head." Like how they reconstructed my head. She bit back a wild laugh. "You were on my detail, weren't you?"

"Supposed to be. Kind of like this morning." He stood just behind her right shoulder now. She smelled his toothpaste, his aftershave, the stuff he put in his hair. Funny how her own shampoo smelled like lemons but she could smell his just fine. "I assumed you'd be in the orchard and was already on my way up here when. The incident occurred." He paused, cleared his throat.

Jules waited, and when he didn't go on right away she said, "So then you got here."

"I thought you were dead," he said. "I've never seen so much blood. Mr. Duncan...I could tell your dad was dead. I found your pulse on your throat and called 911 on my cell. Then my father was here, and security. Mr. Crab had to drag Yorick away and kennel him, he wouldn't leave and the police said they were going to shoot him. He wouldn't let anybody else up here."

"Mr. Crab would've never let that happen. Your father wouldn't either."

"If he had to choose between you and the dog he would. It's what your family pays him for."

"True. And he doesn't like the dogs."

"True."

"Neither does Hector."

Another pause. "Also true."

Do you know where Hector was that morning? She almost asked. There was a part of her that wanted very much so, the bloody vengeful part of her mind that was happy to blame him and be done with it consequences be damned. But she wasn't about to tip her hand to John. And Hector wouldn't have had a security detail of his own, didn't even live on the estate at that time. He was employed by the Duncans, probably something that had rankled, but he was a fairly good corporate lawyer, from what Jules could tell.

"So after Mr. Crab kenneled Yorick?"

"Then the EMTs could come up here and they got you loaded and took you to the hospital. They stabilized you and then airlifted you and Gladys to that place outside Philly."

"My first helicopter ride and I was unconscious for it."

"I'm sure you'll get another sometime," he said dryly, and she smiled. It was true, but from him, it sounded like a threat. Like he'd happily smash her skull in and she'd get that chopper ride back to the hospital.

"Thank you for telling me," she said. Wouldn't it be fun, if he actually cared about her, if he'd been worried about her? He probably did. She held the mental image of John knelt over her prone form, blood on his hands, pulling his phone from his pocket. Smoothly, not fumbling; John did not fumble.

"You're welcome." He touched the nape of her neck, lightly, where she had an ouroboros tattooed. She didn't think he was terribly interested in the tattoo, but it was a very intimate place to touch her. "You're going to get sunburned," he said. It was so normal, so banal, so mother-hen, that she laughed.

"Probably." Jules turned to look up at him. Looked at the faint scar on his cheek, looked at the careful way his tie was knotted, the indifferent way he'd shined his shoes. It was difficult to care about shoe shine when you were walking in the sand. She'd been nice and come to the orchard; she could've gone down to the water's edge, and he would've had to follow her, doleful in his suit and dress shoes. She didn't know how security personnel moved about so well in dress shoes, with their slippery soles. She'd have to ask sometime, but not now. "What am I supposed to do about it?"

"Well, you could've worn sunblock."

"Do you have any? You could help me put it on." There it was, that veiling of his eyes, that disgust and want all wrapped up together when he looked at her.

"No, I don't have any."

Jules resumed walking about the orchard. Far too early for apples in the trees, though bees buzzed about the scant white blossoms. Apples always tasted best after the first frost anyway. He followed her, not so close as when they were standing. She couldn't smell him anymore, just hear him, and Yorick fell into heel with her, smelling sweetly of dry grass and warm dog.

"Where's Una?" she asked, even though she already knew.

"Doing college stuff."

"I can't believe your dad let her stay in the dorms."

"She said it might be safer. Plus, she doesn't like Hector."

"Does anybody?"

"Gladys."

She hadn't expected that. "Touché." She stumbled over nothing, and John caught her by the arm.

"Let's get you inside," he said.

Chapter Four

U na called her that night and Jules sprawled on the couch in the billiard room, listening to bright chatter about college classes and exams and all the clubs on campus. It was the first time Una had spent any time away from home. Less than half an hour away, just a few beaches up the road, but it was like a world away. Jules really was glad she'd graduated college last year. Yorick was sacked out in front of the cold fireplace, legs stuck out straight, snoring.

"Well, Juliet?" Una asked, and Jules had the feeling an important question had been asked. She dangled her flip flops off her toes, letting her eyes unfocus. She'd been wondering where her dad's cell phone was. If she had the password, she could try to track it online. Or could've tried to track it six months ago, when it still had battery. Now it might as well be a rock.

"I don't know," she said, not untruthfully.

"I mean, I saw Ashley the other day at the Inkwell and I guess Gladys is still paying your rent for the apartment? They probably want you to stay at the estate but the estate is where you...got hurt, after all." Una's voice wavered, but now Jules felt like she caught on and her attention focused. A little freedom was good for Una, it seemed.

"I really do want to go back to the Asbury apartment. I haven't talked to Ashes yet, actually. Just some texting. I'm sure Gladys told her not to call. But I've got a doctor's appointment next week, I think, and I'll make them clear me." She wasn't really sure when the appointment was. She pressed lightly on her hip, where she'd made the cut this morning, and that little spark of pain helped. Yes, it was next week. That's when the painkillers would last until. "Have you thought about getting an apartment?"

"Well kind of. It seems like there's lots of apartments close by, so I could walk or bike." A long pause, and Jules pressed the cut on her hip again. She knew, clearly, what was coming, could hear Una's voice as clearly as though she was remembering it. "Don't...you and Ashley have an extra bedroom?"

"Oh, Una, I don't know..." If Una moved in, they could have a third. They'd have to teach her, but with the two of them, it wouldn't be so hard. Una was so earnest, and eager. With a third, they could do so much.

"Dad's more likely to say yes if I'm with people he knows. Especially since they keep an eye on you anyway."

"They keep an eye on me when I'm not at the estate?" Jules sat up, flip flops slapping onto the floor. She'd never noticed anybody watching her.

"Not total police state style, just at a distance if you're out at the bars or a party or something."

"Fucking seriously?" Okay that wasn't so bad. It *was*, but she didn't do anything risky at bars or a party, that she wouldn't want Gladys to know about. In public, that was fine.

"Oh no, I shouldn't have said anything. Don't get upset, Juliet. Are you alone? Are you okay? Don't get upset."

"Well I thought I was alone but I'm sure somebody'll come out from behind the curtains or something if I need help." Yorick sneezed and raised his head and Jules bit her lip and just concentrated on her breathing. For a moment, her vision throbbed, and she breathed and waited. It was uncomfortable to be aware of the capillaries in her eyes. "I'm sorry, that isn't fair to you. I've never noticed anybody watching me, so I guess your dad has people less cold fish than John to take that duty."

Una giggled. "Poor John."

"Yeah. Right."

"I thought he liked you, for a while."

"I think he thought he did. Who's to say what happened there."

"I thought you'd tell me one day."

"Una, honey, nothing happened there." A lie, but so natural and easy. Lying was very easy, very natural, always had been but the bullet to the skull only added to that ability. Maybe it was an unforeseen advantage, maybe some morality center in her brain was already damaged, long ago. Jules settled back onto the couch, almost sleepy, sundrunk from earlier. It would be dinner soon and somebody would come find her. Maybe Gladys, maybe one of the staff. Maybe Gladys and Hector would go out somewhere, go up to the city and give her some peace. Moving back to the apartment, that would be nice.

"That's what John said too. Either you got your stories straight, which I find hard to believe, or you're telling the truth."

"Then we must be telling the truth." It was in fact on this very couch that Jules and John had their most recent encounter, and even then, it was almost a year ago. One of the few times she'd in fact known him to fumble, as they tried to deal with each other's clothes in the heat of the moment, the furtive energy that comes from the thrill of maybe getting caught, maybe not caring. "Turn off the camera," she'd breathed in his ear, right as he got to his belt buckle. Some part of her wanted to just leave it on, she was the lady of the manor, whatever. Part of her wanted to see if he'd think of it on his own.

"What?"

"The security camera. Turn it off." He'd glowered, but moved to the corner of the room and got up on a chair to detach the cable. When he returned to the couch, he was no less enthusiastic. Mentally, anyway. Jules kept an ear cocked for interlopers, and after several unsuccessful moments said "You can pretend I'm Gladys, if that helps."

"Why would that help?" He sat back, still straddling her. The pillows were on the floor, and most of his clothes as well. He'd pulled her shirt off successfully, but her bra was tangled in her hair. Her hair was so long then. It was all so laughable, but not the time to laugh.

"She's prettier. More glamorous. You want to hold her, control her. It's all right." Jules considered a moment, even as John struggled with what she was saying. "I don't mind you imagining my mother. I don't remember what your mother looked like after all." She expected the slap and rocked her head back dramatically with the impact before lashing out with both hands, one nail dragging a furrow down his cheek, the other on his forearm.

"You don't talk about my mother," John said. He wasn't quite gritting his teeth, but he winced at the sting of the cuts.

"It's perfectly normal, John. Attraction is attraction." Jules laughed softly. They remained uninterrupted. The little problem John was having seemed to have resolved itself, and he pushed her down against the couch as he kicked further out of his pants. He just needed to feel like he was in control, facing adversity. Somewhere in there, he still knew Jules was wielding the power, he had to, but still he gave in. Maybe John had once thought of her as a friend, or a possible love interest, or even as a little sister (which made this even more fucked up) but any and all of those feelings took a tremendous blow that night on the couch.

"It seems like the only logical conclusion." Una's voice pulled her back to the present. Jules rolled over and looked at the security camera. The things those cameras had seen. She always tried to be careful.

"It does," Jules agreed. "It's dinnertime, I think I can hear people looking for me. I'll talk to you tomorrow."

"Okay, Juliet. Have a good night. If I see Ashley again I'll tell her you're going to call her. I might be going out tonight, with this guy I know."

"Sounds like fun. Thanks, Una." Of course she'd just text Ashley tonight, but Una's sweetness was hard to reject. Una's friendship and loyalty was potentially valuable, a bargaining chip, a weapon to be used against John and anybody else necessary. Jules ended the call and then looked at the dark screen of her phone. Una going out with a guy? Mr. Poling couldn't possibly know about that. Or John, as he would've immediately tattled. Maybe Ashley knew.

She texted Ashes: //Looking for a new roomie yet?// And then the door to the billiard room opened and Yorick was awake and on his feet instantly. Mr. Poling walked in, and made a face as though he were surprised, but she'd have bet her inheritance that he located her on the estate cameras before he went physically looking.

"Miss Duncan, good evening," he said. She snapped for Yorick, clumsily because she forgot and tried to use her left hand, but he knew what she meant and came over. She leaned on his shoulders to stand up, but Mr. Poling gestured for her to stay seated.

"Mr. Poling. Is it dinner time already?" She settled back on the couch and Yorick pushed his head in her lap for her to rub his velvet ears.

"So I've been told. I think we can make your excuses to your mother, though."

"Do you?"

"John told me what you did today. And you look wiped out, white as a ghost."

"And he was worried about my getting sunburnt."

Mr. Poling sat in the chair nearest to her couch, upright and without relaxing against the back. "Is there anything you want to know about the investigation?"

Jules couldn't help it, she stared at him. "I'm sure my mother wouldn't..."

"No, probably not. But I've known you your entire life, and have been paid to pay attention. You've latched on, and you'll get answers by any means necessary. If you were applying to work here I'd hire you in an instant. Instead, I work for you. So let me." It was perhaps the most Mr. Poling had ever said to her at once. Her phone buzzed in her pocket, but she left it there. Ashley would understand, would even yell at her if she didn't take this opportunity.

"I'll keep that in mind," she said after a too-long pause. "John was able to answer my immediate question, anyway."

"He's a good man, I think, and he'll do well by your family." He paused, considering her. Mr. Poling did make her feel *seen*, for better or for worse. "But you can't possibly have only one question."

"No. I mean, I'd like to know if the police have a suspect, even. I need to read the papers, I haven't been able to."

"They suspected Gladys, of course; that's what one does if a murder victim has a spouse. But she stood no financial or political gain, as it were. Your father had a life insurance policy, with you as the benefactor. Had you died as well, Gladys could conceivably have argued via legal channels that she would've been your heir, in order to recover the money. But that didn't come to pass."

"Is that why Gladys hasn't married Hector yet? Too suspicious?"

"I think Mrs. Duncan thinks even being engaged so soon is gauche. But perhaps part of it, yes. There are few things so sordid as a pointless crime of passion when a bloodless divorce would have proven far less trouble." Not for the first time, Jules wondered about the late Mrs. Poling.

"True. I wonder how long they're gonna wait, though." Mr. Poling remained silent. "Hector's a suspect too then?"

"Of course. Though he may not have been cleared just yet."

"Hector and Dad loved hunting," she said, partly because of the rifle and partly to be able to talk about her father. She didn't really feel like she could, not with Una, who was forever waiting for her to crumble apart in sugar shell pieces, not with John, who examined everything with a sardonic suspicion. And who wanted to confide in

John anyway? Not with Ashley, who would be so receptive, so real about it, that Jules might as well be putting her fingers into an open wound to dig around. No, everything about her father was too raw. Even mentioning the hunting made her mouth dry, made her scalp tighten.

"It's true, they did." Mr. Poling stood again and offered her his arm. "I'll walk you to your room and have somebody bring you something to eat. You still need your rest."

"Thank you." She stood, with Yorick's help, and took Mr. Poling's arm. They walked in silence through the estate. He smelled a lot like John did, but with an underlying tobacco aroma, though she hadn't seen him smoke in years. She hadn't had a cigarette herself since that morning. Once she was back in the apartment she'd take it up again. Or maybe that was it, cold turkey. Probably not an FDA recommended means of quitting, though, a bullet to the head. Bullets were in general not recommended. "Gladys won't like my not coming to dinner," she said.

"Mrs. Duncan is aware that though you are well enough to be home, you're still recovering. Don't push yourself too far too soon. She's also aware, I'm sure, that you'll not remain with us indefinitely but would prefer to return to your apartment with Miss Ward. She's already made sure your lease will allow for that dog."

"She has?" It wasn't so unusual a gesture from Gladys, who at times wavered between being so thoughtful she couldn't be real and so distant she might as well be a stranger. But it hadn't occurred to Jules that her mother would do such a thing, and she was so surprised, and so suddenly thankful that Yorick would be able to stay with her wherever she went, that she found herself suddenly weeping without effort, just tears falling from her eyes as she blinked.

"She doesn't understand your attachment, I don't think, but understands its importance." He pulled a clean white handkerchief from inside his suit coat and handed it to her without looking.

"She doesn't like the dogs much at all," Jules said, wiping her eyes. "But recognizes their utility."

"It's an unusual strength to have," Mr. Poling said, stopping in front of her bedroom door. "Shall I?" He gestured at the ring of keys on his belt.

"I have mine, thanks." She took out her key ring and then remembered and tried to give his handkerchief back. "Oh, here."

"Keep it." He gave her a rare smile and continued down the hall.

Chapter Five

//What do you mean a new roomie? I LIKE having the place to myself ;+) I've been redecorating.// Ashley's text read, when Jules was in her room and flopped onto her bed. Yorick snuffled about the perimeter of the room, as he always did, examining the chairs, the bureau, the closet, and shouldering into the bathroom.

//Stay out of my room.//

//Calm your tits, I didn't touch any of your cards or your book of sinister dreams and whatever else you have in there. Just did the living room and the kitchen. And can listen to all that club music you hate.//

//K. So it'll be a bummer when I come back then?//

//You're coming back? Soon?// Almost immediately.

//Dr. next week & I'll see if it's okay to be on my own (i.e. out from under Gladys' already not so watchful eye). Kind of self-sufficient as it is, just have shadows while I'm here. OK to bring Yorick?//

//Yes! I fucking love Yorick.//

//Oh, but Una said she saw you? And her freedom's making her drunk with power, she wants to get her own place. And asked very shyly if maybe she could come use our 3rd bedroom.//

//Una's sweet, but...//

//Yeah, I don't know either. Think about it.//

//Roger that.//

"Yorick, get my pajamas," she said experimentally. He came to the bathroom door looked out at her, head tilted, thinking. She remembered then that she left her flip flops in the billiard room. Whatever. She rolled off the bed and to her feet, rummaged around in her drawers for yoga pants and a tank top, then went to the bathroom, where Yorick still stood, and turned the tub on for him to drink from. She went through her prescription bottles and removed what she should remove, but only took the painkiller and the anti-inflammatory. The others she dropped into the toilet, flushed. "Don't watch me change, it's creepy," she said to him. She examined the cut on her hip; just a hairline, like a cat had scratched her or a thorn had pricked her as she pushed through bushes. Most days since she woke up felt like pushing through thorn bushes.

Her phone buzzed again, two times one right after the other, rattling across the wooden nightstand, and she left Yorick lapping messily at the tub and went out to check it. It took her two tries to enter the unlock code on her touch screen, and then she was confronted with two texts from "Dad" which was fucking impossible and her stomach felt as though it had either fallen right out of her, or turned to ice, and when it buzzed again she dropped the phone on the floor. It bounced once and came to rest on some of the salt from the night before. It stopped.

Yorick growled from the bathroom doorway, low and deep. "It's okay," Jules said, whether to comfort Yorick or herself, she couldn't say. Both, really. She picked the phone up with her left hand, fingertips numb, beads on her protective bracelets rattling together and sliding around over the cut on her wrist. Her left wrist, with its protective tattoo. Entered the unlock code, swiped to the texts. Three labeled from Dad.

//It was Hector.//

//He'll kill your mother too.//

//He'll try again to kill you.//

Jules swallowed and her dry throat clicked. It had to be somebody fucking with her. Not that she thought ghost texts were impossible. But if anybody found her dad's cell phone, it was either locked up with the police or maybe in Hector's pocket and he was trying to needle her into insanity to get her off the estate and out of his life again. All options seemed equally possible. The last text her dad had sent her before the shooting was a picture of Yorick wearing sunglasses in the ocean orchard, his invitation to come hang out that day. Sometimes she showed up, and they went to the movies, or went fishing, or got in a canoe and drifted about the waterways. Sometimes they just sat around talking about college and her possible plans and the railroad. More than one time she showed up and they went to Great Adventure. There were any number of things they did, they could have done. Then came two shots.

Phone in hand, she went and turned the water off. "You need to learn how to do this yourself," she said. Yorick looked at her, then sniffed at the phone, wet black nostrils quivering. She held it out to him, and he put a big nose print on the screen before trotting past her and getting up onto the bed. She wiped the screen off on her pants leg and turned off the bathroom light.

Outside, the long blue summer twilight still cradled the estate, the crushed oyster shell pathways and marble benches glowing like the moon in the gloaming. It was too early in the year for lightning bugs, no matter how hot it was already, but Jules couldn't help but hope to see their intermittent flicker over the lawns. There was a jangle as the patrol pair of dobermans meandered past. Yorick raised his head when he heard them, eyes on the window, which was open a crack to let the fresh salt air in, but he didn't get up. He was supposed to be one of those patrol dogs, but Jules and her dad wanted a puppy who was a pet, and Yorick latched onto them like it was his birthright. It was, technically; dobermans were personal protection dogs from the start.

A knock on her door, and it was one of the kitchen staff with a covered tray for her. "Thank you," Jules said, and the woman smiled tightly and nodded, eyes on Yorick just inside the door. Jules withdrew and set the tray on her dresser. She wasn't hungry, nothing new there. Another non FDA approved medical advantage to a bullet to the head: weight loss due to natural loss of appetite. She thought about music, and thought about screwing around on the internet, and did neither. Yorick nosed at the edge of the tray, but he'd had his dinner before she went to the billiard room earlier. "Leave it," she said. "You don't want to get fat. Plus, Ashley's the one who gives you scraps." Not entirely true; Jules had also been known to give Yorick scraps. She thought about lifting the lid to see what dinner was, and her stomach did a slow roll over.

Jules got into bed and tucked her phone under her pillow, curling up on her side. She hadn't thought much about her violin until Ashley brought it up. With her hands feeling the way they were, she probably couldn't play anymore. Or she'd have to relearn. She flexed her fingers in the growing dark and sighed. The painkiller started to take hold and smear the edges off things. Yorick made another round of the room and hopped back up onto the bed with her, circling around and stepping on her legs a couple of times before he flopped over behind her knees and rested his head on her hip with a long drawn out sigh. A train went by on the nearby tracks, and blew the long low horn. Not every conductor knew at first that the Duncan house was right on the route, and not every conductor blew the whistle. Those who did tended to be ones Jules and Gladys had actually ridden in the engine with, watching the little beach towns whip by on either side of flashing lights and lowered striped crossing arms.

She should think about Hector's guilt more. She should think about her dad more, think about whether she actually contacted him, or something else. If Ashley were here it would be so much easier, she wasn't going to tell Ashley but of course she had to tell Ashley. They were a coven of two. Three, if they let Una move in. She slipped into a thick and dreamless sleep as the doberman pair outside came past again, tags jangling.

Chapter Six

S he skipped breakfast. She just couldn't face the fake fifties illu-
sion of the Big Happy Family with Gladys and Hector around
the breakfast table, morning sunshine spilling through the windows,
newspaper getting passed around, Gladys' phone pointedly face
down on the table to display how she was having Family Time and
business could wait. Without Jules at the breakfast table, Gladys
would happily be able to answer her Skype call from the German
producer of their new engines or whatever, and Hector could rumi-
nate over the obituaries and the classifieds. Hector fancied himself a
car restorer, among other things, and now he had considerably more
income than when he was just a lawyer in the pay of the Duncans.
And by income, Jules thought, she meant a stipend from Gladys. An
allowance. Jules got one herself, though when her father's life insurance money came through, she'd be free of even that, potentially. The
thought of life insurance money made her queasy, and she went to
perform her ablutions and take, or not take, her pills.

Jules made her way through the dimmed halls to the locked dark
wood door and slotted her key. It was a little hard in the turning, and
then the latch popped. She took a breath, let it out, pushed the door
open.

She was relieved to see the space was unchanged. Snowdrifts of
papers across the broad desk expanse. Old white ashes still in the
little blue and white tiled fireplace. A ledger, for though her mother ran the ancestral business with the iron-jawed determination of
every Duncan who came before her, Jules' father ran the household

accounts himself, meticulously. He'd made a joke of it, said if he was going to be a house husband he might as well go whole hog. Jules spent a lot of time in this office, learned how to build a fire and manage the flue, had help with her accounting homework, just sat and read while her father did one thing or another. She never thought she'd be here without him, about to go through his papers to try and make sense of them, and of the situation. Try to look for clues about deadly treachery from the man who'd been his best friend for thirty years. Yorick sniffed around in the corners of the room, eventually settled on the rag rug, eyes on her.

She spent an hour, then two, but everything on the desk, and in the drawers, was what it appeared it should be. Mundane household stuff, or a book he'd been reading, or a year's worth of National Geographic. Still no phone, somehow. If he'd had it in the orchard that day, to take the picture of Yorick, where did it go? Or was it an old picture and he sent it before going to the orchard?

Jules sighed and turned to go, questions still unanswered, and her elbow brushed three of the pens from the desktop. She bent to the floor to pick them up, in the chair well of the desk, and some strands of her hair brushed against and caught on something. Coming up with the pens, she felt beneath the desk and found a key she didn't recognize taped to the underside of the center drawer. Then she looked at the crooked little fireplace again, and the ashes, and noticed a curl of paper which must have survived whatever small blaze had taken place.

When Jules pulled it out, she recognized the layout of the estate immediately, even from the charred remnant. And the corner that more or less survived was the orchard. But she'd been out there already. She'd been out there her entire life. What did she miss?

She put the key on her ring and pocketed the fragile map shard and left the office with Yorick in her wake, locking it again behind her. She made it to the juncture of halls before Yorick gave a low woof. Jules turned, and Hector was approaching her, eyeing Yorick distastefully. "There you are," he said.

"I didn't know anybody was looking for me. I have my phone," she said.

"You're recovering from a brain injury, we're always looking for you." Hector's face was a mask of concern, but to Jules, his eyes told a different story. He definitely wished she'd died. If she'd died, once he married Gladys he would be the sole heir to the Duncan fortune. She had to get out of this house.

"I feel okay. Just tired."

"You need help back to your room?" It was hard to see Uncle Hector as a bad guy. She'd known him her entire life.

"I think I'm okay," Jules murmured, but really she never felt like she'd ever be okay again. Could she stand it for Hector to walk her halfway across the estate? But somehow they were walking anyway, Yorick shouldering between them. He did not like Hector, but Yorick not liking him wasn't enough of a clue. He didn't like Una either, was all right with Ashley, tolerated Gladys, who regarded him as a bit of drooly and inconvenient furniture for the most part.

"Are you hungry?" Hector asked when they were near the kitchens and dining room.

"Not typically," she said.

"I'll have them send you a milk shake at some point," he said. He really said it like that. Made 'milkshake' two syllables. "You need calories, and it's hard to turn down a milk shake. Strawberry, right?"

"I'm surprised you remember." And she was. Maybe a little flattered. "You always liked chocolate. You and Dad."

"It's true, we did."

They passed Mr. Poling and John talking, and though John was good at keeping a schooled blankness of expression, his eyes widened. Did that mean John suspected Hector as well? Or did it mean that John expected Jules to seduce Hector as well?

"Do you need anything?" Hector asked. "Like I said, I'll order you a milk shake. But I can call your mother if..."

"No, I'm okay. I must really look terrible, if you're this worried. But I'm okay."

"You look better than you did in the hospital. That was...pretty bad."

"I can imagine." Everything was a shock to her, when she woke up. "I wonder what they did with the bullet."

"What, that they pulled out of your head?" Hector seemed both shocked and amused, which was the best kind of reaction Jules would have hoped for.

"Yeah. Do you know?"

"I'm sure your mother didn't keep it with your baby teeth, if that's what you mean."

"That's a shame." Gladys had her baby teeth. She should steal them at some point, so they couldn't be used against her.

Hector laughed. "You are your father's daughter." He put an arm around her shoulders briefly and she felt too shocked, too dulled, to react. "And here we are. Will we see you for dinner tonight?"

"Maybe. What's for dinner?"

"No idea. It's a surprise every time."

"You know Mother sets the menu every morning, right?"

"Is that how it works? It's kind of like the Jetsons, I sit down and people in little aprons bring out the food."

"You're terrible," Jules said, laughing in spite of herself. She had to be careful. Not leap to conclusions. "But I'm going to go lie down. Thank you for walking me to my room."

"You're welcome. Like I said, anything you need, we're here for you."

"Thanks," she said again, and closed the door between them, locking it with a tiny click she hoped he didn't hear. The covered tray was gone from her dresser, as expected. She sank onto an easy chair she had close to the door, because the bed seemed impossibly far away. Either she'd just passed some pleasant time with her father's murderer, and her attempted murderer, or she spent time with Hector who was who he always appeared to be, no more and no less.

It was Hector.

Her father's voice but not his voice was so close, and she felt his breath-not-breath on the back of her neck as though he was right behind her, and she slid from the chair and caught herself on her hands and knees, skull buzzing and vision overcome with throbbing bright white static.

It was Hector.

Yorick barked, and barked, and somebody was going to come and find her like this and it was unexplainable. The room was terribly cold, despite her wide open window and the sunshine outside. Every hair she had was standing on end, arms, neck, head, the pressure in her head like she was trapped beneath pounding waves unable to get relief or take a breath.

Her father's voice, louder than it could possibly be, but trapped inside her skull, raging as she'd never in her life heard him. Her father's voice. He answered when she called him. But was it her father?

IT WAS HECTOR

And then it was all gone again.

Somehow, maybe leaning on Yorick, she made it to the toilet before she threw up burning yellow bile. She flushed and then her gorge rose again and she sat there, panting, for a long time, head against the cool clean porcelain, smelling the slightly-chlorine water smell, her eyes seeping tears as her stomach weakly heaved against her. When that seemed to have subsided, she fumbled in her vanity drawer for the razor, somehow got it out without cutting her fingers, and yanked down the waistband of her shorts. Cutting on her hips seemed the only safe spot, no bikinis this year. Yorick whistle-whined through his nose and she hissed at him and said "Go lie down." He flopped down right in front of the mostly-open bathroom door, still whining faintly through his nose, but even that faded away as she made three small cuts, laddered, breath shuddering, head throbbing with each heartbeat.

She pulled herself up, shaking, and washed off the razor blade, wrapped it in a tissue, buried it in the drawer again. She wiped off the blood on her hip, held her fingers under the water and watched until the sink was clear again, then sucked in a mouthful of water, rinsed, spit it out, did it again. Yorick kept whining and she almost didn't hear the knock at her door. The knob rattled, though, and then the knock came again. She buttoned her shorts, splashed some water on her face, looked in the mirror. Her eyes were so dilated she couldn't really see their brown.

"Who is it?" she called.

"Security, Miss Duncan, making sure you're all right. We heard the dog barking."

"Oh, I'm fine. I was watching a video on my phone and he started barking at a sound in it."

There was a pause, probably as whoever that was reported to the security room base. "Alright, Miss Duncan. Take care, and let us know if you need anything."

"I will." Mitch. That one's name was Mitch, she was sure. Friendly, professional, good with the dogs. She made it a point to know who each and every staff member was. Knowing peoples' names and who they were helped immensely if you needed them on your side, complicit in small ways. She wasn't technically their boss, but might as well be. Jules picked up her painkiller bottle and shook one out into her hand, dry swallowed it.

She had to get out of this house. She might be leaving Gladys with a murderer, but she might die before she accomplished anything otherwise.

Chapter Seven

The doctor was easier than she could have anticipated. Yes, they would refill her painkillers. Did she feel like they were working well, or did she need a different med? Pain was anticipated. How much was up to Jules to report. The numbness, yes. Occasional disorientation. The doctor even listened to Gladys talk about how Yorick had appointed himself nursemaid, and seemed to approve. The doctor also gave her the greenlight to move back to the apartment.

"After an injury, a trauma like you've experienced, it's tempting to withdraw from the world, insulate yourself from other badness that might happen. You should definitely go back to your apartment, spend time with your friends. Go to the beach. Just be aware of your limits. Take the dog with you." The doctor was of indeterminate age, maybe in her thirties, maybe in her fifties, a specialist with a private practice that the place in Philly referred them to. "Your psychological well-being can inform your physical one. Take care with both. But be careful if you decide to go to the bars. One or two alcoholic beverages is fine, but getting drunk on your medication could have long term consequences, and will definitely have immediate short term ones."

"Do you hear that, Juliet?" Jules wished strongly that her mother had simply stayed at home. It was both flattering and smothering that Gladys was taking time off work to bring her to the doctor. She should've had Gladys stay in the waiting room and just didn't think to say it.

"Yes, Mother. May I remind you that I have a degree in psychology, I might be aware of medical interactions. And how often do you think I get drunk?"

"I just want to make sure you get better," Gladys said softly.

"I know." Jules squeezed her mother's hand briefly. Gladys smiled tightly, and then it faded as always when she looked down at her daughter's hand and eyed the tattoos there. There had been many conversations with Gladys about the tattoos, none of them entirely truthful from Jules' side of the table. How do you tell your very banal and businesslike mother that the ink is to aid in magical ritual, and protection from magical ritual? You don't.

"So if that's it, no more concerns, I'll see you next month."

"See you next month," Jules said.

They were out in the car, and the driver got onto the Parkway, before Gladys sighed. "So just like that, you're leaving us."

"You knew I would," Jules said. "Anyway, you were happy when I moved out before."

"I was. But it was different then, I don't think I need to explain."

"Not really." Meaning please don't. Jules got out her phone and texted Ashley //Green light from the doctor.//

//YES!!!// It was like Ashes was waiting by the phone. //Yorick too?//

//That didn't have to do with the doctor. But yeah//

//I'll get the booze! ;+)//

//Can't really booze, but you enjoy.//

"Ashley?" her mother asked.

"Of course."

"Tell her I said hi."

"Will do." //My mom says hi//, she texted dutifully, then dropped her phone in her purse.

"Do you need to stop anywhere?"

"Other than to fill the prescription? No, I don't need to."

Everything was Before. And After. Before her father died. Before she almost died. Before Hector moved in to the estate. After she woke up. After she called her dad. Before and After.

She probably should've told the doctor that her sleep was weird. But she had a handle on what the current medication she actually took made her feel like, how it affected her connections to things, and if she was moving back with Ashley again, didn't want to have to figure that all out again. Maybe she'd sleep normally again in the apartment, in the four poster bed her father had moved there and put together for her, with its protective carvings. He'd known she liked those things, wasn't versed in what they did or didn't mean, but he'd seemed to have an idea. She'd been closer to telling him than she ever would be to telling Gladys. There were always secrets you kept from your parents, however innocuous.

Una sat on the front steps, waiting, when they pulled up. "Jules!" she squealed.

"Una, hi." She squeezed back dutifully when Una hugged her.

"Oh, your hair," Una said, and hugged her again.

"It's growing back," she said.

"I'm going back to work," Gladys said, dropping a kiss on Jules' cheek. "I'll see you at dinner, or if not, I'll come by your room and help you pack."

"Help you pack? Aw, I came home and you're moving out right away? Do I smell?" Una smiled, but her eyes looked hurt.

"It's part of my psychological well-being." Yorick would be around, she thought, looking for him. When she came home from the hospital he climbed into the car to get at her. "The doctor said." The sunlight bouncing off the front steps, the windows in the front doors, started to dazzle her.

"Oh. Well if the doctor said." Una noticed, and made a show of not noticing, the white prescription bag peeking up out of Jules' purse. "John thought you were going to be moving, he just didn't know when. He seemed relieved."

"Well of course." In the house was better, dimmer. Yorick came and nosed her hand, bumped against Una for ear scratches. "I'm taking Yorick with me. I think he thinks he's my shadow."

"He's like Nana in Peter Pan, except he isn't tied up outside somewhere, so he can actually help you."

"Are you saying Nana would've just eaten Peter Pan, if given the chance, and the kids never would've gone to Neverland?"

"Maybe."

"Una, that's dark, especially for you. College is pretty great, huh?"

"I like it," Una said with a little smile, blushing. Jules sat in one of the chairs in the entry, kicking off her shoes on the black and white tiles. "Did you ask Ashley?"

"Not yet, I figured I'd get back to the apartment and settle in, talk to her in person. You've got the whole summer before school starts again."

"I know. I just wanted to be sure."

"Are you leaving us too?" Jules jumped. She honestly had no idea where Hector had come from. He'd probably been waiting just inside the next hall juncture for them to come past, and when they stopped instead, had to make his presence known. Yesterday he'd seemed like old friendly, nurturing Uncle Hector. Today he was a gargoyle.

"I asked Juliet if I could take the third room in her and Ashley's apartment," Una said blithely. "Juniors aren't guaranteed housing at Monmouth so I might not be able to be in a dorm room. And Dad would be much more likely to say yes if I'm with Juliet, right?"

"Right," Hector said, smiling. There was a light in his eyes Jules couldn't abide seeing when he looked at Una, and she took the other girl's hand.

"But right now, Una said she'd help me pack," Jules said.

"I did! Talk to you later, maybe."

"Have fun, girls," Hector said, and Jules felt his eyes on them until they were around the corner.

"Does he talk to you like that often?" Jules asked in a low voice.

"Like what?"

"Like he's the big bad wolf and wants to eat you up."

"I...don't think that's what he was doing."

"Maybe I'm just tired." At her room, Jules tried twice to get the key in the lock and Una took the ring from her hands, their fingers brushing. Jules' hands were cold, Una's very warm. Jules crossed her impossibly large room and sat on the bed, looking down at her bare feet. She kept leaving her shoes everywhere. Una regarded her seriously.

"We don't have to pack now if you're too tired. Maybe you should take a nap."

"It's the middle of the day," she said, sliding her purse to the floor.

Una sat next to her on the bed, put a cautious arm around her shoulders. Her shoulders were cold too, and Una was warm like sunshine at the beach. Jules relaxed into her and their heads sort of knocked together.

"Sorry," Una said.

"Don't be," Jules said, and leaned in to kiss her gently and fully on the lips. Una stiffened just slightly, but closed her eyes and tightened her arm around Jules. Her lips were like John's and not; fuller and somehow firmer, and she smelled like flowers. "I'm sorry," Jules said when they parted to take a breath. They were still just inches apart, eyes locked. Una was breathing hard.

"Don't be," Una said, and she was the one who leaned in this time.

Chapter Eight

Jules did end up sleeping, eventually. She woke partway through the night, still dressed, with Yorick snoring on his back next to her and Una gone. Her shoes were on the floor next to her purse, and a tray with a glass pitcher of water and a covered bowl were on her bedside table. She smiled and fell back to sleep until the gray dawn's light crawled across the floorboards. She sat up and poured a glass of water, drank it slowly. The bowl was fruit salad, and she picked some blueberries out to eat, then fed Yorick some apple slices before she went into the shower.

She'd talked about packing, but there wasn't much to pack. Most of her things were still at the apartment, and the clothes here were mostly the ones she'd left here in the first place. An overnight bag, a laptop bag, and her purse would be the extent of it, and one of the drivers could run her over to Asbury Park and she could be done with it, no muss no fuss. But that would upset Gladys if she left with the dawn. One last farcical family breakfast was perhaps in order.

She wasn't long outside her bedroom when John fell into step beside her. "Morning, Juliet," he said. Yorick looked up at John and seemed to nod, as though it were a changing of the guard, and went off, almost certainly in search of a food bowl and a way out onto the lawn.

"Morning John," she said. He didn't sound outright hostile yet, it was always so interesting to sound out his mood.

"You're up early."

"It's moving day, I couldn't sleep," she said.

"I've never known anything to interfere with your sleep," he said. He seemed more curious than mocking, which made Jules curious.

"I've gone through some changes, John." She paused in front of one of the hall mirrors; she should've picked a different dress to wear. The way the sleeves were cut, the hanged man on her right shoulder was plainly visible. Gladys knew about her tattoos, couldn't have prevented their existence, but a shadow crossed her face each time she saw them. No matter how close she came to telling her dad—no, she was just thinking about that yesterday. She touched her fingers to her temple.

"You okay?" John asked. Jules thought of him with his hands covered in her blood. Finding her pulse.

"Yeah." Jules gave a half laugh. "Just thinking about how much Gladys hates my tattoos."

"Ashley has some of the same ones, doesn't she?" John asked. Wasn't he full of surprises?

"I'm sure she'd be flattered you noticed at all. Some of the same family of symbols, anyway. We both have this one." Jules indicated the brimstone symbol on her forefinger. "She has hers on the first knuckle of her middle finger, though."

"And this one too," he said, touching her on the ouroboros again.

"Yeah, though hers is also the figure eight like an infinity symbol."

"Isn't it already an infinity symbol?"

"Yeah. So now it's like, double infinity." Christ, she just woke up and she was weary again. No painkillers, no cutting, and here John was. It probably wouldn't do to just fuck him on the floor in the hall. "Do you have any tattoos, John? Something your father hates maybe?"

"No, I don't," he said stiffly.

"You can tell me. Or show me." She turned away from the mirror and stepped in close to him. He stepped back.

"I'll keep that in mind."

Eggs benedict again, John gone. Where did those security folk learn to be such cat's paws? Maybe it was just in his blood. The key felt like it was super visible on her key ring, like it must be spotted with blood like the key to Bluebeard's closet of dead wives, but when she glanced down, it looked normal.

Gladys was talking to her.

"What, Mother?"

"I asked if you were ready to return to your apartment today."

"Oh, yes, I am. Though I suppose I should talk to Mr. Crab first about care and feeding." Jules got up from her mostly untouched plate and dropped a kiss on her mother's cheek. She could see the tears in Gladys' eyes. "Don't worry. The doctor said I'm okay to do this. We have cell phones, we have a land line. I can train Yorick to call 911 and bark at the operator, will that help?"

Gladys laughed. "Fine, yes, I'm satisfied. Tell me when you're leaving, I'll ride along."

"I will." She took the long way to the kennels, scrutinizing disused doorways, trying to remember the last time she'd been through them. Until she found the key in her father's office, Jules would've said she'd been in every room in the estate, even the myriad strange and crooked basement rooms, with their wines and cured meats, the constant shush of water reverberating against the bulwark that kept the water back. The cedar-smelling attic, still containing the furs that the Duncan women wore to their parties, sequined dresses, bottles of perfume nobody made anymore.

The kennels were a long low building that probably had once held horses, but the Duncans hadn't kept horses in a very long time. Inside the kennels, though, one dog boomed in a repetitive bark, over and over again. Jules pulled the door open.

"Oh good," Mr. Crab said. "I kept him here, but he really wasn't happy about it." Yorick was in one of the kennels, freshly bathed by the look of him. Probably nails trimmed as well. Raw bone at his feet, ignored. He stopped barking when he saw Jules, yawned gapingly and sat, panting.

"No, I guess he wasn't." Jules opened the kennel door and Yorick walked to her slowly. He had a new collar on, broad russet leather with brass hardware. She spun it on his neck to look at the tags. His old rabies tag, of course, and an Asbury Park registration, along with a dog tag that had YORICK and Jules' cell phone number engraved on it.

"I had to get the number from your mother, of course," Mr. Crab said. He had a black military surplus looking bag on a nearby table. "Some food to get you started, though you know how much he eats and might want to set up auto delivery. A harness, for the car. A six foot leash and a long line."

"Thank you."

Mr. Crab dropped his hand on the dog's head for a moment, between his pricked ears. "He's a good dog, one of our best. He'd die for you, if he thought he had to."

"I hope not," Jules said, blinking away sudden tears..

Mr. Crab cleared his throat. "Anyway. You know where to find me if you need anything."

"Thanks," Jules said, taking the bag. "You're all clean," she said to Yorick with a smile, and he dog-grinned up at her.

Una and John waited on the front steps with Mr. Poling, and Una enveloped Jules in a tight hug. "I'll miss you," she said.

"I'll see you soon, I'm sure," Jules said, a little breathless from the embrace. "I'll think about what you asked," she murmured. Una smiled, that secret smile somebody who's been intimate with a person even a little will get, and stepped back to let Jules pass. She opened the back door to let Yorick hop in, and he leaned forward to sniff the back of Gladys' neck.

"Keep that beast off me," Gladys said.

"Oh, I have a harness for him, to attach to the seat belt." Jules pulled it out of the bag, and spent several minutes wrestling him into it. It probably would've been easier with both of them standing. But she got it good enough, she thought, and then they were on the way. "No Hector?" she asked, in spite of herself. Or maybe to spite herself. Or Gladys.

"He had a meeting with legal. And he said goodbye at breakfast. You can't expect Hector to be sentimental."

"No, of course not." Yorick crawled partway back across the seat to lie half in Jules' lap. Her left leg went to sleep almost immediately.

There wasn't much traffic, but the stop and go at the stop lights started to bother Jules pretty soon, though she never used to get carsick, and she put her window down almost all the way. Yorick strained towards it, but the harness held him back. "Off me, you big lug," she said, and he withdrew to his side of the car, looking at her with sad liquid eyes.

As always, Gladys sighed when they pulled up in front of her building, a huge rambling Victorian, cut into multiple apartments per floor. She'd stopped saying the words 'are you sure you want to live here?' but she clearly thought it.

Ashley sat on the front steps, smoking a cigarette, her ferret Puck nestled in her dark hair like a fur collar, his little black-nosed, champagne-masked face pointed away from the smoke. She stood and came down the front walk as Jules began the process of extricating harnessed Yorick from the back seat. The driver popped the trunk and got out to carry the bags. Ashley reached in for the turntable. "I'm so glad you remembered this," she said around her cigarette. Puck perched on her shoulder now, holding on with his little hands, staring down at Yorick, who strained his nose upward towards the ferret. They'd met before.

"How could I forget it?" Jules asked. "I'm glad you brought it to me."

"I thought it might help."

"I think it did," Jules said, and she caught Ashley's eye for a moment. They both smiled; Ashes got it. She stubbed out the cigarette in the sand filled metal pail on the porch and led the way upstairs. The hall was blessedly dim, all the wood was dark-varnished wood. A worn blue runner led up to the second floor landing, and following the bannister, they went up to the third floor. The first and second floor apartments were all just a few rooms, one or two bedrooms, one bathroom. The third floor must have been where the original landlord lived, because it was the entire top of the house, once you got through the white painted door, the only hallway door like it. They had a circular eastward facing room on one front corner, the top of the partial tower, and the other front corner was where the kitchen was, that let out onto the fire escape-cum-balcony. Two of the bedrooms shared a small half bath, and Jules' bedroom was the one that had a big enameled cast iron claw foot tub, which she grandly allowed Ashley to soak in whenever requested.

Jules unclipped Yorick's leash, and he made the rounds. Ashley took the turntable to the third bedroom, currently the de facto book and album library. There wasn't even real furniture in there, just boards with cinder blocks, bean bag chairs, and some end tables they'd picked up at various curbs. It was also the room in which they frequently smoked pot and, far less frequently, dropped acid. But Gladys really really didn't need to know that, or even be thinking about it in Jules' current medical state. Okay enough to live on her own. That's what they were focusing on.

It only took the one trip to bring everything in. The driver went back outside immediately, and Jules peeked outside, just for her own peace of mind. She didn't see any other black cars that might contain lurking security personnel.

"Your refrigerator is almost empty," Gladys said.

"Jules and I shop recreationally, Mrs. Duncan. I couldn't take that away from her, and I've been subsisting on the oyster crackers my customers don't eat."

"Don't they give you a meal at Perkins?"

"Nothing in life is free, ma'am," Ashley managed to say with a straight face. "And Perkins closed, I've had to seek other employment." Puck left her shoulder and climbed the carpet covered, floor to ceiling cat tree they had in the corner of the living room. The crown molding had a space at the top for reasons unknown, and he used it as a little ferret clubhouse. Once a month they got out a step stool that they balanced on one of the end tables to get up there and recover any stray items Puck may have purloined because they caught his fancy. He never seemed to eat or damage anything he shouldn't, but he did steal things.

"Well let me give you girls some money," Gladys said, unzipping her purse. Jules rolled her eyes, but was unsurprised. It was part of the process. Like she didn't have her bank card and a credit card.

"Thanks Mom," she said, and Gladys put a bank envelope in her hand instead of the expected couple of twenties. "Oh Mom, this is too much."

"What good is it if I don't spend it?" Gladys said with a rare, mischievous smile. "Don't spend it all in one place. No tattoos."

"I promise I won't spend this money on tattoos," Jules said, and Ashley nodded.

"I'll pinkie swear."

"That's not necessary," Gladys said, and she hugged both of them. "Call us any time if you need anything. Any time."

"Mom, you're twenty minutes away. It'll be fine. I'll probably come home Sunday for dinner."

"Good, that's good." Gladys even gave Yorick a pat on the head before she left.

"Wow," Ashley said as they watched the car pull away.

"That could've been worse, really."

"How much did she give us?"

Jules riffled through the bills. "Couple hundred. We could take the train to the city." Not that they'd see MaryAnne. Still no more texts from her.

"Well, once we get you a beach badge, that'll clear most of that out. I got mine on sale at Christmas."

"And you didn't get me one? Geeze." Then she saw the look on Ashley's face; at Christmas, she was still unconscious. They didn't know if she was going to be alive for beach season. Jules turned away and picked up the pack of cigarettes from the coffee table, shook one out, and Ashley got out her most recent purple plastic Bic. Ashley had fostered an affinity for purple plastic Bics when they first started smoking, her rationale being you could always find one. Jules, on the other hand, had hunted down a Vietnam era Zippo lighter, on the rationale that she could always refill the fluid and put another flint in it when it stopped working. Plus Zippo would always fix their products, she'd heard.

The first breath of smoke was familiar, smooth. The second caught somewhere, somehow, and Jules ended up coughing until tears leaked down her face and her ears rang. At some point, Ashley plucked the cigarette from between her fingers and smoked it herself, going to get a glass of water.

"I wondered how that was gonna go," she said.

"Me too," Jules said weakly, sipping at the water.

"Science." Yorick climbed up onto their decrepit couch, and it creaked audibly, like a ship at sea. "That's going to be interesting."

"I could tell him to get off."

"Nah. Not like we paid for it." Ashley flopped sideways into one of the armchairs, so her legs were over one side. "We could buy a hundred dollars' worth of hot dogs and cheese fries at the Windmill and then eat it for the next three days."

"When do you work next?"

Ashley shrugged. "I dunno. When somebody calls me." It was still kind of a shock that Perkins closed. It was still no easier to find a job, college degree or not. Ashley had her bartender's license at least.

"Will you think I'm lame if I tell you I'm tired?" She was and she wasn't. She felt like she could breathe more easily in the apartment, with all the sunshine spilling through the windows, than she could in the estate. Without Hector's shadow lurking. Without all that blood in the—

"Oh you're totally lame, but I won't hold it against you. We can do stuff tomorrow."

"I mean, I'm not going to bed right now or anything. But I don't feel like going out."

"I understand, Jules. Just take it easy." Ashley smiled. "We'll order pizza and drink beer and watch the Great British Bake Off or something."

"Perfect."

"And you're gonna tell me about the turntable."

"I promise."

Chapter Nine

A shley let her sleep in the next morning, more or less. More or less because Jules wasn't really sleeping, she had only slept a few hours and then just remained prostrate in the dark staring at the swirls of plaster on the ceiling. Who thought to swirl the plaster on the ceiling? Who did they imagine was going to look at it? "You going to sleep all day? It's beautiful out, sunny, not too hot."

"I'm thinking about it." She was thinking about staying in bed all day, anyway. Sunny wasn't such a great thing right now, she needed to buy sunglasses. Find her sunglasses. She always had such a hard time keeping track. No John to constantly be ready to needle, no Hector to be on guard with. No ghost of her father prowling the halls. When she had slept, no dark dreams had come, no pale hands and faces in the night, no rough voices in her ears telling her over and over *It was Hector*. It was a relief.

"Come onnnnn. I missed you. Puck missed you." Ashley cracked the door and held Puck through, then poked her head in. "See?" Puck looked at Jules and Yorick with bright interest, dangling like a sack of potatoes. Yorick hopped off the bed and trotted over, snuffling at Puck, and Ashley, before nose poking her knee.

"Take Yorick out, and I'll get up and get dressed?"

"Out of your room? Oh, you mean out out...Yeah, sure. Come on, buddy." Ashley didn't leave the room until she was satisfied Jules was actually getting up, though. Jules rummaged around in her dresser, found cutoff shorts, a Stone Pony t-shirt she (or maybe Ashley) had cut into a tank top, a bikini. She considered the bikini only

56

briefly, then found an old black halter one-piece and brought that with her into the bathroom instead.

Jules dropped her pajamas on the floor and opened the medicine cabinet to look at the amber row of bottles she'd arranged there. She took a painkiller and put the rest back. Maybe it would've been better to just cut. But no, the cutting had to have a purpose. She had to have things under control, or she'd be back at the estate in no time, with her mother's disappointment and Hector's leering laughter and Una's worry and John's smugness.

Jules found Ashley in the kitchen, drinking a cup of coffee and smoking a cigarette while she stared out the open window. Yorick lapped noisily at a mixing bowl full of water. "Not a lot of action today," Ashley said.

"People have jobs." Jules hunted around for shoes. She found and rejected numerous flip flops and sandals, and then found a pair of red Converse she jammed her feet in. "Okay, ready."

Ashley put her cigarette out in the sink and ran water on it before putting it in the garbage. "Is that my shirt?"

Jules shrugged. "It was in my dresser."

"It doesn't matter. Come on, the world is our oyster!"

"Ever think about what a weird phrase that is?" Jules jammed her wallet and her phone in her back pockets. "Do that many people even like oysters? They're like snot, in seashells."

"Shut up." Ashley grabbed the beach bag and hustled her out of the apartment and fiddled with the keys until she'd locked the door and the deadbolt. "I know you've thought about it. You probably wrote a paper on it. But I don't want to talk about Aphrodite and clams and shit for the next three hours, so we're going to behave like normal people and go up to the boardwalk where we will buy fried food and get sand everywhere and maybe play skee ball and go on some rides."

"Is that what normal people do?"

"Until the bars open, anyway."

"Oh the bars, of course."

"You're the one wearing a shirt from the Pony."

"Which may or may not be your shirt."

"Yeah, I can never remember if you bought it and I cut it, or vice versa. Whatever. We could go to the salon and get your hair dyed or spiked or something."

"I think I'll just let it grow again."

"It was really long before." For just a moment, Ashley's nonstop smile fest was overshadowed.

"And it'll be long again, it's just hair. Come on Yorick, let's have a constitutional."

"No dogs on the beach still, I thought?"

"And it's not season yet right? But we can take him on the board-walk anyway, I think."

"If we can't, we'll walk around and bring him home. No big." Puck was in his open doored cage, sacked out in his purple ferret hammock. He was saving his energy for later hijinks. They left their creaking empty house and walked up to Asbury Avenue, past the empty lot where the Palace had been. No more carousel rides.

Somebody waved at them from up the street and they waved back.

"Do you know who that was?" Jules asked. Ashes grinned.

"No. Better safe than sorry."

They crossed Ocean Avenue and hit the boardwalk. The sky and ocean were almost the same color blue, white caps on the ocean and big fluffy cotton ball clouds in the sky. "I never want to leave here," Jules said.

"Here the boardwalk or here Asbury Park?"

"Either. Both." Jules laughed, just a little. "The beach. I can't imagine leaving the beach. How do people in the city breathe?"

"I don't know."

There were a few surfers out on the water, sitting on their bobbing boards as the waves came past. It was between high and low tide, Jules thought, not many waves worth talking about. Some umbrellas dotted the beach already, and a small herd of kids ran around on the sand. They were trying to get organized, all work on the same big sand castle. Their mothers or babysitters or whatever sat in chairs under an umbrella, sunglasses almost as big as their faces, smoking and swapping magazines and talking. No police in sight, so they proceeded with Yorick, who walked with Jules like he'd been leashed his entire life, the leather slack from her wrist to his collar. She hadn't really considered before whether he was leash trained; before, she'd mostly left him at the estate, where leashes certainly were not necessary. Before, she hadn't needed him the way she did now. The way Ashley needed Puck.

It was low tide, and they waded in the surf for about an hour, shoes and bags and towels up on the sand, until a police officer came down from the boardwalk to talk to them about Yorick and they cleared out. Maybe they would've gotten a ticket, if he didn't recognize Jules. She wondered how many front pages of papers her face was on. She wondered how long it went on for. They walked back to the house, stopping for a bucket of fries along the way, which they shared liberally with the dog.

"Are you supposed to drink on your medication?" Ashes asked as they walked back to the Stone Pony.

"No."

"Are you going to drink on your medication?"

"Yes."

"Jules."

"Ashes, it's okay. I'll probably just have one beer, two, something like that. I'm not getting blasted." And I'm not taking all my medication, she wanted to say. But maybe not even to Ashley. No. She had to be able to trust *somebody* and if it wasn't Ashley it wasn't anybody. "I'm not taking all my medication."

"*Jules.*"

"I'm taking the life-saving, don't drop dead stuff! But they've got me on an antidepressant too and you would not believe how awful that feels. How cut off from everything. Everything. And my dad just died, I *should* be depressed. It's not normal to feel normal after that. After what I've been through. I just can't do it." She started crying at some point in the middle and was mad about it but pushed through until Ashley hugged her.

"Hey, hey, we're in this together right? I've got your back, you've got my back. We'll figure it out." Ashes sounded a little unsteady; neither of them were criers. "You going to tell me about what you used the turntable for?" She asked when they separated.

Hector, it was Hector. Jules shook her head, arms prickling with goosebumps. "Later, okay?"

"Pinky swear?" Ashley held up her hand and Jules hooked pinkies with her.

"Pinky swear."

They hung out at the Stony Pony for a while, listening to the band onstage that they'd never heard of. They didn't know anybody, though, and it was a drag buying their own drinks. Not even the mythic quality of 'maybe Bruce will show up' was enough to keep them there. Under Ashley's watchful eye, Jules had one beer.

They went up the street to the Wonderbar, where Ashley knew somebody in the band, and that was a little better. Jules knew most of the people Ashley did anyway, and they did some shots. Jules could never remember that beer and liquor rhyme anyway. The crowd was a good one, happy not rowdy, and it was one of those perfect early local pre-summer nights where the light was bright enough and soft enough, and there were just enough drinks.

Jules was sitting at the corner of the bar and had the bowl of peanuts. She'd been given change in silver dollars at some point, that didn't really seem modern and normal, and she poked them around on the bar, clinking them together. Ashley was talking to somebody Jules didn't recognize, a tall skinny guy with straight dark hair pulled into a ponytail. He had a tattoo on the side of his neck that she couldn't figure out at a distance, and was wearing jeans and a leather jacket, though not the biker kind.

A girl Jules kind of knew, though couldn't remember where she recognized her from, came over and hugged her and bawled just a little bit for a few minutes. She'd heard about the accident, she called it, and was so sad for Jules that her father was gone and was so glad Jules was all right. Jules kind of froze, rabbit in headlights style, and nodded once in a while, and the girl bought her a shot of tequila in memory of the good times and then her other friends found her and pried her away from Jules and they went out into the humid windy night.

"This is Jenner," Ashley said, suddenly at her elbow. Jules took note of her 'look what I found' tone and turned slowly, keeping a neutral expression on her face. Really, though, her immediate thought was 'isn't Jenner a character from that cartoon with the rats?' It couldn't be his real name.

"Pleased to meet you," Jenner said with a smile that didn't seem to hang just right, reaching out a tattooed hand for the peanuts. Jules slid him the bowl and pocketed her silver dollars.

"What brings you here?" she asked, because Jenner wasn't a local. Maybe not even from New Jersey. Not a Benny, though. She was past her "maybe one or two beers" and was drunk enough to know it.

"I heard it was a good scene," he said with that same smile. His teeth were...small? Too pointy? He was maybe thirty, maybe older. The light was weird. The band wasn't onstage anymore, either gone for the night or taking a break, and the jukebox was rocking instead, nothing she knew. As Jenner offered Ashley and then Jules a cigarette from his too-pristine pack of Marlboro reds, her eyes were caught on the tattoos on his fingers, Norse runes she thought. Different somehow. She didn't like them.

"Asbury Park is only the tip of the iceberg," Ashley said, and Jules recognized the gleam in her eyes. This was the predatory Ashley, taking-this-guy-home Ashley. Something about Jenner didn't sit right with Jules, from the tattoos to his careful accoutrements. Maybe he was like them, or maybe he was a poseur. Or maybe he was just a regular guy who just unintentionally checked the right boxes.

The lights were starting to hang in her eyes even when she wasn't looking at them anymore, and she started thinking about that amber bottle in the medicine cabinet again. Or the razor, wrapped in a handkerchief in her bedside table. Maybe she'd buy a straight razor. That would make it more ritualistic, and deliberate. "Let's go in the water," she said. She couldn't stand this bar, any bar, much longer.

"What, now?" Ashley asked, but she sounded more excited than doubtful. Jenner, he looked doubtful. Maybe he was wondering what kind of chicks picked him up. Maybe he would go away. That would be very nice.

"Yes, now. And then I want to go home."

The stars were bright as they could be with all the lights, no clouds Jules could see. The air was heavy, though, wet and heavy, with the pound-roar of the waves just across the street and the stutter-roar of straight pipes down the block. She crossed the road without looking, Ashley trailing behind. She didn't care if Jenner came too. She left her shoes just next to the stairs down to the sand, didn't take any of her clothes off. She just walked down across the sand, cool now with the sun long gone, and the water was so cold as it slapped her legs, spray splashing up onto her lips. She walked right in, low tide, and walked out next to Convention Hall until Ashley caught up with her and grabbed her arms. Her scars stung, her scabs lit up in the salt like little trails of fire.

"You're crazy," Ashley said, but she was laughing. Jules glanced back; Jenner was still on the beach. His cigarette flared occasionally.

"What's the deal with him?"

"He's interesting." Except for occasionally, at certain meeting places, certain festive environments, they'd never met anybody else like them. With their interests. Ritualized. Tattooed. In contact.

"I don't think he feels right."

"That's why you wanted to come out in the water? To yank my chain about Jenner?"

"No. I just wanted to." Jules was glad to be away from the lights and music. She'd wanted it, earlier. She'd probably want it again sometime soon, but it was hard to tell. "He doesn't feel right," she said again. They stood in silence for a moment, water wet silk around their hips and thighs. Ashley had taken her shirt off and was in her bikini top and cutoffs.

"I didn't notice," Ashley said. "No big, there's other fish. I'll cut this one loose."

"Thanks." Jules looked out further, to the water in front of Convention Hall. "Do you think people ever see the Morro Castle?" Was that moonlight? Was it pale shadows like she saw, or thought she saw, in the apartment? Like she sometimes saw from the corners of her eyes in the estate.

"What, like a ghost ship?" Ashley wiggled her fingers in a way she must have thought was spooky. When Jules didn't laugh, she let her arms flop to her sides, splashing a little. "Yeah, I don't know. Maybe. Didn't some other ship run aground in the same spot?"

"The New Era."

"Why are we talking about shipwrecks? It's freezing in here, let's go back."

"Is it?" Jules asked. Ashley was always a wimp when it came to the temperature. Anything cold was too cold. She turned around and took Ashley's hand, and they walked back, lifting their feet high over the knee deep waves. There were lights there too, from the boardwalk, from the big full moon, but it was different. Jules wondered if Jenner's cigarette was the same one or if he'd lit another. They hadn't been in the water all that long.

Ashley said, "Anyway, he has other plans tonight. I gave him our number, he'll call when he has a number. He's staying around town awhile I guess."

"Weird he doesn't have a cell," Jules said, and then they were up on the sand again.

"You ladies enjoy your dip?" he asked, and his smile hadn't really improved.

"Refresco," Ashley said, taking her shirt from him and pulling it on. It immediately clung to her wet bathing suit top. She rummaged in the beach bag for towels. It seemed improbable that she'd brought the beach bag back out with them as they came to the bars, but there it was.

"It must have been," he said, and Jules was too tired to figure out why he was still talking.

"Here's your towel," Ashley said, passing it over. Jules rubbed her head for a minute, then wrapped it around herself sarong style.

"Thanks." Jenner offered a cigarette, and she took it, leaning into his flickering lighter. She was shivering, she must be cold.

"Okay, nice meeting you," Ashley said, linking her arm through Jules'.

"You too. Maybe I'll call you this week," Jenner said. He watched the two of them, a little bemused.

"Or next Friday. But this week is probably fine." Ashley said, and Jules laughed.

"Goodnight!" Jules said, and Jenner gave a small wave.

"I don't know where he's staying," Ashley said as they crossed the sand.

"He's a big boy, I'm sure he's got something lined up."

"Yeah, probably." Ashley bent to pick up Jules' Converse and glanced back at Jenner. Jules looked too; he had his back to them, and was looking out over the ocean. "So you really don't like him?"

"I do not." Jules tied her laces together and hung slung the shoes over her shoulder. The cigarette didn't taste the way normal Marlboros did; maybe the box wasn't red after all. Or maybe he'd cut some weed into them or something, but it seemed strange to just hand out your weed to girls you met at the bar. People don't just give away their drugs. "Did you know him before tonight?"

"No, but Susan did. She met him at a Monmouth party."

"Is he a student?"

"Graduate student, maybe. Or maybe an adjunct professor, I don't know. She said he did tricks at the party, though."

"What do you mean, tricks?"

"Card tricks. Coin tricks. Hypnotism stuff."

"Before or after everybody got high?"

"Before, during, and after." Ashley scraped her hair back into a ponytail. They could still hear the bar sounds, people partying, but nobody else was on the street with them.

"That's kind of wild." Jules swung her shoes on the ends of the laces, just to feel the momentum. "He didn't look like a parlor tricks kind of guy. He looks like he's...serious."

"Oh he very much wanted me to think he was serious. Without saying too much obviously."

"Obviously. Maybe he left the top hat and bunnies at home until he knew we believed."

Ashley giggled. "Did you see the symbols on his fingers?"

"They're part of what bugged me. I wonder what he practices, and with who."

"We could've asked him."

"Why didn't we?"

"Because you thought he was a creep."

"Oh yeah." Jules thought a moment. Was an educated creep better than trying to initiate a novice? No. "Besides, we know we need to be careful."

"We do." Ashley dug in the beach bag again, this time for their house keys, as they stood on their honeysuckle smelling front porch. No, it was too early for honeysuckles, why did Jules smell them?

They crept up the shifting stairs, giggling because they were trying so hard to be quiet, hushing each other, giggling more. Despite having walked from the beach barefoot, Jules was still leaving sandy footprints through the foyer and on the carpet, and Mr. Donofrio wouldn't be happy about that. Not like she could vacuum now, that would start a revolution. Everybody else was asleep. They stumbled around their dark apartment, knocking into end tables and as they felt along the wall for the light switches, Yorick tripping them as he bumped his head into their knees and hips. "I need a shower," Jules said.

"It's up to you." Ashley was somehow sand free, Jules didn't know how she did it.

"Goodnight." She took Yorick out first, smoking a slow and careful cigarette on the front lawn as he did his business. She'd forgotten to leash him, but it didn't matter at the moment, in the quiet dark. He led the way back up to the apartment.

Jules forgot the cardinal rule of post beach disrobing, that you did it in the shower, and dropped her suit and clothes on the floor in a shower of sand and tiny shells and rocks. She turned the water on and waited for things to steam up, wiggling her toes in the residual grit. She'd drag the vacuum in here tomorrow.

Chapter Ten

Jules woke to the smell of fresh coffee and rolled over, pawing her phone off the night stand. 9:30. Not exactly the crack of dawn, but what was Ashley thinking? She opened her crooked bedroom door and let Yorick out first while she went to take her morning meds; an experiment, she took the anti-inflammatory only. Maybe she wouldn't need the painkiller. Yorick padded heavily across the hardwood sea of the living room, no nail clicks, and started crunching kibble. So not Ashley, then. She wouldn't have fed him.

Ashley appeared in her doorway with a mug of coffee. "What's going on?" Jules asked.

"Una's here," Ashley said, rolling her eyes.

"Why? How?"

"I don't know. But she made us coffee. So far."

Out in the kitchen, Una was putting away the dishes from the rack. "Good morning, Juliet," she said, and had coffee poured before Jules did much more than stare at her.

"What's...going on?"

"Oh, I had John drop me off. He was going up to Fort Monmouth for something and will grab me on his way home."

"I've been gone a day, you missed me that much?"

"Well, I know you girls aren't much for cooking, so I made him stop at the store too, and thought I'd make you some whirlybirds!"

"Some what?" Jules asked, glancing at Ashley, who was leaned over the stove to light her cigarette, hair held back with one hand. Ashley shook her head and went out on the balcony.

"Whirly birds. Pork roll sandwiches?" Una paused with the grocery bag in her hand and laughed.

"Oh. Why do you call them that?"

"I must've gotten it from Dad. I think he said that's what they called them in high school?"

"Oh." Jules sipped her coffee and Yorick came to stand against her, head pointed up to look into her face. He didn't love Una, but he liked being fed. And he liked pork roll. "Yeah, that'll be fine. Good, I mean. Thanks."

"You're welcome!" Una was already getting out their singular nonstick frying pan, the cutting board, a wooden handled knife. Outside, the street was starting to hum, passing cars, people walking. It was hard for Jules to remember it wasn't June or July yet. It was hard for Jules to remember it wasn't still that Indian summer day in October. It was hard for Jules to remember—

Yorick poked his nose up under her elbow, hard enough she almost dropped her mug.

"Whoops, forgot to take my meds," Jules said.

"Oh no! Can I get you anything else?"

"I can take them with coffee." Well she did, anyway. Maybe she wasn't supposed to.

Ashley poked her head in as Jules left the kitchen. "You okay?"

"Handling it," she said. Ashes nodded, withdrew. Jules closed the bedroom door before Yorick could follow her in, set her coffee cup down on the edge of her big white porcelain bathroom sink and went to her nightstand for the razor. She folded the waistband of her yoga pants down and considered her uncovered skin, the cat scratches she'd made there. Why did it help? She knew better. But it helped. Fuck it. Her father was dead. She'd almost died. Somehow, it drove the weirdness in her vision back to the edges, let her breathe easier, made her head pound less. None of it went *away*. Just subsided. She rinsed the razor with alcohol, patted the new cut briefly with a tissue.

Remembered to bring her coffee back to the kitchen. Ashley was at the table, her coffee topped off.

"So Una, am I crazy, or did you say you'd met a guy when I was talking to you the other night?

"No, I said I met a guy. I mean, it's not we're 'dating' or anything yet." She actually made air quotes, despite the spatula in her hand. "But I've talked to him at some parties at school."

"Does your dad know?" Ashley asked.

"Well, no," Una said. "And...I might be going to see him tonight, and might have used you guys as an excuse, actually, and said I was staying over don'tbemad." She pulled the last of the pork roll from the pan and turned around to look at Ashley and Jules, who looked at each other for a moment, and then burst out laughing. Una blushed tomato pink and turned her back on them to make the sandwiches. "Stop, you guys," she mumbled.

"Una, no, sweetie, we're laughing with you. Or we're laughing with relief. Something like that. You'd get in so much fucking trouble, well I guess you wouldn't because you're free white and twenty one, but you know what I mean. Conrad would be *livid*," Ashley said. Una plopped the plates on the table, sat in one of the chairs.

"I know. That's why I lied."

"Well there's only one way to fix it," Ashley said, insouciant all of the sudden. Jules picked up her sandwich and gave Ashes a sidelong glance.

"What's that?" she and Una asked at once.

"Well, you take us to the party, and we tell your dad and other individuals involved that *we* strong armed *you* into going."

"I didn't say anything about the party!"

"But you didn't say there wasn't!" Ashley crowed. "I knew it! Where is it?"

"I don't know if I should..."

"Come on, Una, we're complicit now. Might as well take it all the way," Jules said with her mouth full. "And this is really good."

"Thanks."

Chapter Eleven

J ules had been under the impression that The Empress performed as a normal hotel, not as a venue for a building-wide party, but maybe somebody just rented the whole thing. She could do that if she wanted. Or, the party just got too big, too much of a monster, and the overnight staff of the hotel were battened down somewhere. But it felt like a huge house party.

Una led them there, but once inside, she looked positively tharn.

"What's the occasion, anyway?" Ashley asked, a beer suddenly in her hands. Jules blinked at it for a minute; she literally did not see Ashley acquire said beer.

"I don't know. Somebody got out of jail or is going to jail. Or maybe it's a graduation party. Oh wait, no, Sam's going into the Army, that's what the party is for." Una babbled for a while, and then stopped.

"So it's a Monmouth party, here? Who's Sam?" Jules asked, even as Ashley was nodding. Mostly to be obtuse.

"No, it's not a *Monmouth* party. But you know, Sam. Straw colored hair? Gets his jeans at the tack store out on 34?"

"Oh, right." Big Sam was said to run a rope through the belt loops on said dark-dyed, very stiff jeans and hang them off the jetty into the ocean for a week or so to get them broken in. Jules was unclear on whether he washed them or not after they came out of their Atlantic baptism. Jeans like that used to come from the Army-Navy store, her dad told her, and were broken in the very same way. "*Big* Sam."

"Yeah, see, you know who he is. I think he's wearing a Varsity jacket today."

"I didn't think Big Sam was on the Varsity team. Any Varsity team."

"He's not, he got kicked off for drinking, and then beat somebody up and took his." Even though she was right next to them, Una seemed to be fading in the crowd, like a magazine picture left out in the sun.

"Ladies, a pleasure to see you again." Jenner was there with them, offering cigarettes. She took one, and then pulled back when he tried to light it, squinting. There was a line of text painstakingly written down the side of it in black pen, in a language she didn't know.

"What's this?" she asked. Ashley was already smoking hers, and if there was writing, it was on the other side. Probably smoking hadn't been allowed in The Empress since the eighties. Probably somebody had rented the whole place and was going to pay for the deep cleaning. It's the kind of thing Jules could afford, if she did that kind of thing.

"Just a thing I do to pass the time."

"I've never seen anybody write on cigarettes before." Would it be a big deal if she smoked his cigarette? What could he have charmed it to do, anyway? She had protections.

"Like I said, it's a thing I do." Jenner seemed pleased she had even noticed, and offered his lighter again, an all-black Zippo. Jules took hers out, lit her own damn cigarette. Cleansing fire.

"Jules knows all kinds of poetry. She's always reading; Shakespeare and Shirley Jackson and Stephen King and stuff." As always, Una was happy to talk about everybody but herself. She was flushed across the cheeks; so that's why she wanted to come to this party.

"The classics," Jenner said with a smile.

"Yeah, sure, the classics." The estate library was stocked with the classics; maybe they were the contemporaries, when the books were purchased. Jules hadn't read anything since her father died; it just dried up.

"Whereas I'm more into music," Ashley interjected. "Well, Jules does that too."

"Oh, do you ladies play?" Jenner asked. What a weird grandpa question.

"Piano some," she said. "I don't have one, so I'm probably horribly out of practice. Jules plays violin, when she feels like it."

"There might be a piano here somewhere," Jules said with a wicked grin. Ashley looked at her with wide 'you shut your mouth' eyes. "And the Pony does, obviously, but they don't let just anybody on stage there." It had been years since Ashley played the piano, Jules happened to know. Somewhere between one and five. She'd somehow acquired a beer as well. There was a beer fairy around, it would seem, who behaved as a reverse tooth fairy. Jenner did not ask her to whip out a violin and go to town. Good. That would've been a little too The Devil Went Down to Georgia.

"Anyway, Jenner, you didn't say you'd made new friends here already," Ashley said playfully, with a pointed look at Una.

"I do apologize. I thought we were of like interests, not that you had romantic designs." He draped an arm across Una's shoulders. His right arm; there were snake fangs down his first two fingers. A chill crawled down Jules' spine despite the hot crowded room. "I've already been bewitched, you see. What a coincidence that the three of you know each other, though. Can I take you to dinner tomorrow?"

"I'll have to see if I'm working," Ashley said casually. Jenner looked at Jules.

"What about you, can you come? I think Una's more comfortable with friends around." Una nodded, eyes pleading with Jules.

"Out to dinner tomorrow? I don't know if I'm up for it, but the rest of you should go. Excuse me." Jules set down her empty can and went in search of the nearest bathroom.

It was like edge-of-summer Mardi Gras or something. There were a lot of green bead necklaces draped on people and left in broken desultory piles on the hall carpeting, maybe a stray box of St. Patrick's Day paraphernalia unearthed for the occasion. Almost all of the room doors were open up and down the halls, with people in and out, smoking, dancing, drinking. Radios were on in a bunch of the rooms, some of them tuned to the same station, some not. The whole place rented or not, this was A Lot.

She found a room with people watching The Wizard of Oz with the sound off, and with Dark Side of the Moon on and thumping the walls on a turntable that was perched on top of the television and looked to Jules like it might slide off the back at any moment. Who knew there'd still be CRTs in the rooms and not flat screens, wasn't this whole place remodeled lately? Jules felt like she'd somehow slid into the very edge of another time, maybe back when her parents would be partying in the same town, as though Gladys had ever deigned to do such a thing. Dad and Uncle Hector then. The group was five girls and three guys, all piled together like sleepy puppies on the still-made king sized bed, eyes fixed on the flickering screen, mouths open just a little. Some of them were smoking, and the yellow cut-glass ashtrays on the bedside tables were overflowing with butts.

"Can I just use your bathroom?" Jules asked.

One of the girls, a redhead, looked up. "Yeah, it's empty. You cool?"

"No."

"Too bad. This is great on shrooms. Or just pot."

"I'm sorry."

"It's okay, you can still use the bathroom." Nobody else even looked up. Jules wondered if they had already used whatever they were holding, leaving the redhead sober.

The bathroom was pristine, every individually wrapped thing still wrapped, including the towels. The sink positively sparkled, the toilet and bathtub the same. Jules had never seen the Empress bathrooms, or rooms before, she wasn't sure if they were usually like this or not. This time and place. She closed the door and locked it, looked in the mirror. Her eyes were a little dilated, a little bloodshot. She looked okay, though, calm. The way she typically hoped she would look. She dug a single painkiller out of the watch pocket of her jeans. She didn't want to open any of the cups, they just looked too right like that, in their little wrappers. She cupped her palm under the faucet and swallowed the pill with just-cold water.

Maybe if she only took them one at a time, she didn't have a problem.

Maybe if she only took them one at a time, she wouldn't feel so much like she needed the next one. There were razors here on the countertop, and a spot in the wall to put the used ones. Just like the olden days. She wanted to drag Ashes into the bathroom and describe what she saw. She was afraid Ashes would see a different bathroom. Pink Floyd thumping in her ears like a heartbeat, she pulled a razor out. She left the water running and looked at herself in the mirror, then undid her jeans and pulled them down, just a little. She did it just below where the waistband of her underwear rode, three quick cuts, stinging but sparkling and making everything more real. Everything a little more focused, even through the comfortable painkiller cotton wool fuzz. She pushed the razor into the throw-away slot, looked at the blood beading on her skin. She hadn't gotten any on the pristine bathroom surfaces. She flushed the toilet, ran her hands under the water, pulled up her jeans and buttoned them. The bathroom was still pink.

Jules wiped her hands on the seat of her jeans and walked out; none of the people on the bed had moved. "Thanks," she said, and the redhead's eyes flicked to her for a second.

"You're welcome! Enjoy the party."

"I will. You too."

Ashley, Una, and Jenner were almost where she left them. Closer to the door, in a quieter corner amidst the chaos. Jenner reached over and didn't quite touch one of Ashley's tattoos, and Jules wished she could read lips to see what he asked her, and what Ashley answered. She was laughing when she did, though. Una said something too. There was no telling what they talked about. She almost left without saying anything.

Instead of walking away, she went back to them. "This place is crazy," she said.

"Isn't it, though?" Ashley answered with a grin.

"Kind of loud for comfortable conversation," Jenner said. Jules was still trying to figure out the tattoo on his neck without staring. A circle with lines through it. Not a pentagram, she knew what that looked like, there were more lines than that, and kind of hooked at the ends. Like he thought the stuff in Lovecraft was real.

"Well who needs comfortable conversation? What does that even mean?" Ashley had a red Solo cup.

"It means it's hard to talk about anything serious in an atmosphere like this."

"I don't know where you come from, where serious and comfortable equate to the same thing. That's just bizarre." Ashley looked at Jules; oh hah hah, talk about something serious.

"Maybe I'm not putting my point across." He spoke earnestly, looking into Ashley's eyes. His eyes were very dark, Jules noticed. Almost completely black, like Heathcliff's.

"Oh, you just need to not take Ashley seriously," Jules said. "She's broken more than one heart that way. Sonnets have been composed on many a men's room wall about Ashley's fickle nature."

"You stop that!" Ashley squealed with laughter and gave Jules a shove. They both dissolved into laughter. Jenner smiled like a man not getting the joke but unwilling to ask, looking between the two of them.

"You two have been a pair for quite some time," he said.

"Ages." Jules said. "We were degenerates who smoked by the fence together."

"So what do you do, then?"

"Mostly bum around Asbury Park and pick up guys."

"Oh, so you're roommates?"

"Sure are," Jules said, pulling Ashley's cigarettes out of her hip pocket. Jenner obliged with a light again, and Jules let him this time. She looked at the tattoos on his hands and arms, not bothering to be discreet about it. What the hell, anyway. Una took a cigarette too, and Jenner lit it for her without hesitation. Una didn't smoke; Jules watched this with interest.

"Do you have any tattoos?" Jenner asked, looking from Jules to Ashley and back again.

"No." Jules said, cigarette held between tattooed fingers.

"Yes!" Ashley said at the same time, waving her same tattooed fingers. She and Jules locked eyes, and then burst out laughing. Squeals near the front door and sudden flashing lights confirmed that the party was in fact illegal, and over.

"This way," Jenner said, catching Una's hand in his and pulling her away from the front door, through a hall past the check-in desk. Ashley and Jules followed, and soon they banged out a metal fire door in the back which did not sound an alarm and were running across the nearly deserted street, asphalt still hot from a day in the pounding sun, as thunder scattered across the sky above them and cold rain droplets began to fall. They cut across a block, through backyards and across fences, then were back on the sidewalk and up the street to Ocean Avenue again, Convention Hall suddenly across the street from them, cars tooting their horns, people lined up on the boardwalk in front of the restaurant that was Howard Johnson's for so many years and Jules could remember as nothing else.

"Pity Madame Marie's isn't open this late," Ashley said, breathless, lighting a cigarette.

"She'd make a killing if she only opened at night, I'd think," Jules said.

"It isn't even the original Madame Marie," Jenner said dismissively.

"Like you'd fucking know. It's her niece or something. Whatever. Even a fortune telling old Italian woman isn't going to live forever." Jules stuck a cigarette between her lips and leaned in to light hers off Ashley's. "They foretell the bad shit and then leave future generations to deal with it."

"Oh do you have much experience in that?" Jenner asked. Of course he didn't like her tone. Good.

"Sure, we're three generations deep into some kind of curse, the Duncan family is."

"Duncan?" Jenner looked at her narrowly. He was still holding Una's hand.

"Ooh, I don't get to say this often enough. Don't you know who I am?" Jules grinned.

"I do not."

"She's Juliet Duncan. Of the railroad Duncans," Una said in a somewhat crestfallen tone. Jenner kissed her hand, his eyes still on Jules.

"I didn't know we were amongst a legitimate descendant of American robber barons, it's extraordinary," he said.

"I'm sure you've been in the presence of illegitimate ones," Jules said, drawing on her cigarette. Lightning flashed out over the ocean and the thunder rattled through again. Why were they still standing here with this guy?

"Yes, but they probably didn't know it. And they didn't have the strange distinction of following matrilineal lines."

"Oh yes, the Duncan Habit." Gladys was born a Duncan. The Duncan women were the queens, as it were, and the Duncan husbands, consorts; either they took the Duncan name or kept their own, but all the children would be Duncans. The first railroad Duncan, Adele, was an 1800s widowed suffragette, lawyer, and entrepreneur. There wasn't actually a curse. Or, there hadn't actually been a curse. Who was to say anymore. "Surprised you know."

"Studying an area's local history is of interest to me."

"He won't tell me where he's from," Una said. She still held a cigarette, but it had long since gone out.

"A history hobo," Jules said. Maybe the running plus the booze plus the painkillers were why she couldn't really feel her hands. It wasn't alarming, it wasn't a cold disconnected numbness. Kind of a warm encompassing fuzziness, like whatever her hands and fingers were doing was probably okay. Her right hand was managing the cigarette adroitly. No words written on this one, no symbols either. Through the cold rain, the heat billowed from the street still. The ocean crashed with the thunder, and Jules looked across the street; at least they'd finally torn down that steel skeleton of everybody-forgot-what-it-was-supposed-to-be.

They didn't talk more. Or they did, but Jules just watched the lightning spider across the sky and light up the clouds and the waves. It wasn't raining much anymore. It wasn't any cooler out, either. Instead, the humidity had reached a state not unlike standing in a giant's mouth. Una still looked a little bit panicked, and was clutching Jenner's hand.

Jenner maybe didn't like being called a hobo, and studied Convention Hall for a moment before leading them down onto the beach and over to the stairs up to the promenade.

"I don't think we're supposed to be out here after dark," Una said dubiously.

"Don't worry, we can escape into the ocean," Jules said.

"I just thought sitting for a little while might be nice before I took you girls home," Jenner said, and Una smiled.

"So what do you do for fun around here?" Jenner asked.

"You didn't realize this was it?" Jules asked.

"I would have thought a railroad robber baroness would have higher brow diversions," he said.

"Well the hellfire club isn't something we talk about with the uninitiated," she said distractedly. She was still looking out over the water, imagining a ship on the sandbar there, smoke billowing from it. There wasn't any particular reason she was hung up on the story of the Morro Castle. It had just come into her brain and stayed there, like when a song was stuck. Ashley elbowed her nonchalantly, making it look like they were just fumbling for cigarettes.

"I knew it!" He gave her a too-slick grin, a practiced in front of the mirror grin. She wondered how he'd chosen the ponytail, or if it had something to do with his practice. Maybe he pulled it loose and let it hang when he was intoning things he read from the book of the Mad Arab Abdul Alhazred. Shit. She burned her fingers on her cigarette and dropped it onto the promenade, twisting the toe of her Converse on it to make sure it was properly out. The pounding surf was soothing to her. Womblike, a heartbeat.

"What next?" Ashley asked. She sounded far more sober than Jules felt, and disappointed by it. Jules stole a look at Una, who seemed mostly content. She probably hadn't drunk the beer she'd been holding. Una was a cipher, and not. Jenner was the first guy she'd really been involved with, certainly the first guy Jules knew her to lie to Conrad about and sneak around for. But Una also seemed uncomfortable with Jenner, like her skin didn't fit right, and she was on uneven footing. She seemed like she was smiling because he thought she should smile, not because she felt like smiling.

"The night is young, isn't it? We could go to one of your storied bars again. We could go to the restaurant right outside. Any number of things are within our grasp."

"I might just go home," Jules said, straightening up.

"Not alone you're not," Ashley said immediately.

"Well. Yorick is there."

"We don't let each other walk home alone."

"You could still have a fun night, I'll be okay."

"It's the rules, Juliet," Una said primly.

"Oh not you too." But yes, especially Una.

"You can walk us home, Jenner, and we'll figure out dinner for another night," Ashley said. The rain was done now, the pavement steaming gently in the street lights as they left the beach. Jules didn't want Jenner to know where they lived. Jenner probably already knew where they lived. Jenner came here for a reason.

"Okay, that's fine," Jenner said, his tone carefully good natured but Jules saw a flash in his dark, dark eyes that she didn't trust or like and couldn't quite read. Jenner was one of those random outliers she felt she needed to be careful around, not because he was a particular danger to her specifically, though maybe he would become one, but because he seemed like he was a danger to Una and thus a calculating predator, a manipulator, in addition to fancying himself some sort of mystical figure. She hadn't seen anything yet to prove or disprove, just the tattoos, just some heavy-handed conversational hints. Maybe he knew something real. Maybe he didn't.

What she and Ashley knew was real.

Jules always forgot about the smell of wet concrete until it was all around her. It was impossible to describe, like salt and sand but not, a rough and callous scent that was somehow comforting, and made her think of hopscotch chalk washing away, of leaves turning inside out in sudden summer storm winds, of rain steaming up off hot asphalt, all the summertime things. It was too early for any honeysuckles to be blooming, but she smelled those too, especially climbing their porch, where the honeysuckle bushes encroached on the slate front walk. Maybe a neighbor had honeysuckle shampoo or something.

"And this is where we leave you," Jules said, as Ashley got out the key for the front door. Of course it was late enough for every other tenant to be asleep. Why did they pick the third floor again? "Carry me," she said to Ashley, holding out her arms.

"Sorry, babe." They closed the door quietly behind them. Jenner still stood on the sidewalk in front of the house and Una wiggle-finger waved at him.

"See, we should've kept John. He could've done it."

"Ah, but would he have? That is the question."

"Whether 'tis nobler...oh, fuck it."

Chapter Twelve

Ashley and Jules took Una home the next morning, in the Bug, a vintage model Volkswagen Beetle which had been manufactured only a couple of years before. Ashley's mom had gone to Mexico on a "business trip" (air quotes were always employed) and bought the car to drive home. It was Ashley's twenty-first birthday present. It was red and had those silly long eyelashes decals on the front headlights. Yorick and Jules sat in the back seat and took in the sights, Yorick's ears folded back. Airplaned, her dad used to say.

"We need to get him Doggles," Ashley said.

"I'll ask Mr. Crab sometime." Jules waved at the security guys as they pulled up. They waved back, and Una climbed out of the car.

"Aren't you going to come say hello to your mother?" Una asked.

"I'm sure she's working," Jules said. "Tell her I said hi and I ate food and whatever else you deem appropriate. I trust you."

"Okay," Una said dubiously. The front door swung open as she climbed the stairs, and Mr. Poling walked out with Hector, who put his hand briefly on Una's shoulder before looking past her to the car. Ashley had already pulled away, so Jules didn't feel like it was necessary to move and acknowledge him. He'd think she hadn't seen him.

"So what do you think?" Jules asked as they rolled back down the driveway. Juno ran on the grass alongside the car, and Yorick barked at her companionably, face split in a big doggie grin.

"About what?"

"About everything. Whether Una should move in with us. Whether Jenner is a big terrible creep."

"Well. What do *you* think?"

"I think Jenner is a big terrible creep and he might be dangerous or know enough to be dangerous. Una should absolutely move in with us. She'll make us three, which we've needed, and it'll get her away from Hector. And we can keep an eye on her while she's running around with Jenner, until we can run him off."

"Get her away from Hector?" Ashley said, craning her head to check for cars as she turned into traffic.

"Hector's a bigger danger than Jenner," Jules said.

"Aw, what's wrong with Hector?"

It was Hector.

Jules didn't say anything for a long moment. Maybe too long.

It was Hector.

"Jules, what is that?" Ashley glanced over her shoulder.

"What is what?"

"What did I hear? And my arm's all goosebumps, look." She held up her right arm.

It was Hector.

"Nothing." *IT WAS HECTOR.* Her head pounded, and Yorick licked his lips and yawned. "Not right now. When we're home again."

"Jules, seriously." Her voice strained thin.

"When we're home, Ashes." She slumped in her corner of the backseat, sunglasses pushed so tightly up the bridge of her nose they slipped when she blinked. Yorick lay down and shoved his head under her hands, and she pet him reflexively, scratching her fingers into his ears and the back of his neck until he groaned and kicked his back foot a little, eyes half closed in pleasure.

Ashley went through the McDonald's drive through and got them fries and iced coffees and a twenty piece. She ordered Puck and Yorick each a cheeseburger, just the burger and cheese, no onions or ketchup or anything. He twitched his long nose towards the front seat once the bag of food was there, but otherwise didn't move from Jules' side.

Once they were home and settled on the couch, Ashley peeled the papers and stuck both straws in the drinks, handed Jules hers, then settled back into the couch, eyes intent. "Now spill."

"It isn't as easy as that," Jules said, but of course it was. She'd meant to earlier. It was just easier not to. "I couldn't just...I had to know if dad knew what happened, who did it. So I called him." She paused, and breathed, and then sipped some of her coffee. It coated her throat, milky and sweet. Ashley waited. "He said it was Hector," she said at last.

"I cannot believe you did that on your own," Ashley said.

"I drew a circle. And Yorick was with me."

"That's not good enough. It's dangerous, Jules. You don't know if you actually called your dad. Well, you called your dad, but you don't know if he's who or what answered."

"I know that. That's the only reason Hector is still alive. Because I don't know if he really did it."

Ashes was quiet for a long time, long enough for Jules to consider what she'd just said. "Is that what was happening in the car, you still heard him? It?"

"Yes. And you heard it too, which makes me a little more comfortable in my sanity."

"Glad I could help. I'll be more happy right after I hose the Bug off with some holy water."

"Might not be a bad plan anyway. Protection is never a bad plan."

"I know that. You know that. Which is what makes this so fucked up. I can't believe you didn't call me for this."

"I was home. I needed to know and Gladys would never have gone for a sleepover. So I got the rotary phone out of his office and did a circle and...did it."

"The rotary phone?"

"I couldn't find his cell. Still can't."

"Well you're not gonna find it here."

"No shit, Ashes. Thanks."

They sat in silence for several moments. "I can't believe you didn't tell me sooner," Ashley said in a smaller voice.

"I think I needed to process it." It was still hard to remember, from minute to minute, that her dad was dead.

Ashley nodded a little. "Or you needed to know you could trust me."

Jules grabbed her hand. "Of course I could trust you."

"So what else is going on? What's this about Una?"

"Well, he's being kind of creepy uncle with her, I think. But probably not Una. I think he might hurt Gladys. If it was him. If he got Dad out of the way so he could be with her. But at this point he might want her out of the way so he can just have lots of money and a railroad. The problem is, I didn't die. So he'd have to try again for me too."

"So Una's the one you can get away from him. Obviously Gladys makes her own decisions, and probably wouldn't understand your accusing him. He's been such a help to her, always there for all of them, et cetera." Ashes fed Yorick his burger in slow pieces. He took them delicately, like a gentleman. Puck hovered on her shoulder, a lock of hair grasped in one of his tiny ferret hands, and he watched the goings on with his ink drop eyes. "And you're here now."

"Yeah. Which might not be safer for me, really. If somebody kills me now, it just looks like they came back to finish the job. Maybe the cops will get lucky and whoever the murderer is will leave enough forensic evidence to get caught this time." Jules drank more of her coffee. The room was doing a slow spin, and she couldn't tell if she was hung over, if it was the head injury, or both. Or talking about murder. She hadn't planned how she'd kill Hector, if it came to that. Maybe it was better not to plan. Less to go wrong. "But Una might be safer here. Especially if she's going to be sneaking around. And anyway, with Jenner, especially with Jenner, we can help her."

"Did you tell anybody else about this? John?"

"Fucking no, of course not. You think I can tell John anything?"

"He might listen."

"Listen and then go and tell Gladys and Hector so they can have me committed. Hey, then he wouldn't have to kill me, right?" Jules sighed and lit a cigarette. "Let's talk about the Jenner thing. I can't talk about home anymore right this second."

"Okay. I can't get a read on him. Other than my initial one," Ashley said. "And now I'm wondering if I should be suspicious of that. He hasn't really said much. Said much, with words, he's still being really fucking coy. But his tattoos say an awful lot."

"They're pretty scattered thematically. Well, I guess the runes and the snake can be linked. The snake dripping poison on...Loki's face? When he's tied to the roots of the World Tree for being a dick. But the thing on his neck?"

"Yeah. I think he thought it was a Key of Solomon."

"Well I did when I first saw it." Jules thought a moment. "Or maybe it's better to think he was mistaken, than to think he's actually following the Necronomicon?"

"Maybe. But it's made up, seriously. What are you gonna get if you try to use the Necronomicon?"

Jules shrugged. "People say the Bible is made up."

"Well, yeah, but in the case of the Necronomicon we had Lovecraft say 'yeah, I made that shit up. Creepy, right?' And everybody was like, 'that rascally ol' H.P.' and had a good chuckle. Nobody has a good chuckle over the Bible."

"Well. They do."

Ashley rolled her eyes. "Okay, few people believe the Bible was written by a racist horror writer in the early 1900's."

"There you go. Though I guess we should just maybe not talk about Scientology at all right?"

"Right." She slurped some coffee. "So wait, what were we talking about?"

"Una moving in. The Jenner problem."

"I don't know if Una is exactly ready to learn any of the truths we have a handle on."

"Maybe not. But do you want her to learn from him? Or us?"

"If she's got to learn, us. We don't know what he does. Or if he knows what he's doing. The snake fang hand thing isn't exactly friendly." Ashley picked at her french fries, feeding the occasional one to Yorick.

"We've just run into so few...others...it's hard to anticipate what he's all about. It's not like we all fucked off to Harry Potter school or Brakebills and had teachers and classrooms."

"We had a teacher." Fries finished, Ashley moved on to the chicken nuggets. "They only give four sauce packets for twenty nuggets? Stingy bastards."

"You can have mine." Ashley wasn't wrong. They'd met MaryAnne entirely by accident, and she'd overheard some quasi occult conversation they'd been having and either decided she needed to be part of three for a little while, or that they were close enough to the truth that she needed to set them on the right kind of path. "Have you heard from her?"

"No. We're having our solo period of learning or whatever. She'll come back when it's time, she said."

"She didn't text or anything when—"

"No, she didn't." Yorick snuffled his nose closer to the chicken nuggets and Jules snapped her fingers at him. It didn't quite work, the noise wasn't terribly sharp as her fingers mostly worked, but he got the picture and moved away to spread out on a bare portion of the wooden floor with a world-weary sigh.

Ashley tested the warmth of Puck's burger, unwrapped it, and set it on the floor for him. Yorick rolled his eyes towards it without lifting his head, and sighed mightily. "I'm not sure there's any way to know when MaryAnne will think will be the right time. Especially since it seems like now."

"You're right about that." Jules watched Puck eating. "So what then? How?"

"Well, we let her move in first. We'll make the tower room the bean bag, music, and 'incense' room instead, give her the other bedroom."

"And then once she moves in start watching The Craft all the time and do each other's make up and Tarot cards?" Jules grinned.

Ashley threw a french fry at her. It spun onto the floor, and Yorick stared at it, ears forward and mouth closed, until Jules pointed at it, and he crawled over to pick it up. "Light as a feather, stiff as a board."

"We need to get her a deck. Your first deck should always be a gift."

"We should get a yard sale or thrift store one, not an Amazon one."

"Obviously," Jules said. She finished her coffee and watched Ashley eat most of the chicken nuggets. "Do you think Hector killed my dad?" she asked, hating how plaintive her voice sounded

"Honey, I don't know either. I wouldn't've thought so. Best friends for how long? But jealousy is one of those things I guess." Ashley pushed the bag to Jules. "The rest are yours. You didn't eat anything yet! Do you want me to melt cheese on your fries?"

"Sure."

Ashley took the bag and went to the kitchen. When she dumped the fries into a bowl they rattled like kibble, and Yorick trotted out to investigate his food bowl for offerings. Their downstairs neighbor must think a small elephant moved in, Jules thought. Maybe they should get more rugs. The microwave roared like a mini jet engine, and Ashley rattled around in the silverware drawer for a moment until it beeped.

"I think the kitchen threshold is kinda weird, do you?" she asked, coming back and handing Jules the bowl of melty cheese fries and a fork.

"Weird how? I don't think I'm the best judge of weird right now." She got up, though, and wandered over. The thing about looking for weird was confirmation bias; either you found it because you were looking for it, or you didn't, because why would you find it? But no, that threshold was weird. She didn't smell anything she shouldn't, the floor didn't wiggle, her skin didn't tingle or go numb. But it felt like any one of those things could happen, or could have happened before. "Okay it wasn't always weird, right?" It was so hard to doubt herself so much.

"Nope." Ashley pushed past her and back into the kitchen. "Where's the sea salt?"

"You think I know? You're the one who's been here."

Ashes opened the cabinet nearest the fridge, and stretched on her tippy toes. "Found it!"

"I don't have the energy for this right now."

"I'm just gonna put a line down, we can worry more about it later. We'll figure something out."

Jules laughed. "That's our motto, after all."

"We'll figure out what it means in Latin and get matching tattoos!"

Chapter Thirteen

The first time Jenner came for dinner, he bought flowers and a bottle of wine. Both liquor store specials, Jules thought. After the food was eaten and the dishes in the sink, he took out a dented Altoids tin with a couple of joints in it and offered them around. Maybe it was his idea of a real hostess gift. Where was he from, anyway? He seemed kind of like a California guy, but a nineties TV version of a California guy, like on Buffy the Vampire Slayer where some people were in shorts and tank tops and other people were in jeans and leather jackets and you just had to wonder what the temperature in LA really was like anyway.

Una wasn't done moving in yet, and things seemed to be moving slowly and quickly. Jules and Ashley hadn't gotten her a tarot deck yet, but all of her boxes were in her room. Jules wished she could've been there for the conversation with Mr. Poling about Una's desire to move. Or maybe it wasn't bad at all.

John helped with the move, of course, and it was strange to see him out of his security suit again, in jeans and a T-shirt like a real boy. Jules wondered, sometimes, if she could just be happy with him. That might be impossible by this point, with all her manipulations and machinations to bait him, watch him squirm and get angry, see how far she could push him.

Jenner walked around with a glass of the wine, a red of course, and inspected the art on the walls. Their room doors closed, so the field of play was mostly the living room and the tower room. A bunch of it was vintage band posters Ashley's mom gave them, new versions of what she had in her dorm when she was a kid, Zeppelin and Pink Floyd and Jethro Tull.

Their one framed piece of actual art was their one open but not open concession to being witches. A dark haired woman stood barefoot next to a smoking and bubbling brass cauldron, tracing a circle into the ground with a hot poker, or a sword. Some days Jules thought it was a sword more than other days. Five crows or ravens were outside the circle, and she had flowers tucked into the cloth belt of her flowing dress. Were the birds helpers, or were the birds harmful, kept away by the circle? Was the nearby caravan's open door where she had come from or where she was going?

"Interesting choices," Jenner said as he finished his rounds. He'd also scrutinized all the items on their shelves, assorted metal chalices because once you start buying them at thrift stores, you just keep finding more at thrift stores. The old rosaries that filled them, for the same reason. Jules especially couldn't just leave a secondhand rosary in the store where she'd found it. A Tibetan singing bowl, Ashley's collection of incense burners, ornate glass vials of holy water. The stuff on the shelves was okay for public viewing; their chalk, their tarot cards, their real candles, those were all locked away in their rooms. It was better for those items to not be casually handled, though Una was the only innocent in the room, which made her valuable in her own way.

"Ashley's mom is quite the world traveler," Jules said, nursing her own glass of wine. The turntable was on the coffee table for the occasion, and Puck perched nearby on the couch, watching the vinyl spin, mesmerized.

"Janie got me a necklace in Ireland," Una said. "It's what, Connemara marble?"

"I think so," Ashley said. "Why don't you wear it?"

"I don't really wear crosses," Una said, blushing a little.

"Well, you might get attacked by an atheist," Jules said. Yorick was laying on the floor by her feet, head up, watching Jenner. It was partly a letdown and partly a relief when Jenner walked through the door and all the dog did was sniff him all over intently and then dismiss him. Jules wanted very much to just dismiss him. Yorick watched him, though. So, not an immediate threat but.

"So Jenner, what do you do?" Ashley asked, with all the pointed interest and hostess politeness of a housewife whose knives were freshly sharpened.

"I travel a lot, though not so globally as your mother, apparently. I work when I can. Just lately I picked up a job as a short order cook. And I...educate myself." All three girls, as if on cue, waited and sipped their wine. "I was born in California, but haven't been back there in years."

I knew it, Jules almost yelled.

"Educate yourself?" Una asked, before anybody else could, a teensy frown puckering her normally untroubled brow. "Like online classes?"

"Sort of. I do have a degree in philosophy." Of course, Jules thought. "But I've also worked on history, and religion, and ancient studies. It's amazing where you can find teachers."

"It sure is," Jules said dryly. Like a coffee house. Like on the train to Manhattan. Like in a used book store.

Jenner added some more wine to his glass and held the bottle around. "More?"

"No thanks," Una said. She'd barely touched her first glass. Ashley also shook her head.

Jules held her glass out. "Sure." She wondered if that was the moment the pieces finally fell into place for Jenner. He caught her eye as he poured the wine, and then looked at her tattoos again, from her fingers to her wrist, to the Hanged man on her shoulder. All of her silver jewelry.

He held the bottle out to Ashley anyway, an excuse to look her up and down again as he said "Are you sure?" with that stupid smarmy smile plastered on his face. Ashley's shoulder tattoo was the queen of swords.

It was so petty, Jules' satisfaction at watching his realization that she and Ashley were not just Jersey Shore girls with mismatched furniture and mismatched families. She watched him tally the symbols, the lights going on in his eyes, and while she respected that he was educated enough to finally notice, to realize that two thirds of the girls he was in the room with were also magical practitioners, that made him both all the more laughable for not noticing sooner, and all the more dangerous to Una as a target for him to claim.

They'd just broken bread together, which should make them all safe to be around each other. If he knew that in the first place. If he could be trusted to respect that.

She drank more wine and grew more tired, and when the others moved to the tower room to light incense and light joints, while Una almost certainly just watched, she begged off to bed.

"Are you okay?" Una asked. "We can have Jenner over another night."

"I'll be fine, I'm just going to lie down. You won't bother me at all."

"If you're sure..."

"I'm sure. Go." Jules smiled, and mostly meant it, and took Yorick out one last time before they retired. Of course she lay awake, staring at her pale swirled ceiling in the silver moonlight. She could hear the murmur of voices, but not the words. She assumed they'd talk about her, but whatever. Jules trusted Ashley with her life, no reservations.

The next time Jenner came over, Una was all moved in, little white lace curtains on her windows, everything that was boxed unpacked and put in its place, cardboard broken down and stored in some mysterious place. Or maybe recycled. It all happened when Jules was sleeping, like Una was some kind of little helper elf.

Jenner brought more wine. He also brought a bead curtain, that he presented to Una. "A housewarming gift, for your kitchen threshold. It feels kind of strange."

Jules and Ashley exchanged a glance while Una thanked him. She still didn't know. Ashley rummaged around through their junk drawers until they found a hammer and some tacks and hung it immediately, with Jenner steadying the wobbly chair she'd selected to perch upon.

"What's the pattern the beads make?" Una asked, standing back with Jules to watch the proceedings.

"It's like a spider web. It's a dreamcatcher, to trap bad dreams and only let good ones through."

"Who's been dreaming in the kitchen?" Jules asked.

"I don't think its proximity to the dreamer matters," Jenner said. He was using his Important Explanations Are Being Made voice. He hadn't yet wised up enough to respect them; maybe he never would.

Jules sniffed and ashed her cigarette. "Then why would there be more than one dreamcatcher in the entire world? You'd only need the first one that was ever made."

"Maybe you just don't understand," Jenner said, and Jules wanted to slap his infuriating face.

"Or you don't," she said. She ground her cigarette out in the ashtray and went to her room, lay on her stomach on the bed and shoved her head under the pillow. Yorick sat on the floor next to the bed and grumbled at her, occasionally poking her with his nose, occasionally resigning himself to chewing a toy. For once, she could cry, and did. She never knew when she'd feel like it, or when she'd be able to. Not sobs right now, just fat hot tears that welled up and spilled out, soaked up by the pillowcase. Her head felt hot and stuffed with cotton, and her nose was all plugged up.

There was a knock on her door, muffled by the pillow and the crying. She snuffled, quietly, and lifted her head. "What?"

"We're going to get ice cream, do you want to come?" Ashley called.

"No thanks. But you can bring me back something."

"Aye aye, captain."

Jules waited until she heard them all leave the apartment, heard the door close, and then went back out into the living room. She stood in the center of the room and considered the bead curtain, head cocked first one way, and then the other. She knew what a dreamcatcher was, but the thought of a spider large enough to go with it gave her the shivers. It wasn't her dreams that were the problem, anyway, it was her awakes.

She turned to go back to her room, and for just a second, she smelled her father's aftershave and felt him next to her. She spun in a full circle, expecting him to be there, somewhere, like maybe he'd just gone out to buy some beer and decided to drop by and see her, but she was alone in the apartment with Puck and Yorick.

"I miss you, Dad," Jules said, rubbing her face and then rubbing her hands through her hair. She sat on the couch and drew her legs up, and both animals curled up with her as she cried some more. She saw shadows in the corners of her eyes and didn't know if it was her father's ghost trying to find her, or whatever thing she'd called up that wasn't her father's ghost, or other ghosts entirely. There were things other than ghosts in that divide between the living and the dead. They needed to fill out a checklist before they started hanging around people.

Hours later, she woke up when Ashley and Una stumble bumped their way through the apartment door, Jenner close behind. "Jules, why are you on the couch?" Una exclaimed, laughing like it was the funniest thing in the world.

"Una, why are you shitfaced? Ashley?" She glared at Ashes, who was supposed to know better. Who was supposed to be watching out for their babe in the woods. Why didn't they tell her yet? Why was it so hard to do anything?

"Una makes her own choices," Ashley said. Her eyes met Jules' and she shrugged just a little. She tried, anyway.

"Well, we went to get ice cream, but we weren't sure where to go, so we drove around for a while. And we drove past a tattoo parlor that was open, in Long Branch? And we stopped and Jenner paid for me to get a tattoo. See this? It means brimstone, just like you and Ashley!" Una pushed her hand at Jules' face; there was a symbol tattooed on the third knuckle of her index finger, black linework puffy and red at the edges. "So then we got drinks to celebrate. And then we got ice cream and I got you a banana split and I hope it didn't all melt but if it did you can just put it in the blender and it'll be just as good."

"It wouldn't be the first time," Jules said, lips feeling numb. She took the cold paper bag from Jenner. "I'm just going to go ahead and put it in the freezer, and I'll either blender it or just eat it tomorrow. Thanks for getting it."

"Una said that a banana split was the way to go," Jenner said. "Ashley did not disagree."

"Do you disagree?" Jules asked. She found she was loathe to go through the bead curtain. Maybe it was part of his own personal web, placed here to trap them.

"I'm not a big fan of bananas. That, and as soon as the word banana entered the conversational sphere, Una kept singing some ridiculous song."

"You cannot tell me you don't know the banana man song. Or banana boat song. What's that song called, Juliet?"

"Day-O. It's in Beetlejuice."

"See, Juliet knows things."

"I'm well aware that Juliet knows things," Jenner said.

Oh I'm not sure you are, Jules thought, finally pushing through the beads and going into the kitchen, if only to get away from Jenner. She shoved the banana split container into the freezer and spent some time smoothing out the paper bag and folding it. She remembered covering her school textbooks with paper bags every year during the first week. By the end of the year, the paper bags would be fuzzy at the seams and the clear block labelling would be superseded by hearts and doodles and song lyrics and things, but the textbooks were still pristine when unpackaged. The importance of a public school education, when raised with generational wealth: the ongoing Juliet Duncan saga. Jules smirked to herself, shut the freezer.

"So why is brimstone important?" Jules asked in her best Teacher Voice, returning to the living room. Ashley was smoking and looking at the records, trying to pick one to play. Una kept looking at the titles and shaking her head. Jenner sat in the easy chair watching them with a bemused expression on his face.

"It means as above so below."

"Did Ashley tell you, or did you watch that cartoon?"

"Ashley told me!" Una protested. "What cartoon?"

"Did she tell you what else it means?" Jules asked, eyes still locked with Una's. Jenner took a breath, maybe to intercede, and she waved her left hand at him, evil eye bracelet clacking against her rosary.

"Ummmmm...what happens one level happens on all of them. Emotional, physical."

"Okay good, you learn well while drunk. Was that a college thing?"

"Don't be mean, Juliet," Una said, real hurt in her eyes. She went and sat on the arm of Jenner's chair, and he patted her leg. "It itches," she said.

"Sorry, kiddo," Jules said. "And there's tattoo stuff in the medicine cabinet." There should be a bandage on it still, probably, but she went to get the ointment anyway, right as Ashley dropped the needle on a Baroness album, and she couldn't hear if they were talking about her again. In the mirror, she was very pale, and her eyes very large and dark. They were making mistakes and she couldn't fix things fast enough.

"Thanks, Jules," Una said, but when she reached for the aforementioned tattoo stuff Jenner took it instead.

"I'll do it."

"Thanks Jenner."

Ashley caught her eye and smiled apologetically. Explanations would be forthcoming. Really, if Una was going to get a tattoo, one of theirs was far better than one of Jenner's. It actually rather suited Una's fine-boned hands.

"My dad's going to be pissed," Una said after a few moments.

"Yeah, probably. But you're an adult, and both of you have to start remembering that." Jules went to bed. Her dad was not pissed about her tattoos. Curious, because he never felt the impulse, but he was curious every time she put another hole in one of her ears too.

She did not dream about her father.

Instead she dreamed about a big spider web spread across the Garden State Parkway to catch all the bad things. Anybody speeding, anybody transporting drugs, guns. Jules wasn't in the dream, not precisely, she was somewhere outside the dream watching it like a movie. The spider web caught a couple of trucks trying to go further north than they should. The spider web caught a bus driver who was having a heart attack. And then a giant spider, shining black, climbed up from underneath the roadway and cocooned all of the vehicles. The ailing bus driver, it let the ambulance crew take, but it cocooned the other drivers, and bit their heads off one by one. Jules watched their pale white ghosts, like steam, pour out of their bodies and wander around on the blacktop, the "good" vehicles passing through them like mirages, protective symbols spray painted on their roofs. Which they were. They were sad, confused mirages, and once enough cars passed through them they were just gone.

Jules woke up with her face wet, and she sniffed and wiped her cheeks. Yorick was snoring and gray light filtered around her curtains, and she heard the shush of a steady rain. The apartment smelled like coffee and bacon, and though it seemed possible Una had sprung up from her drunken sleep renewed, it was unlikely. As far as she knew, Una had never actually been drunk before and was going to have to face the consequences. Jules wrinkled her nose at the thought of having to deal with Jenner first thing in the morning. She wished the Parkway spider had eaten him. Then she shook her head and wiped her face again; there was no Parkway spider. How weird she was so upset.

The kitchen table was set when Jules padded out there after downing some painkillers. Her head was pounding, her vision stat-icked over, and sometimes coffee helped. The shower was going, and she'd bet the answer was Ashley, not Una. Jenner was there in the clothes he'd worn the night before, a kitchen towel hanging from his front pocket. He handled their small stove and mismatched cook-ware with aplomb, not a big deal, but with a style Jules hadn't no-ticed before, a deep seated familiarity with the rhythm of cooking it-self versus the environment in which one cooked.

"Good morning," he said, with just a shade of hesitation. Or Jules wanted him to be hesitant, maybe a little bashful, and imagined it. He probably slept on the couch. It didn't occur to her to look for pil-lows or a sheet or anything.

"Morning." She poured a cup of coffee and stood with the refrig-erator door open to pour milk in it. They should really get half and half. "How did Una come through?"

"Alive but with a pounding headache and an itchy tattoo. The rain doesn't help."

"There are a few specific things rain helps. Headaches do not tend to be on the list."

"That is a fact. How do you want your eggs?" Eggs. She mentally shuddered; apparently today wasn't an eggs day.

"I'm just going to make a bacon sandwich, I think." Jules rummaged for a bit and came up with individually wrapped American cheese. Well, cheese food. Jenner looked a little bit disgusted.

"You ladies are questionable in your food shopping choices."

"At least it isn't Velveeta. It's cheap and has a really far out expiration date. I'll thank you to take your food snobbery elsewhere when you're a guest in this house."

A shadow crossed Jenner's face and he straightened up. Jules hadn't realized he was in an almost perpetual slouch. "I apologize for insulting you while I am a guest," he said with gravity.

"Apology accepted." Jules looked him in the eyes; he was dead serious. Good. Of course, that meant she'd been behaving very badly indeed, towards said guest. Shit. She closed the fridge and busied herself with some questionable sandwich making.

The shower turned off and Ashley emerged about five minutes later in shorts and a WRAT concert t-shirt, a towel wrapped around her hair. "Thanks, this smells great," she said, settling at the table. "Where's Una?"

"Jenner's making her breakfast in bed."

"Somebody should." She craned her neck to check the stove clock. "Shit, I've got to get to work."

"It's hard to imagine you as a waitress," Jenner said.

"You don't really know us," Jules muttered around her sandwich.

"I'm brunch bartending today, actually. But oh, how the people love me. I tease the old men and compliment the old women. I hush the cries of toddlers and win the hearts of all the teenage boys. I get the best tips in the house."

"She does," Jules agreed. "She's like a goddess. The Platonic Ideal of Service. She needs epitaphs and such."

"I'll have to come see you in action sometime."

"Oh, I'd rather you didn't. I'd get self-conscious and drop a tray for eight on somebody's head or something. I'd Coyote Oh God instead of Coyote Ugly."

"I don't think you'd be that bad. You're pretty lucky." Jenner was putting the finishing touches on Una's plate.

"Do you think so?" Ashley smiled and frowned at the same time, one of her particular gifts, and looked at Jules, who shrugged.

"You girls met me after all," Jenner said with what he had to think was a winning grin, and went out through the bead curtains to knock on Una's door.

"Oh Christ," Jules said.

"Looks like we're in it for the long haul," said Ashley.

Chapter Fourteen

E ven with Una in the apartment now, she was alone more. Either Ashley was at work, or Una was out with Jenner, or taking summer classes. Jules would lie on her bedroom floor, Yorick lying next to her, and think about her father and cry until she felt like she couldn't anymore. There were always more tears, though. It was like when she had a cold and thought more snot could not possibly come out of her head. There was always more. Was grief like being sick? Maybe. It wasn't something she felt like she could get away from.

The last pack of cigarettes she could find was on the floor next to her, a lit one stuck from the corner of her mouth, and she had her tarot cards out. Marlboros, not cloves. Well, the clove equivalents, little rough tasting cigarillos. Apparently people thought clove cigarettes made kids think cigarettes were candy. Did it matter how she got there? Jules didn't think so. She shuffled, and pulled. The Lovers, of course. That was Una and Jenner, though Jules sat and thought for a long time about what the Devil might mean. They might not have anything in common. Jenner might be truly controlling.

Jules pulled the Nine of Swords, the Nightmare card. That was her, plagued with dreams on a recurring loop, the sun twinkling off the inlet, her father's blood in the grass, her mother telling her in the hospital he'd been killed. She looked around, worried for a moment that she'd left the razor out somewhere while she was in whatever fugue state led her to the living room floor with her tarot cards, cigarettes, and a bottle of rum. No razor visible. She took a drink from the rum. Yorick grumbled and licked her face with his big warm washcloth of a tongue. She scratched his ears for a moment and wondered where Puck was. Probably asleep in one of his little hammocks.

The next card was the Ace of Cups, and she almost just put the cards away. Was that joy on the horizon? She wasn't really doing a spread, just pulling cards after shuffling, letting the drawn ones fall to the floor around her. She wasn't experiencing any joy. Maybe it was reversed, was it upside down when she pulled it? That would mean fear of connection, and she was having that, for sure. Or lack of interest in connection. She took another drink, finished the cigarette while looking at the disembodied hand holding the overflowing cup. My cup runneth over, said the Bible. My cup runneth dry, said Jules when she reached the bottom of the bottle of rum. Was she getting sloppy drunk, sitting around alone on a weekday, fucking around with tarot cards? Maybe. Sitting on the floor was like sitting on a cloud, and the air was a cushion around her. Maybe she'd reached a transcendental state, wouldn't that be a bitch when she had to go have dinner with Gladys and Hector tomorrow at the estate?

She lay back on the floor and looked at the bead curtain again. Web, but no spider. Or Jenner was the spider. Jenner was the devil. Or it really was to catch bad dreams. Or maybe it was full of bad dreams and that was where all of hers came from. But that wasn't true either.

Jules was still on the floor when Una and Jenner came home, but had evidently put her tarot cards away somewhere in the interim. Una sat on the floor next to her. "So what are you doing?" she asked. Jules thought about the time they'd kissed, spent hours kissing, and wondered what Una thought of it. If Una thought of it.

"I was listening to music," Jules said, which had been true at one point in the day. The speakers hissed and the spent needle knocked. Born to Run was still on the turntable, if she remembered right. Jenner seemed to be hanging around on the periphery, she couldn't really see him, and after a moment he went to the kitchen. The water ran, and then a few minutes later the smell of brewing coffee.

"Are you hungry? You can have my doggie bag if you want it."

"I should eat, probably. What did you get?"

"Manicotti and garlic bread. I'll get you a fork."

Jules sat up and put her back against the couch, listened to Una and Jenner murmur at each other in the kitchen. The speakers still hissed, and the turntable still knocked, unanswered.

Una and Jenner rattled back through the bead curtain from the kitchen, and Jules obediently took the silver foil doggie bag, pulled the paper lid off the container. It still gently steamed, and she forked a piece of red sauced pasta into her mouth. "Water or coffee?" Jenner asked. He was holding a glass and a mug. He was pointedly not looking at the empty rum bottle.

"Water right now," Jules said. He handed her the glass and drank from the mug of coffee as he crossed the room to the record player and turned it off. "I'm fine. You guys don't need to take care of me." Yorick circled the room, then sat down so he was between her and Jenner.

"We don't mind," said Una. "I have to go study now, though." She kissed Jenner on the cheek, shyly, and retired to her room.

"I miss those days and I don't," Jenner said, watching her go.

"Me too. Where did you go to school, Jenner?" Jules asked in a bright tone. A muscle in his jaw twitched and he eyed her for a moment. His eyes were very dark. She should've waited until Ashes was here for this, but couldn't miss the opportunity.

"Oh, a prep school in California."

"A prep school, how very upper crust."

"I didn't know you went to a prep school," Una said from her bedroom. She'd left the door open "Did you go to college too?"

"No, I apprenticed under a master of the occult," he said in a deadpan. Jules waited to see if he'd laugh, maybe to cover up for

Una's benefit, but he did not laugh. We're really doing this then, she thought.

"Well that's cool." Una sounded a bit flustered.

"For what?" Jules asked.

"Excuse me?" Jenner asked, blinking.

"What did you apprentice under a master of the occult for? Was it a Faust sort of situation or what?" Jules picked up his pack of cigarettes from the coffee table and shook one out. Tiny black script crawled down the side and she reached for her pack after all. Maryanne always called them students, even herself. Never a 'mistress of the occult.' They would be students until the day they died, because learning, all learning, was a lifelong endeavor. There was always more to know, and always somebody who knew more. What fucked up people the most, Maryanne told them, was hubris. The idea that with this power they could do anything they wanted.

"I don't think you're prepared to have this conversation," Jenner said. "I don't think you would understand—"

"Bullshit," Jules said. "You said it to impress us and didn't have an answer prepared when I inquired further."

"I'm sorry that you feel that way," Jenner said steadily.

Una appeared in her bedroom doorway, looked back and forth. "Guys, come on."

"No, I think you need to know who you're getting involved with. Who we're letting into our house." You don't know anything about what he's claiming, Jules wanted to say, I do. Ashley does.

"It's been a couple of months, I'd like to think I have some idea who Jenner is."

"All right. Then who is he?" What's he been doing to you? And she didn't mean anything about sex.

"I...well you can't just..."

"You didn't even know he went to prep school. Or some prep school in California somewhere. Vague as possible, that's good." Una wasn't who she was mad at. She didn't need to yell at Una.

"I didn't assume you would be versed in California prep schools. I can probably get a copy of my transcript to you, if necessary."

"No, I don't think that will be necessary," Jules said in her iciest tone, the edges of her vision crackling. Yorick pushed himself under her hand, insistent, and she rested her hands on his back. Maybe she was ready to pass out. Her mouth tasted like pennies and ashes and sometimes chocolate. "Maybe you should stop *assuming* what people are *versed* in."

Una was practically in tears. "I don't know what's wrong with you, maybe you're just *jealous*. But you can't talk to him like that. We're going back out and I'll see you tomorrow or something." So yes. Una had thought about their kissing quite a lot.

"So I just showed you that you don't know anything about your boyfriend, and he acted all superior about it, and you're going to pick his side and storm out?"

"Yeah, I guess I am," Una said, newly defiant. This was not a thing Una had ever done in her life.

"Right on," Jules said, and lit another stolen cigarette. What else was she going to do?

Una didn't slam the door, but she might as well have. Jenner made sure to give Jules a smug look before the door was closed all the way, and she gave him the finger. Fuck him anyway. Ashley would be home from work soon enough and they could talk about it, get a game plan. Or talk about it in the morning. Apprentice to a master of the occult. Maybe it was somebody they'd heard of. Maybe they could text Maryanne and she'd actually answer them, because this 'master' shit was bad news.

Jules took the empty rum bottle to the kitchen and pitched it into the garbage can, where it broke. She looked at the glittering jagged edge of the bottle neck on the top of the pile, and thought about drawing it across her skin. Thought about the fine blood beads which would rise to the surface afterwards like dew, and then spread until they touched each other and started to run like little rivers. With all that blood, with some chalk and some salt, she could—

She turned off the lights and went to bed.

Chapter Fifteen

When Jules got up the next morning, Ashley sat in the kitchen, drinking coffee and flipping through the local free paper. "So what're we gonna do?" Jules asked.

Ashes raised her eyebrows. "About?"

"About Jenner. About Una. What do we tell her and how and how soon?" She scooped kibble into Yorick's bowl, the sound of the food hitting the metal bowl driving little iron nails into her skull. She sat across from Ashley.

"The problem is that it needs to be a lot, to protect her. And it'll be too much too soon."

"We've got our books still." MaryAnne's teaching wasn't book-specific, but still, they had a collection of things to reference.

"We do. But she's got homework, she can't split her attention too far." Ashley set her coffee down. "Una told me you picked a pretty lame fight with Jenner last night."

"It was lame," Jules agreed. "I wasn't ready, and he's such a smug fucking bastard. But it felt important. It was the first real time he'd said enough to open the door. Interestingly enough, after his declaration that he studied under a master of the occult, he didn't ask about my studies. I don't know if he thinks I'm a rich girl who's just playing around or what."

"You did mention hellfire clubs."

"Well. They're a thing. Not our thing, granted, but a thing."

"We're getting away from the point."

"Yes, what is your point?" Una had finished in the shower and come into the living room during their conversation, standing just outside the dreamcatcher beads with her hair still dripping.

"Are you still mad at me?" Jules asked.

"Kind of. But what are you talking about? And what does it have to do with me and Jenner?"

"Come sit down with us," Ashley said.

"Okay." Una rattled across the threshold and Jules shuddered a little, thinking of shiny spider carapaces. Maybe Puck had the same thought, he ferret-galloped into the kitchen and looked around at all of them before climbing Ashley to sit on her shoulder and pull on her hair. She scritched him absently with one finger.

"Okay, you know how Jenner said last night he studied under a master of the occult?" Una nodded. "Well, me and Ashes did that same kind of study. But the thing is, it's bad news to call yourself a master. Or mistress."

Una looked from Jules to Ashley. "You guys are playing a joke on me."

"We're not. You thought we got bff brimstone tattoos for fun?" They held out their hands. "Symbols like this have power. And there's lots of ways to use power; we hope to do it the right way, the responsible way."

"So you're saying Jenner isn't responsible."

"I have no idea, but he knows you're uninitiated and seems to assume Ashes and I are ignorant, even though he seemed like he put the pieces together. He could just be an asshole."

"Don't call him an asshole!" Una pushed back from the table.

"Hey, hey, Jules doesn't mean it. She's just frustrated, and worried that something could go really wrong really quick. We wanted to have this conversation with you a while ago, but didn't know how to do it. Now that you're here, it's time. And three is a good number, y'know?" Ashley smiled, and Una was smiling back. All Jules had to do was concentrate on not ruining it.

"Three?"

"Three witches, it's a thing. We wanted you to be our third." Ashley was so much better at this. So patient.

"Me? You mean, you thought of me before I asked to move in?" She looked at Jules, softening, her unaccustomed anger falling away.

"Yes, we did," Jules said, and managed a real smile. Because Una was innocence and sweetness and light, always. Because she and Ashley were so much like one another, always the dry sarcastic cool kids, they needed tempering. Because she'd grown up with Una and the three of them were as much like sisters as Jules was going to get. And then an alarm went off on Una's phone.

"Oh no, I have class! Can we talk more about this when I get home? Should I get anything from the library?" It was so hard not to laugh at her earnestness, so important not to laugh at it.

"See if they have anything on the Keys of Solomon, for a start," Jules said. "And Aleister Crowley." She knew they did. She'd wandered the hallowed halls of the Monmouth University library before. There were things more modern, more important, not published but passed around from hand to hand, but that would come later. Who knew zines would be the modern grimoires?

"Okay." Una went to her room to finish getting ready.

"Well that could've gone better," Jules said.

"You're such an asshole," Ashley said, but she laughed and got up, coming to give Jules a hug. "But it also could've gone much worse. Do you want coffee?"

"Please."

"I see you finished the rum." Ashley had her back to Jules, pouring the coffee. Her tone was neutral, but Jules could interpret. Worry. Annoyance that the rum was gone.

"Captain Morgan ran aground, yarrr. I'll get a new bottle, maybe something different." She took the mug. "Thanks."

"You're welcome. Now, what shall we do today?" As if they were ladies who would put on gloves and bonnets and sally forth to go calling.

"I don't know. Garage sales? It seems like I had..." Her phone rang. "Something. Hello?"

"Are you going to keep me waiting all day?" John. Why would John be calling her? He sounded pretty normal: irritated with her everyday existence and how it inconvenienced him.

"What do you mean? Where are you?" she asked.

"Parked out front. You're supposed to have lunch at the estate?"

"Oh. Shit. I thought that was dinner? Okay, I'll...be out soon." She hung up before he said anything else. "I have lunch at home," she said.

"Oh, was that John? He's such a miserable bastard to you."

"I know, it's refreshing. He's waiting for me in a car outside."

"He's such a creep, why didn't he just come in?" Ashley opened the door to the fire escape and leaned out to wave. "Go get dressed!"

"I don't know what to wear," Jules muttered, taking her coffee cup and her dubious black and rust shadow with her back to the bedroom, Yorick licking his chops, the food bowl ravaged. She rifled through her drawers and then pulled stuff along her closet rail, settling on yet another black sundress. Really, most of her options for this season were black sundresses.

All tattoos on deck, but at this point, whatever. She'd kind of been considering a new addition, no decision yet. Maybe after this Jenner thing was handled, to celebrate. She ran a brush over her hair, threaded silver hoops into her ears, and chained a chiming silver ball around her neck. A serenity ball, like those pairs of enameled balls you could get. They were supposed to be soothing, calming. Jules thought maybe she was just belling the cat. She jammed her feet into flat leather sandals she remembered were uncomfortable, but not until after she'd already said goodbye to Ashley and gone tralala down the staircase with Yorick in tow.

"Do you really have to bring him?" John asked, as he watched Jules harness and buckle Yorick into the back seat. He waved awkwardly at Ashley, who still perched on the balcony, smoking. She gave a laconic wave with her cigarette hand.

"I do," Jules said, plopping into the front seat and slamming the door after waving to Ashley. Why did she have these sandals anyway? Maybe she'd throw these ones into the ocean where they could become fish food. They were probably very expensive, and probably Gladys bought them for her for some function. "What kind of mood are they in today?"

"Just peachy, that I could tell. Should I have inquired further?"

"No, that wouldn't have been necessary," Jules said. She was unprepared to needle John today. It was simply too much effort. Maybe that on its own would throw him, diminished behavior. The drove in silence for a while. "Remember getting stuck at the draw bridge?" she asked.

"A specific time?"

"No. The fact that you could."

"Of course I remember getting stuck at the draw bridge."

Jules could think of nothing else to talk to him about except for Una, and she wasn't exactly about to go blabbing that all over the place. "At some point, I'd like to go to the orchard."

"I don't know why you'd want to."

"I feel sort of a compulsion." And that was the closest she'd get right that second to telling John the unvarnished truth. She had to do it. Maybe she'd find her father's phone, for all the good it would do her if it had been out in the weather for that long. Maybe she'd find something else. The key from his office was still on her estate key chain. "You don't have to come with me."

"So far as my employment obligations go, that isn't true."

"I have Yorick."

"Mmmm," he said, making the turn up the drive, to their little bridge.

"I'm sure Mother and Hector will be thrilled to see me. It's been a couple of weeks after all."

He looked at her a little oddly. "They invited you. They'll be happy to see you."

"John, are you honestly comforting me?"

"Don't let it get around," he said. Another miracle, an attempt at a joke. He was still useful after all. She could use a drink.

"Your secret's safe with me. I'm excellent at keeping secrets."

"I'm sure you are." He and Yorick flanked her through the halls to the dining room, in a different wing from the airy light breakfast nook. The dining room had big glass doors as well, and opened onto a big courtyard tile black and white checkerboard style. An Alice in Wonderland tile, she always thought, because of the illustrated copy she'd read as a child. It also had one of those long tables in it that the movies made fun of all the time, and that Jules might have once used her cell phone to call the other end of the table to pass the salt. Her mother didn't think it was very funny, but her dad did.

Then she was in the dining room and seated. Yorick wedged himself under the table near her feet, displacing one of the empty chairs. She'd air kissed with Gladys and awkwardly hugged Hector, wishing for a dagger to plunge into his back. The orchard after lunch, then. It was hard to countenance the fact that perhaps she had changed but everybody else stayed the same. Or Hector had always been a wolf in sheep's clothing. She was still so unsure. She drank her water rapidly, until the serving staff just left a glass pitcher by her place setting. She kept expecting a voice she couldn't get away from, couldn't answer, couldn't satisfy, saying *it was Hector.*

Couldn't satisfy *yet.*

"And how do you like having an extra roommate?" Hector asked between courses. Jules could not say what her appetizer had been. Something light.

"Una's great. She's taking a summer class so she's still at the college a lot."

"Is she going to pick up a preposterous pet as well?" Gladys asked, smiling the way she did when she was being insulting but meant only the best.

"What's so preposterous about Yorick?" Jules asked, and rubbed him with her foot under the table.

"Perhaps nothing, on his own, other than his size and the amount of energy he has. The whining. But then there's that thing Ashley has. A weasel?"

"Puck is a ferret. And I don't know if Una wants to get a pet. What do you think suits her, a hedgehog? Or maybe a bird."

"A white kitten with blue eyes," Hector said, sitting back in his chair as the main course was brought out and the wine was poured. Jules shook her head at the wine bottle, and looked at the plate in front of her, tried to fix it in her mind. Some kind of fish. Risotto. Asparagus. She drank some more water.

"That would probably make her really happy," Jules said. "Una loves kittens."

"I don't know how you can stand it. Don't ferrets smell?" Her mother shuddered minutely.

"Puck is neutered and Ashley feeds him really high quality food, so I think that helps."

Hector gave a short laugh. "I'm surprised Yorick hasn't made a snack out of him."

"What? Why would you say—"

"Hector, don't talk about things like that," Gladys interrupted, and it seemed she was looking at Jules with concern. Jules managed the smile she thought her mother was looking for, and that was that.

They ate for a time in silence. Sometimes, if there was a to do, there was a string quartet the Duncan family would hire, or a harpist, or a pianist. Nothing this afternoon, it would have been very strange indeed, but the silence was very loud. She turned her head a little to look out at the courtyard, a little too bright in the sunlight, with a staff member sweeping the tiles. The last time she ate here, it was with her father. Gladys was someplace else on business. Maybe presenting hyperloop stuff to congress, or whatever it was railroad people were most excited about lately. They'd had a rack of lamb, and a million tiny little potatoes that were roasted crispy-soft, and—

"Juliet, Hector asked you a question." Gladys reeled her back in.

"I'm sorry, I didn't hear." She turned back to the table, sun speckles dancing in her vision, obscuring Hector's face, Gladys', as though they had mirrors balanced on their necks. Mirrors in their eyes, and she could only see herself reflected, her anger, her grief, her hope.

"I asked what your plans were."

"Plans?" she repeated stupidly. She knew how she sounded.

"Yes, plans. Will you be working with your mother? Returning to school for a further degree?"

She stared at him, stared daggers she was sure. What possible reason could he have for asking her things like that? He was quite happy to sit about spending the stipend Gladys granted him, or plan trips to go to exotic locales and shoot wildlife. Maybe he was planning the wedding.

"I'm not certain why you're asking me that. I thought we already discussed my future tattoo apprenticeship." She drank more water, wished it was wine, though wine would really do nothing to improve her demeanor in this situation. Just make her feel swoopy and flighty. She had to keep her shit together around Hector and Gladys. She couldn't act like a wounded animal here. "But what about *your* plans? When is the wedding?"

"We haven't set a date yet," Gladys said in an even voice, the sunlight glinting off the silverware, the glasses, her giant emerald. That was a chink in the armor, though. They probably wouldn't, with the case still open. It would be gauche.

"Do you have a maid of honor picked yet? Will it be Catherine again? Hector, do you have a best man?" Hector was a little bit white around the lips. Catherine was Gladys' best friend from college, a sorority sister and now a man-eating lawyer in Manhattan. She came to estate functions once a year at least, and Gladys frequently rode the train up to the city to spend a few days with her. Girls' vacations.

"Yes, it will be Catherine again," Gladys said, still in that even voice. Patient, even. The voice she'd occasionally read books to Jules in, when her resolve had worn down and she'd had a couple of glasses of wine after dinner and was guilted into spending quality time with her small daughter. "Beyond that, I really couldn't say."

"Gladys Duncan leaves no event unplanned," Jules said. "Unless...you're just going to elope? I mean, I know you couldn't throw as big a gala as your first wedding, that would just be in poor taste, though you definitely could still fit into your dress. But I at least expected a justice of the peace and maybe a small reception on the terrace here, with those little white lights strung on everything?"

Hector laughed, abruptly and too loudly. "Maybe you should be a wedding planner, Juliet. Asbury Park is where a lot of entrepreneurs set up now when they're just getting started, isn't it?

"Oh, I can't stand weddings," she said, baring her teeth at him in a smile. "I do think I've finished with my lunch, may I be excused?" Her plate was untouched.

"Are you all right?" Gladys pushed away from the table as well.

"I'm fine, just had a large breakfast. I confess, I forgot about our lunch and had to throw myself together when John called. I'll just get some things from my room and have him run me back." Yorick got up with a jangle of tags, sniffing the air hopefully. When no food fell

from the sky, he went to the door and waited. "Plus, Mr. Crab wanted to see Yorick, trim his nails, brush his teeth, make sure I wasn't
making him fat."

"You weren't here for very long," Gladys said, hugging her and
dropping a kiss on her cheek.

"I know, Mother, but I'm just up the beach. I'll be back soon."

She brought Yorick to Mr. Crab first. "I'll pick him up when I'm
leaving," she said. She shouldn't go to the orchard alone. She didn't
want to go to the orchard with John. It was easier to sneak without
the dog.

"He looks like he's in good shape," Mr. Crab said.

"I'm hurt that you doubted me."

"He's the one I didn't trust." Mr. Crab slap-patted Yorick on the
ribs, and the dog half closed his eyes in pleasure and leaned against
the dog man's knees. "You can go on about your business."

"Thanks." Jules went back inside, trailed along the hallways to
her room. Partway there, she stopped and took off her terrible sandals, dangled them from her fingers as she counted security cameras.
Did they add any to the orchard? Maybe. Not that it would've
helped.

She locked the door behind her and then opened the window
and pulled the screen out. It wouldn't be the first time she'd climbed
out her room window, but it was the first time since having a bullet
fragment removed from her skull. She kept forgetting to ask Gladys
what they'd done with it; she could've used that instead of the wedding. It was probably in a landfill by now somewhere, medical waste.
Kind of a disappointment.

As she climbed over her windowsill and reached her toes for the
little ledge beneath, Jules concentrated her thoughts on the look that
was on Hector's face when she asked who would be his best man.
He'd been her father's, of course. Could that look on his face be considered guilt? Because the mansion was built in a funny way, because

their little island was built up in a funny way, her window wasn't a full two stories up from the ground. From the ledge beneath, if she moved over a bit, she could then lower herself down to a portion of mostly decorative wall and from there, the sandy soil. Then up the path to the ocean orchard.

No alarm sounded from the house, and Jules noticed no new cameras as she made her way through the stark summer afternoon, no changes at all to the landscape. It didn't seem as though anyone was following her, though John could appear at any moment. It felt to her as though it ought to be evening, that long blue summer beach twilight punctuated with a ribbon of orange sherbet of sunset on the horizon. Gladys and Hector were probably still drinking their coffee, wondering what they were going to do about her. Hopefully nothing. It would seem that perhaps they had done enough.

The orchard was as she'd left it, sun-blasted, cicadas buzzing mystically somewhere. She checked again for cameras, for followers, nobody. This was her house, formerly her home, she shouldn't need to sneak around. She shouldn't need to answer questions about why she might want to spend time in her father's orchard. What had they done with him? Was he buried in the Duncan plot? Was he cremated and his ashes in the house somewhere? She stopped, toes gripping the short grass, almost to the mysterious spot on her scrap of burned map. Her stomach was shivering, her spine cold and tight. Had she not asked? Had they really not told her? Jules ransacked her memory, wishing it was as easy as putting the right word salad into Google and getting a correct or even plausible response. No, she didn't know. Or didn't remember.

On her hands and knees then, in the shadow of the big old apple tree in the center of the orchard. Sheltered from any number of prying eyes, on the estate and off. She hadn't noticed any boats on the water, any curtains twitching in the mansion. John's telltale footsteps were not yet in evidence. She scrabbled with her bare hands in the dirt amongst the roots, her nails were always cut short anyway, and found what the x marks the spot must be, a metal box that the tree had partially grown around, that dirt had partially covered.

The keyhole was saved from being dirt clogged by a swinging metal disc that took more than a little leveraging to move. Jules kept looking up, vowing not to be one of those people concentrating so hard on whatever was suddenly at hand that they forget they were being sneaky. Nobody apparent. Had that rock always been there? Was it a camera? Two of her nails tore and then she gained access to the keyhole. She didn't know a whole lot about tree growth, but it seemed impossible for her father to have been the one to place this box here, unless he did so when he was very young. And he didn't know Gladys then. And Gladys had never in Jules' life shown interest in the orchard.

There wasn't any way she could pull the box loose without tools, and she opened it where it was, the lid struggling against the body of the tree, wood creaking and bark splintering. It wouldn't open all the way, but Jules could see several items inside, and then a door slammed on the side of the house facing the orchard, and thank god her dress had pockets, she pulled them out and stowed them away without really looking at them, just a few things clinking together in an aged jumble. She closed the lid again, twisted the key, and the plate fell in front of the keyhole again. The tree was darker in that spot, as it wept sap, and she kicked some dirt around to make it look more normal. Probably nobody would notice even if she hadn't done it.

She looped around through the orchard until she reached her father's bench again and stood over it, closer than she'd gotten the last time. She touched her fingertips to the bright chip in the top, edges still jagged, where the bullet that found her skull first struck. Her hand was still bleeding where her nails had torn, and she felt a nearly electric jolt when her blood touched where the marble was stained from her father's fatal wound, and her vision clouded and the world swam away from her.

She saw the orchard in flashes, the green grass, the blood and brains splattered upon the ground, the white shards of skull, the blue blue sky with its serene pulled-cotton clouds drifting lazily by. Her own pale face, pressed against the sun warmed grass, the damp earth. The black suited security personnel, their own sidearms drawn, scanning the area while trying to skirt the fallen Julian Duncan, his eyes staring sightlessly. John on his knees next to her, bloodied hands holding his phone, pressed to her neck. He'd smeared blood on his face too. The EMTs arrived, and he rode with her in the ambulance. Mr. Poling stopped Gladys on the pathway, before she could see her fallen daughter and husband. Jules wished she could've seen the look on Gladys' face. She should look for the shooter, she should look where her father was—

Then she was in her body again, in the orchard in the summer sun with her father eight months dead, struggling against John's strong arms. "Jules, Juliet," he was saying over and over through gritted teeth. She stopped moving so abruptly John almost dropped her, and she peered up into his face with curiosity. Which was it? Did he care about her or did he hate her? Did it matter? It surprised her to consider that it might matter.

"I'm okay," she said. She wiped at her face, tried to slow her breathing.

"What's the matter with you? How did you even get out here?" he asked. He pulled a handkerchief out of his suit coat pocket and wiped her face; it came away, red, pinkish. She looked at it, and then held out her bleeding hand. John sighed and wrapped the handkerchief around her fingers.

"Let's go inside, okay?" The plea in her own voice surprised her and she couldn't see his face at the moment, through the sun static. He supported her with one arm as they walked, and she leaned on it a bit more than she would normally have wanted. Whatever had just happened left her feeling wrung out like a once-wet washcloth. Well. She knew that she'd been transported to those moments in some way, unplanned, no ritual or failsafes. Anything could have happened. She only wished she'd had the time to turn and to look out across the inlet as well, to try and get a glimpse of the shooter. Maybe she could recreate it, make it happen again. Or maybe she blew her chance. *It was Hector*, the voice whispered thoughtfully, and her eyes throbbed in time with her pulse. "I walked," she said.

"Of course you did." John sighed, held the door and ushered her back inside, blessedly cool, blessedly dark. She stumbled on the threshold as though something (someone?) grabbed her ankle, and John caught her by the arm again. She was going to have a bruise.

"Take me to my room," she said, though she wasn't sure if he heard. The clanking in her pockets seemed very loud, but John didn't act like he noticed. *It was Hector* was the refrain of their walk, the rhythm of their steps. It didn't grow louder, didn't threaten to burst the confines of her skull, except once when it boomed so loudly she staggered, the world askew like a run aground ship, and didn't know how John didn't hear it. When she felt steady again, she was lying on top of her made bed, John sitting on the edge watching her. "Did you call anybody?" she asked.

"No."

"Why not?"

"I wanted to see how long it lasted. You just kind of...swooned. It didn't seem like a seizure, more like a bad dream. I thought maybe being out in the sun without eating got the better of you."

"Without eating?" Had he watched the farcical lunch? Was watching them a popcorn affair for security? Did the off duty guards have a drinking game they played while they scrutinized the Duncan family? She would, if she were one of them. It would be one way to keep sane.

"You could hook clothes hangers on your collar bones, I made a leap of logic." He picked up the hand he'd tied his handkerchief around and unwrapped it. "What were you doing out there, that you did this to your fingers?"

"I tripped and fell," she said. "I put my hands out and landed stupid."

"You need to be more careful, or stop going out there. You tripped last time too. I don't know what you think you're going to accomplish." John got up and went into her bathroom and the water ran for a moment. He came back with a wet washcloth, and wiped the caked blood and dirt from her skin, surprisingly gentle. She watched his face as he did it, imagined him reading the lines in her palms, something she and Ashley dabbled in for fun, that MaryAnne never commented on. MaryAnne just let everything flow, be personally meaningful, possibilities endless. Protections, that's what she was the strictest about. Always protect yourself. "I can't do anything about your dress," he said.

She looked down; there was dirt up her front, most heavily on her knees and the hem of the dress, but also on her belly and breasts. "Wow," she said. "I'll get changed when my head stops spinning. Gladys would lose her shit if she saw me."

"She would," he agreed.

"Really, John, I expected you wanted me ordered home again. I'm surprised you'd foster my freedom." She smirked, and he frowned and returned to the bathroom to rinse out the washcloth.

"It would disappoint Una," he said.

"You're so sweet with your sister." She swung her feet to the floor and stood experimentally. No voice, no pounding, everything seemed solid. She pulled her dress over her head and dropped it on her bed, rummaged in her closet as he came back from the bathroom.

And after a moment he came and put his hand on her shoulder, turned her so she was facing him. "What?"

"What's this?" he asked, running a light finger across the ladder of cuts above her panty line. "Did you do that to yourself?"

"What does it look like?"

"That's fucked up, even for you." Jules expected him to be disgusted, but mostly he seemed curious.

"Add it to the list, right?" She turned away again, pulled another dress over her head. "Did I mess up my hair?" she asked, turning. She wanted him to laugh, frown, something, but he remained impassive. Interesting.

"It looks fine. How long have you been cutting yourself?"

"A couple of months, I guess." It was inexplicably touching that he was handling her like this. "Are you going to tell on me?"

"Are you going to keep doing it?"

Yes. "I don't know."

"Fair enough."

"Are you going to tell on me?" she asked, finding an overnight bag and stuffing her dirty dress in it, some other dresses from the closet.

"No." He went and sat in the wingback chair. "If it was worse than that, maybe."

"Thanks." She zipped up the bag. "So have you spied on the apartment at all?"

"Not recently. Why, have I missed anything?"

"We all strip down to our underwear and have pillow fights while doing drugs. Nothing major." Oh yeah and Una has a boyfriend.

"Well that's good." He checked his watch. Now Jules was almost certain he had cameras in their apartment, if he had zero reaction to her and Ashley having pillow fights in their underwear. Was there anybody who *did* strip down to their underwear for sleepovers with their female friends? Other than Lena Dunham?

"Do you have somewhere to be? I can get somebody else."

"No. Gladys has got some gala in Manhattan this evening. She'll be leaving for her train shortly."

"She didn't mention it. Is Hector going?" She said his name without thinking and then winced in anticipation, but nothing happened this time. She looked down; there was still some salt just inside her closet door, that the maids had missed.

"Of course. Has diamond cufflinks for it and everything."

Maybe she should stay over, prowl around more. Sit in the chair in her father's office. But she had those items to examine. Jules closed her closet door. "Okay, let's get Yorick and go."

Chapter Sixteen

They were most of the way there when John broke the silence. "It feels dumb to ask you this, but just keep an eye on Una, okay?"

"Unlike you and I, John, Una and I *are* friends, and friends watch out for one another."

"Yeah, sure you and Una are friends. Ashley's the closest thing I've ever seen you have to a friend, and I'm not sure you care all that much about her."

"Well that's a thing to say to a person."

"You just don't have the capacity. It's like how the mutt in the back seat doesn't really care about anybody but you. Mr. Crab said he took apart a crate when you left him in the kennel to go gallivanting."

"I thought I heard him barking."

"They heard him barking in New York." John parked the car. "Do you want me to carry your bag up?" he asked.

"No, I've got it."

"Even with the dog?"

"He's fine with me." Jules got out, unbuckled Yorick. "You know, for hating me, you sure care an awful lot."

"I don't hate you," John said with a sigh. "Go get some rest."

"Yes, Doctor." Yorick stopped and lifted his leg on the maple out front before they went up the stairs. John didn't drive away until after the door closed behind her.

She smelled incense in the hallway, and wondered if Ashley was just burning incense for the sake of it, or if she had smoked the pot without her. It seemed unlikely.

The apartment door was not locked. The lights were not on, but a number of candles were lit in the living room, yellow flickering tongues in the growing darkness. Ashley was bent over the plastic milk crates that held their records, taking care to pick one out as she always did, holding back her loose dark hair with both hands. Jenner sat in the easy chair, Una perched on the arm, a glass of red wine in his hand. He looked up as Jules came in and smiled. "Welcome home," he said.

"Thanks." She was a little mystified, took her purse and bag to her room. She wasn't going to look at the things from the orchard with Jenner here, no way. Ashley finally picked a record and put it on, Pink Floyd, big surprise there.

"How was lunch?" Ashley asked, when she came back to the living room.

Yorick turned to stare at Jenner right as he said "No, pick something else. Classical?"

"It was okay," Jules said. "We've got the Bach."

"Whatever." Ashley shrugged. "Jenner brought acid," she added, smiling over her shoulder a moment. Jules looked from Ashley, to Jenner, and then to Una, who had the fixed smile of somebody who was determined to have fun if it killed her.

"Just for fun?"

"That's one way of looking at it. Some people also use it to expand their minds," Jenner said. "I wanted to talk to you, all of you, about magic. About the possibilities of what we can do."

"Oh for fuck's sake," Jules said. She almost laughed, then looked at Ashley, who was not laughing. "Does this have to do with your occult apprenticeship? And ours?"

"Una has yet to begin her education," Jenner said. "There are things people can do, frequently through ritual, that is more than most people have dreamed of."

"A lot of people dream about flying and stuff. Are you saying we can fly?" Una asked.

"No, we can't fly. This isn't an after school special," Jules said, and Jenner scowled at her.

"We can fly, maybe. I've heard of it, certainly. We can know the previously unknown, speak tongues, communicate with the dead. Perform feats of otherworldly strength."

"You have not heard of people flying."

"Jules, stop making fun." Una shook her head, then Ashley dropped a record on the turntable. The speakers hissed, and then a string and piano piece started playing, Chopin's Nocturne.

"I'm not." She wasn't. But she was. At least she was distracted, at the moment, from the terrible murderous puzzle with which she was confronted. Jenner was so fucking insufferable, and she didn't want him interfering with what she and Ashley could *safely* teach Una.

"A first step to opening your mind to such possibilities is dropping acid," Jenner said, ignoring her. He took an Altoids tin out of his pocket and opened it, displaying the blotter paper style tabs. It was like he couldn't conceive of transporting his drugs any other way. He held the tin out to Una, who picked one up slowly. He held it out to Ashley, who took one, and then to Jules, who didn't move other than to take the final drag off a cigarette she didn't even remember lighting.

"I don't know how it'll interact with my painkillers." She wasn't precisely lying, anyway.

"Oh, sweetie, was your head bad today?" Una asked, brow wrinkling

"Off and on. Hector is fucking insufferable. But if you three want to do your thing, I can just vacate to my room." She didn't want to leave Jenner alone with them, but she wanted him to prove he wanted her to stay.

"It should be perfectly safe with your painkillers. It would mean a lot to me to share this with you, all three of you. I feel drawn to you girls like no other people I've met in my time here."

What a line of bullshit. "I appreciate the thought..." Jules was interested in seeing how far he would go.

"I'm taking it too, if we're talking about trust. I'll even go first." Jenner took one of the tabs and placed it on his tongue like communion, where the edges went transparent immediately. He took a sip of wine, and then stuck his tongue out again, gravely, to show the acid was gone.

"The drugs aren't what I don't trust," Jules said.

"Oh, come on Juliet," Una said in a small voice. She looked very scared, but also resolved, and Jenner took her hand.

"I'll be able to help you if there's a problem. The point is to reach the door that unlocks your higher consciousness and allows you to view the magic in the world with fewer inhibitions." Ashley already took her tab and stretched out on the floor, her preferred acid-dropping posture. Second favorite was a bean bag chair, the bigger the better.

"I know what the fucking point of—"

Una interrupted. "It's okay isn't it Juliet?" Jules sighed.

"Oh fine, what the hell." She reached out and took one of the tabs out of the tin. Jenner snapped the tin closed and set it on the table, and Jules put the tab on her tongue. It tasted very slightly sweet, like the paper from underneath button candy. It dissolved slowly and left her tongue sort of fuzzy feeling. "And now we wait until the walls change color and flying cats come through the windows?" she asked with a smirk.

"Quit making fun," Una said again, but she was smiling too. Maybe she liked the idea of flying cats. Jules could just think of

The Birds. She took a breath and let it out slowly, tried to clear her thoughts. She didn't want to psych herself into a bad trip, wouldn't that just be her luck, after the day she had.

"For now, concentrate on the music," Jenner said in his slightly deep, newly soothing voice.

"Where did this album come from, anyway?" Jules asked, sitting in one of the armchairs. Yorick lay on the floor next to her with a dis-approving sigh. Una had moved to the couch.

"I thought it was yours," Ashley said.

Jules waited until she thought the drug was supposed to be tak-ing hold, didn't feel anything, started to turn to Jenner, to ask if he was just trying to trick them with mind over body, and then froze and closed her eyes for a long moment. Jenner's face, or the glimpse she'd caught of it, had elongated. His dark ponytail was grown longer, slithery in the shadows behind his head. She wasn't re-ally sure what that ponytail was up to.

She turned away and was distracted by the pattern on the wall-paper, as it seemed to be moving. Or maybe something behind the wallpaper was moving, like the snake ponytail behind Jenner's head. There were a few wafts of cigarette smoke and incense still in the air, and when Jules squinted and looked from the corners of her eyes, she saw silhouettes first, and then they seemed to take more solid form, though still made of smoke. People, smoky reflections of peo-ple, not really taking notice of the three of them but people all the same. Walking through the apartment, pausing at the mirror by the door, carrying glasses to the kitchen.

"Do you see them?" she asked Ashley. Or maybe she didn't. She heard her voice in her head, but Ashley didn't react as though she'd spoken. Nobody did.

One of the silvery smoky ghosts stopped by her, and she looked into its face or tried to look in its face. Were they really ghosts, or were they hallucinations? Ghosts existed, ghosts and demons and other things most people didn't think to believe in anymore.

Una was crying, for what reason Jules couldn't say. Jules realized that Jenner was talking, maybe he'd been talking all this time, and Una was listening to him, Una was with him on whatever guided tour thing he was doing for her, spirit journey dream catcher bullshit, armchair philosophy and sophomoric alternative drug ideologies, but Jules wasn't. She wasn't buying it, wasn't listening, wasn't sure of what Jenner thought he was selling. His ponytail was fucked up, very black and far too long and with a dark corona of shadow. It was as though his tattoo had come to life and uncoiled up and off his arm to hover behind him and hunt for the essence of others.

The ghosts gave him and that snaky ponytail a wide berth, even if they didn't seem to be paying attention to the small gathering of the living. She looked at Ashley, who appeared to have just dozed off, wasn't looking around at all, wasn't talking, just breathing while lying on the floor, Puck curled in a little ball on her belly. Nothing unusual there, Ashes was Ashes.

The record finished playing, the arm knocking, the speakers hissing again and for a moment Jules could only look at the snake wrapped around Jenner. She wondered if he knew. He didn't give Jules and Ashley enough credit at all, if he gave them any, didn't think they'd see him for who he really was. Jenner was with Una on the couch now; he stroked her hair while she lay on her back and looked at the ceiling, or his face, and he still talked. He never shut up, not when he thought he was imparting some kind of wisdom, teaching some kind of secret only he could dole out.

Instead of trying to talk anymore she watched the ghosts have a tea party, or a regular afternoon tea, something like that. She was a little unclear. They reacted to things she could not see, and walked right through the furniture, because of course the furniture was not there to the smoke people just like the smoke people were not there to Una and Jenner. Maybe they were to Ashley; they'd talk about it tomorrow, probably. Yorick saw them, though. He moved his eyes but not his head, his ears twitching occasionally. The blur and drone of Jenner's voice made her sleepy, even though his words didn't reach her, and after a while she went to sleep, or went further into the trip.

She checked the dream catcher for spiders, either in her sleep or in her thoughts or in the trip, but there were no spiders there and it looked pretty much the same way it always had. It was just a bead curtain in a dreamcatcher pattern. Jenner's intention for it, ill or not, didn't matter. It was a regular object. She slept deeper, slipped deeper, and saw sunshine on her eyelids like she was laying out on the beach with clouds chasing across the sky. She turned her head because she thought she heard her father calling her, coming out of the water or coming down the beach, and she sat up, and slid off of the chair and onto the floor with a thump.

The apartment was quiet, the soft grey light of dawn just patting the windowsills. Jules stood up and stretched; she was strangely clear-headed and for the moment, free of pain. She looked around the apartment, but either there were no ghosts, or the light made them hard to see. Una and Jenner were not on the couch anymore, and Ashley's room door was closed. Jules took Yorick out, creeping across the creaking thin-carpeted floors. Every noise seemed far louder than it probably was in actuality. The other tenants were getting up, getting ready to go about their days, clinking their forks and brewing their coffee. Yorick sniffed at each of their doorways both on their way out, and on their way back in.

She brought her purse and overnight bag to her room, locking the door behind her. She rummaged in her bedside table until she found a pen and a blank book, and wrote everything she could remember from the night before, the acid, the ghosts, Jenner, before she could forget any of it. She and Ashes always compared notes, after; she wondered if Una would remember anything. She filled six pages with black ink in handwriting that Ashley had once declared code and then tossed the book back into its drawer.

Next she pulled her dress out of the overnight bag, took the orchard items from the pockets. There was a stoppered and lead-sealed glass vial filled with what looked like apple seeds. There was a tarnished black silver chain with an equally black cross on it. The cross had a tiny glass bubble on it, with an equally tiny scrap of white cloth in it. The cross also seemed to have a teensy bit of wiggle to it, and with a bit of fiddling, Jules pulled it apart. The arms of the cross formed the cross guard for a small knife, the blade whitish metal and looking wickedly sharp. She looked at the blade a long time, thought about trying it on her flesh, thought about John's fingers on her skin. She set it aside.

The next object was a hand sized book bound in crackling dark oxblood leather which seemed to be an old fashioned Bible with ribbons in the bindings. She opened it gingerly; there was handwriting in the margins, passages underlined, and the endpapers were filled with close-written cursive. The letters swam across the page when she tried to look at them; tomorrow, maybe.

The final item was small, smaller than the book, a hard leather case kind of like what binoculars came in. A glint of metal was visible inside, and Jules unsnapped it and slid out a double barreled derringer. It looked like the kind a dance hall girl in a Western would keep in her corset for personal protection. It was a little greenish, and there were corroded bullets in the chambers that she gingerly shook out, finger well away from the trigger. Was there a safety? How would she even know? She stared at it for a moment, small like a toy but heavy like truth.

She carefully placed the derringer back into the case, not loaded, and went into her bathroom. She put it on the top of the light bar over the vanity. She considered the duo of greened brass, then pulled her painkiller bottle out of the bathroom cabinet, shook out the last two, put them in her mouth, dropped the bullets in and replaced the bottle on the shelf. Jules filled a cup with water and swallowed both the pills at once, round edges hard in her throat all the way down. Then she returned to her room.

Jules opened her jewelry box and poked around until she found the silver cleaning cloth she kept there. It took a while, but she cleaned the chain, and the cross. The cross, it turned out, had delicately filigreed markings on it which had been obscured by the tarnish. They looked sort of like they might have a purpose rather than just being decorative, maybe some kind of symbolic language like Enochian, but she was still residually twitchy from the acid and the edges of things were getting smeared away with the additional painkillers, seeing shadows from the corner of her eye, and she couldn't concentrate on it right now. Yorick was already a bundle of paws on the foot of the bed when she tucked the vial, the Bible, and the cross into her nightstand drawer and flopped onto her back on the bed with a squeal of old tired springs. She fell asleep promptly, and it was deep and dreamless.

Chapter Seventeen

Ashley saw the ghosts too. Weird they hadn't seen them any other time. "Do you see them now?" Jules asked. They were in the tower room, reclining in bean bags with Yorick between them as they both scratched his sides, bare feet up on the windowsills. Honeysuckle wafted through the open window and mixed pleasantly with their clove smoke.

"No. It's hard to believe we accidentally arrived at the correct confluence of events to see them though, right?"

"Is it? Maybe it's what Jenner wanted. Maybe he had special ghost-viewing acid."

"That would be fucking weird. Plus, they didn't pay any attention to me. Did they to you?"

"No."

"I wish we could call MaryAnne."

"Me too." When MaryAnne left, she left. No Facebook contacts, no phone number, no email, nothing. She'd explained herself, sort of. She showed up at the right time for the three of them, the right place in their lives for them all to be together, study together, learn together. And then the time passed and she had to find others. And she'd come back if and when the time was right. "Maybe she'll know somehow, and call us."

"Maybe." Puck scrambled across Jules, looked into her face, hopped onto Yorick, walked up Ashley's arm.

"Okay, so let's assume we were going to reach the ghost seeing state the next time we did acid anyway. What else did he accomplish? Did you talk to Una yet?"

"Una seems fine. She got up and went to college like normal. I guess he talked her through whatever unicorn fairy world was going to be best for her to deal with." Ashley picked Puck up and flew him through the air slowly like an airplane. "The question is what comes next. He keeps saying he wants to talk but he doesn't want to talk. He wants us to go along with whatever he's doing. He just needs bodies for it, not even aware ones, and that goes against..."

"Pretty much everything," Jules finished. They both sighed.

"We can protect ourselves. We can try to protect Una."

"We can probably protect Una," Jules said, like repeating it would make it more true. They smoked in silence for several more minutes.

"Need more smokes soon," Ashley said.

"Do you work today?"

"Nobody called me."

"I'll take Yorick for a walk and get some," Jules said, sitting up.

"Are you sure?"

"Yeah. I need exercise. Maybe I'll get something delicious and terrible for us as well."

"I like the sound of that."

"I knew you would." Yorick was standing at attention, looking between them as they talked. He knew his name and he'd learned the word walk since coming to the apartment. Other understandings varied. "And then we'll do the protection. Us first. Una when we can."

Ashley nodded. "I mean, we can kind of include her, but it wouldn't work the same way as if she knew and was here."

"Some is better than none."

"True. Hey, where'd you get that?" Ashley pointed at the cross. Jules didn't remember doing it, but she must've put it on when she got up in the morning, like it was part of her routine.

"Oh, it was in some stuff I went through at the estate. But, I'd better go before he gets too excited." Yorick waited by the door now, and spun in place when she said that.

"Neat. See you later!"

It was sunny but the salt wind was cool. They headed towards the ocean first, Yorick's leash dangling from her left hand as she smoked the clove with her right. She'd thrown her purse over her shoulder and shoved some plastic grocery bags in the pocket of her cutoffs in case she needed to pick up after him.

"Who's walking who?" Somebody joked from a porch, and their companion laughed. Jules sort of turned her head in their direction and made a gesture at smiling. She didn't think of where exactly she was going to buy cigarettes until she was mostly up Cookman, the Empress in sight. She could remember a time not so long ago when restaurants and hotels both had cigarette vending machines in their lobbies, with coin slots and pull knobs. There had been a brief blurb in the paper about the party at the Empress having been broken up, but no arrests listed. Wawa on 33 had cigarettes, though probably not cloves. Opposite direction. She sighed, cut a block across, and went back the other way. She didn't want to pass the porch people again. What a stupid thing to say to somebody walking a dog. Yes, Yorick was big. But he wasn't dragging her down the sidewalk. Really, he didn't need a leash at all. He walked sedately, kept bumping into her left leg and then looking up at her face.

"You're a clown," she said to him.

"No dogs," the cashier at Wawa said, dead boredom to complete alarm rapidly blooming on his face. "You can't have a dog in here."

"I can't leave him outside. I just need a couple packs of cigarettes, do you sell Djarums?"

"Uh yeah. Yeah we do." The cashier spun to the cigarettes, found the right ones. He kept looking at Yorick without looking at Yorick, like he might get eaten or fired or both. "How many?"

"Three," she said. Just the right number, obviously. He rung them up and she uncrumpled a few twenties to give him. She never meant to keep her cash in a crumpled mess but, well. "Thanks." Through the transaction, Yorick sat serenely at her side, taking in the sights. It occurred to Jules that she knew none of his official commands. She talked to him, he listened.

They walked back to the apartment. A few times, Jules stopped in a puddled shadow on the sidewalk and leaned on Yorick. She should've gotten a drink at Wawa, but then like an oasis in the desert, there was a garage sale ahead, and some kids with a lemonade stand, and Jules happily bought and drank three icy cups before her throat stopped feeling like a dried out sponge. She gave them a twenty too. Yorick smelled the kids, obligingly licked one of them and allowed himself to be pet, and leaned against Jules' leg. Thirst crisis past, she browsed the garage sale. She had a hard time *not* browsing garage sales, who knew what she might miss.

It was mostly junk. Baby stuff the kids had outgrown, clothes nobody was going to want, boxes of old magazines. But then on one of the folding tables, Jules hit the jackpot and found a Thoth deck. One corner of the box was faded like it had been on a windowsill for a year, but when she opened it and gave the cards a cursory shuffle through, they seemed to all be there and in good shape. Also on the table was a box of incense, a brass elephant, and a big Ziploc bag filled with beads that she couldn't tell if they were all bracelets or necklaces but she couldn't leave them. The haul came to ten dollars, and the woman who took her money seemed like she'd been hanging out on this stoop for the last twenty years.

"That's a huge dog," the woman observed.

"He sure is," she said, because what else was she going to say? I grew him myself? "Thanks."

"Have a good one," the woman said, and returned to her conversation on her bluetooth. So, some things changed, then. The bluetooth looked like a cybernetic cockroach crouched in her ear, and Jules' palm actually itched to slap it. Yorick pulled her away, the first time he'd ever done that, and they went back to the apartment.

"Figure we'll use the last of the Himalayan salt?" Ashley asked as they came through the door.

"What?"

"For the protection ritual."

"Oh. Sure. You just want to use the little grater that came with it."

"Of course I do. What other salt comes in a block with its own mini grater?"

"I'm not qualified to answer that question."

"Of all of us, I thought you'd be the one."

Jules kicked off her shoes and Yorick went and spread out on the cool linoleum in the kitchen. Puck gamboled over to him and lay on the floor next to his head. "Look what I found," Jules said, as Ashley finished laying out the items on the coffee table, the salt, a stick of chalk in a silver cigarette holder, a vial of dried herbs. "I'll go through the beads later, but I found Una's tarot deck."

"You don't think the Thoth art will weird her out?" The Thoth art weirded Ashley out.

"I'm sure any of the art will weird her out. Una is very vanilla."

"Because tarot reading is so edgy." Ashley examined the incense, smiled at the elephant.

"To her it is."

"True." Ashley ran the chain and the deadbolt on their door. Jules picked up the chalk and Ashley picked up the salt, and while Ashley did the circle Jules wrote the names of the Magi on the lintel for the apartment door and protective symbols on the entries to the room. The chalk was epiphany chalk from Our Lady of Mount Carmel Church and was specifically for blessing and protecting the home. "You don't want a hat?" Ashley was wearing her bowler. MaryAnne had frequently worn a top hat, like Death in the Sandman comics. Jules never felt particularly drawn to covering her head.

"No, I don't."

Ashley shrugged, and they continued. Puck and Yorick watched them intently from outside the circle.

Their ritual used the 23rd Psalm but they probably could've made up their own words, picked a different prayer, used song lyrics. They burned myrrh incense and lit white glassed-in candles with paintings of saints on them and drew their circles and symbols, and then finally Ashley started the words. Not everything they did had words.

"The Lord is my shepherd, I shall not want. He maketh me lie down in green pastures, he leadeth me beside still waters. He re-storeth my soul; he leadeth me along the paths of righteousness for his name's sake."

"Yea, though I walk through the valley of the shadow of death, I will fear no evil. For thou art with me; thy rod and thy staff, they comfort me."

"Thou preparest a table before me in the presence of mine ene-mies, thou anointest my head with oil; my cup runneth over."

Then both together, meeting in the center of the circle, their symbols drawn, the candles all lit. Ashley had the blade, and they nicked their fingertips, dripped blood into the candle with the Vir-gin Mary on the glass: "Surely goodness and mercy shall follow me all the days of my life, and I will dwell in the house of the Lord for-ever."

They stood there for several moments, listening to the candle siz-zle, a calm settling over Jules. It had been too long since they practiced together. Maybe they should've done it sooner, even just this little thing, and she would've felt far less angst for so long, or far less alone in her angst. Or maybe it wouldn't have changed a damn thing.

"What about Una?" Jules asked. "I've got one of Mr. Poling's handkerchiefs, maybe—" Ashley thought a moment, then took the chalk and the handkerchief and went into Una's room; Jules followed. She crawled under the bed, knocking her bowler off, and the chalk scraped for a moment.

"Best we can do right now, I think." They couldn't perform rituals on an unknowing or absent target. There were probably people in the world who could, a sinister thought, but not Maryanne and not them. Not couldn't but wouldn't. Ashley got up and they went to the living room to clean up. The chalk faded on its own, always did. Jules looked for the ghosts, but didn't see any still.

"We'll do one with her here. I don't like not knowing what Jenner's doing here, what he wants."

"I don't either, but it's best if we don't alienate them, because then we'll never know and we lose the chance to stop him if it gets out of hand."

"I'll try to be good," Jules said, blowing out the candles. "You make it look so easy."

"It's a gift, what can I say?" Ashley scooped Puck up and put him on her shoulder. "Now, you're sure about the Thoth deck? I can give her one of mine."

"If we're gonna do it that way, I can give her one of *mine*. It's just the first deck I've seen free range. We can wait until we find another one."

"Let me think about it. I'm sure I'm just being silly and it's fine."

"Stop. You're not being silly."

"See? Playing nice is easy." Ashley smiled. "Now let's go to the beach."

Chapter Eighteen

Jules walked around town with Yorick, going a little further each time. Not a whole lot of people tried to talk to her; it was amazing what social armor a big dog provided, regardless of his behavior. She perused garage sales, bought booze, brought home sushi for lunch. She was frequently up early enough to sneak onto the beach with Yorick to get their toes in the surf and be gone again before the badge checkers showed up for the day. She should look into what kind of fine it would be to have a dog on the beach in season like that. Whatever. Hector was a lawyer, he could deal with it. A gift from her to him.

One day she walked all the way to the Inkwell, in Long Branch, where they'd first met MaryAnne. They'd bought Dutch coffees and were screwing around with tarot cards on one of the tables when she sat down with them, hair a purple pixie cut, a ladder of silver hoops up her left ear. "Good old fashioned Rider-Waite," she'd said in a conversational tone.

"It sure is," Jules said, not exactly welcoming. Ashley, though, was always far better at interacting with people like a normal human being. Plus, MaryAnne was not going to be driven away that easily.

She couldn't go in there with Yorick, though, and didn't really know what to do otherwise, so walked back along the boardwalk until she found a bar with a patio where she could sit. It was too bright, but she didn't feel like sitting in the apartment. She wore the cross from the orchard, and had the Bible in her purse. The derringer she wrapped in a bandanna and had under her mattress, though she felt like she was aware of it, cosmically. A burning beacon of a question, too old to have anything to do with her father but then why did he have the key, the map? Did he open the box and then leave the stuff there, also at a loss as to their purpose?

She wasn't confident the corroded bullets she had would fire, even if she cleaned both them and the gun, and didn't want the gun exploding in her hand if she was trying to kill Hector with it. She wasn't confident she could research these things without the FBI or somebody paying her a visit, no matter how rich her family was.

And those goddamn *seeds*, what was she, Nancy fucking Drew? She looked at Yorick, pulled out her phone, and googled "are apple seeds bad for dogs?" It seemed the safest way to phrase it. Apple seeds, you see, contained cyanide. And cyanide was the leading cause of death in old fashioned mystery novels, to hear people talk about it. That would be a sort of poetic justice, using cyanide to poison the person who shot her father in his apple orchard. Poisoning Hector was less risky to her than shooting him, anyway. Did she have the stomach (hah hah) to poison somebody? She thought she might.

"Whatcha doing here?" Ashley asked, dropping into a chair across from her.

Jules shrugged, shoved her phone in her pocket. "I was just walking around."

"And our mothers tried to say Converse and flip flops were no good for walking in and would damage our feet. Well, your mother said. My mother never said anything about it."

"Your mother's opinions were most often expressed if we were sticking it to the man," Jules said dryly. "So what's up?"

"Get a load of this shit. Jenner wants to go to Essex Road."

"Why does Jenner want to go to Essex Road? Did he hear about the albinos or something?"

"I have no idea. He seems to think it's the best place around here to do the ritual he has in mind."

"Oh, one LSD experience and we're doing rituals together now? He thinks that now we're the weirdos together?"

"Just all magical besties," Ashley grinned. "Oh, I found a garage sale on my way here, found two more decks. Rider-Waite and Morgan-Greer."

"A Morgan-Greer? Wow." Jules finished the last of her hard cider, flat and warm now. "Somebody's going to be pissed their mom sold their stuff."

"It's the American pathos of the garage sale. Crumpled dollars made, souls damaged, life goes on. I think Una will like that one a lot, though."

"Yeah, I think so too. But anyway. Do people even still believe anything about Essex Road?"

"There's all sorts of tales on the internet, so probably."

"Well, I guess we have to go, because Una'll go, and we can't let her do that alone with him." Jules looked for the end of Yorick's leash; she'd just kind of dropped it on the ground next to her chair. "When?"

"Now. He's parked out front."

"It's the middle of the afternoon, nothing's going to happen on Essex Road in daylight."

"Sweetie, it's after sunset." Ashley looked at her with barefaced concern, and she looked away from Ashley "We'll tell him to fuck himself. You should just come home and rest."

"I won't sleep even if I lie down now. Let's just go." She'd rather have Yorick there if this was going to happen, anyway. If they went home first, he wouldn't be in the mix. "I'm going to make a pit stop, take him with you."

"No problem. See you outside."

Jenner parked right out front, and Una was leaned against the passenger door. His car was an old one, some kind of blank gangster cars that still actually had running boards, and suicide doors, and nothing like AC or computerized anything. "I didn't know you had Al Capone's car," Jules said. "Did it cost a lot to fill in all the bullet holes?"

"I think you're thinking about Bonnie and Clyde, who went down in a hail of bullets. That car is in a museum. Al Capone was ultimately arrested for tax evasion." Jenner smiled at her, the smug bastard..

"I don't think you can convince me that Al Capone's car never took a bullet," Jules said, sliding into the back seat. Ashley slid in next to her and handed a paper bag and a plastic fork over, heavy with a solid piece of apple pie, moist and flakey and cinnamon smelling. "You got me apple pie? You do love me."

"You're welcome. We looked for you at the Inkwell first."

"Solid strategy."

"Now, Jenner, you said you'd tell me what we were going to do after we got Juliet," Una said primly from the front seat.

"Plus you need to tell me how you knew I'd be here," Jules said. Jenner glanced at her in the rearview mirror, his gaze sliding over to Yorick, who sat bolt upright next to Jules, ears erect, eyes locked on Jenner.

"We're going to go to this Essex Road place to see if there's an appropriate crossing there."

"What do you mean, crossing?" Una asked.

"Running water, or a crossroads."

"There's no crossroads at Essex Road," Jules mumbled around a mouthful of pie. She and Ashley exchanged a glance. "Don't you know how to read a map. And why, are you going to make a deal with the devil? Didn't some rock guy do that, Robert Johnson?"

"Robert Johnson is known for blues. Robert Plant is known for rock, but is not said to have sold his soul at a crossroads. Robert Johnson is."

"I know who Robert Plant is."

"I didn't say you didn't." Jenner didn't ask for directions once; he must have already found it at least once and this was just part of his act.

Jules had been down Essex Road at night before, probably every kid in the area had after reading about it on Weird NJ's website, windows up and doors locked and at a speed that was not strictly safe. It was hard to pinpoint what the real spookiness of the place was. The legends, so far as they went, were varied. Some people said that a village of albinos lived in the underbrush there, but it was hard to believe that any number of people would be able to hide along a road like that, even a twisty and namelessly creepy one. It wasn't in woods, there was an office development or something there. And what was scary about albinos? They were just people.

Now, when people said Essex Road was *haunted*, that was far less specific. Somebody hanged himself there once, maybe. Or there was a horrible car accident, maybe. Or some girl was murdered there on prom night. Or Satanists lurked there. Or somebody saw the Jersey Devil, a goofy cryptid in the hypothetical, but in practice, Jules could die happy if she never saw such a thing. In reality, Essex Road was just a road, maybe a little bit pointless, just a kind of long curve of a Point A to Point B road, short, with trees that were kind of overgrown. The Parkway loomed over it, and hearing that kind of constant traffic probably took some of the mystery out of things.

Jenner turned off Asbury Avenue onto Essex Road right about the same time Jules finished her pie. She almost wished she hadn't eaten after all. Maybe such things were not to be faced on a full stomach, the better to nervously vomit with my dear. There weren't many building lights on, though they passed under a number of street lights. Jules closed her eyes when she thought she saw ghostly faces out in the underbrush, only to find them gone when she opened them. She was the only one to see, she was sure of that; if Una thought she saw anybody in what woods were there, she would have shrieked already. If Ashley saw anything, she would've tipped Jules off.

After the first couple of gentle curves, Jenner slowed, and then stopped. Yorick growled, low in his throat. "What are you doing?" Jules asked.

"If there's water nearby, this is the right spot. If the road crosses over water, it's definitely the right spot, for our purposes."

"You're not going to tell us at all, just be all mister mysterious?" Una asked, the playfulness of her tone straining.

"Maybe he brought us out here for human sacrifice, and thinks we'll cooperate better if we don't see it coming," Jules observed. 'Our purposes' her ass. Jenner gave her an impatient look.

"It's impossible to explain everything and still get anything done on time. There are certain alignments of the stars and planets tonight, and phase of the moon, and the ritual I want to perform is brief but requires three people at the very least, even if said people are not all knowledgeable. Enlightened."

"Oh are you finally acknowledging that I told you me and Ashes were in the know?" Jules asked, getting another impatient look for her trouble. "You could've taken the time to explain it to us even a little on the drive over without all this cloak and dagger shit."

"I feel like we need to sign disclaimers, like when we went to Girl Scout Camp," Ashley muttered. Jenner got out of the car and opened the trunk. "You're just going to park in the middle of the road?"

"If another car comes, it's more likely to see my car than us standing here in the dark. But another car isn't going to come while we're here."

"I'm glad you're so goddamn certain."

"I do nothing without being sure," Jenner said.

Jules leaned over the seats and poked Una. "You're just okay with this?"

"He wouldn't do anything to hurt us."

"We met him what, two months ago?" Jules asked, lighting a clove and offering the pack to Ashley, who also took one. "We have the right to say no to this."

"I'm sure it'll be fun. Or interesting." Jules' resistance was only hardening Una's resolve, an interesting thing to see.

"Come on," Jenner said, opening Una's door. "I can do it with just us two but—"

"Oh fuck you," Jules said, and angrily climbed out of the car. "You can do it just the two of you and it's that much more dangerous. Yeah we get it. Fucking bastard."

Jenner didn't even look at her, just indicated where they should each stand on the pavement, just kind of in a row. Jules looked around. No faces peered at her from the night, and she heard no hoofs or clawed feet approaching. So far so good. The night was starry and she wondered which stars and planets were doing what, that had Jenner all excited. It was a good thing she and Ashley had done their ritual already. Her stomach was jittery, like a glass of water set on a speaker that was playing really loud. Jenner walked this way and that, placing candles in tall glass holders, shaking stuff out of bottles. Yorick moved around Jules, keeping himself between her and Jenner, the hair between his shoulder blades ruffled.

"These candles have been specially blessed," Jenner said, as though answering a question. He returned to the trunk of his car, and came back shaking a can of spray paint, the metallic rattling almost sending Una out of her skin. Ashley and Jules looked at each other, eyes meeting in the starlight, whites flashing. Should they pull the plug on this? "Not much longer."

"If you say so," Ashley said, sounding pretty surly herself by this point, throwing her cigarette away. Jules realized she couldn't hear any cars on the Parkway, even though it was within a literal stone's throw. She also couldn't hear any cicadas or whatever else screamed and buzzed and croaked in the night all summer long were. It was dead quiet on Essex Road, except for their breathing, and Jenner's preparations. He was spraying some patterns on the road, and then a big one. The little ones, Jules couldn't see all of, but the big one was a pentagram. They weren't at all standing how Jules thought they should be, to make use of a star. Even though four people to fill five points wasn't mathematically correct anyway, the three of them standing at the little point didn't make much sense either. Maybe it wouldn't work, because of that. She and Ashley exchanged another glance.

"I'm not on board with this at our current disclosure level," Jules said. Everything she felt and saw was held at an arm's length.

"You're perfectly safe. No harm will come to you because of what I'm doing here tonight. But you can wait in the car if you're scared."

He's bluffing, she thought. He wouldn't want anything to upset whatever shit he's pulling. Then she saw movement from the corner of her eye and turned to look. She wasn't sure if anybody else saw them, but there were people there, ghosts maybe, made of moonbeams and starlight and mist and smoke, but human forms all the same. They gathered outside the pentagram painted on the blacktop and stood there, watching. The susurrus of the Jumping Brook reached Jules' ears, and she looked at the car, beyond the ring of ghosts. She looked at Una's pale face and wide eyes.

"I'll stay," she said, much more quietly. She reached out and took Una's hand, squeezed it in what she hoped was a reassuring manner. Ashley took her other hand.

"All right then." Jenner walked to the car for one last thing and came back with a frayed piece of rope, the end knotted into a noose. "This rope was used in a hanging," he explained.

"Bullshit," Ashley said. Jules almost started laughing, but bit her lip firmly. She wouldn't be able to stop if she got going. Her fingertips tingled and she looked at the forms without looking too hard. No telling what she might see, and she might not like it. She wasn't sure if he knew what he was playing with, or if she and Ashley could stop it at this point even if they wanted to. Their best bet was to try and protect themselves and Una, try to keep anything he called here from breaking loose and doing some damage.

"What's it for?" Jules asked.

"Contacting the spirits of the dead," Jenner said, with more theatrics than were strictly necessary.

Well hell, I can do that, she thought. "For what?"

"To ask them questions." Funny, he didn't seem to be a big fan of questions. He stood at the legs of the star.

"What do you need us to do?" Ashley asked.

"Just stay where you are. Your presence alone helps my conduit to the world beyond."

Yorick was stiff, watching Jenner, and Jules watched the ghosts as Jenner spoke. They didn't react to anything. It seemed mostly like they were watching, but occasionally there would be ripples in their small ring. Jules couldn't see what the darkness in the darkness was, but she had a feeling it might be Jenner's real goal. After all, she could see the ghosts, and they didn't seem either communicative or all that interested in him. Maybe he should've brought a Ouija board. Jules stifled her laughter again, and Jenner cast his dark glance on her for a moment. Una was all but crushing her hand, but it was her left one, so she didn't much feel anything but pressure.

There seemed to be something else beyond them, something bigger and darker, and maybe that was what Jenner was after all along. He began to speak in what sounded to Jules like German. It wasn't Latin, she'd been to Latin mass a couple of times, on special occasions and MaryAnne taught them some. The big darkness past the filmy ghosts seemed to get more focused, and Jules stared at it until she couldn't stand it anymore and she looked at Ashley to check the situation. Ashley's lips were moving in her own silent prayer, or ritual, or riposte. Una seemed rapt by whatever Jenner was doing, but Jenner was all she looked at, nothing else, like a rabbit frozen in headlights.

Even without looking at Jenner, Jules was also starting to feel the tenuous thread of a connection to him, and she grimaced. In general, she was starting to feel very disconnected and connected all at once, feel the slow spin of the world around them, feel the thrum of life force through her and through Una, and Jenner and Ashley nearby, feel the crackling-frost cold of the adjacent dead. She knew what Ashley would think was the best protection in the moment, and mouthed those syllables herself. She could only hope that Jenner meant it when he said he'd protect Una, but she was trying. She and Ashley tried.

At one point in that interminable time under the stars, Jules felt the direct attention of the thing in the darkness fall upon her. It probably also considered Ashley and Una in turn. She wished like hell she'd taken German in high school, not French, apparently not nearly as useful in Jenner's dubious occult arts. Or her own, to be quite frank. Its regard passed, though, and nothing new seemed to touch her, and she remembered the Bible in her purse. She couldn't touch it without letting go of Ashley or Una, though, and had to settle for picturing it in her mind. The ribbons in the binding. The cracks in the leather. Yorick looked up at her and then back to Jenner, a clear question; he didn't just have his hackles raised, but a whole swathe of hair from neck to nub, velvet stroked in the wrong direction.

Jenner seemed to be directly involved in a dialogue now, his ponytail rising and swaying gently of its own volition, and Jules wondered what this might look like to Una. Jenner's voice was louder and softer in turns, and Jules wondered how much longer they would stand there, and what the logical conclusion of such an interaction could be. Either the big thing in the darkness would go away or it would what? Take one of them? Engage Jenner in a game of chess?

She looked at Yorick and said "Wait" very softly. Not a yes, not a no. How lucky he listened, stayed with her; she didn't have enough hands to keep her shit together if he decided to just bolt.

She looked at the ghosts again, tried to focus and really look at them. While she still had a cigarette burning, the smoke seemed to strengthen them, make them more solid, but she couldn't see any of their faces, and though their hands fluttered once in a while, and they pressed in around the pentagram, she couldn't get a sense of their mood. Her cigarette burned to the filter and she had to spit it out. The susurrus of the water in the pipe beneath the road made it hard to think. It was a small relief in the shit show that the thing in the darkness didn't feel like whoever, whatever, answered the phone when she called her dad.. She felt like she might be nearing the point at which she'd say "yes" and let Yorick tear into Jenner.

Jenner's pose changed abruptly, and the candles all blew out. The ghosts and the black thing in the darkness were gone too, like they were also blown out. He started to pick things up, the supposed hangman's rope, the book of matches, the spray paint, the candles.

"Was that it?" Jules asked. Una dropped her hand and she flexed her fingers; Ashley held on a moment longer and they exchanged an unhappy glance.

"Yes, we're all done." Jenner wasn't grinning, exactly, but there was a light in his eyes that hadn't been there before. A secret, satisfied light.

"Well that was spooky," Una said with a little shiver, an uncertain smile. "Essex Road at night. I didn't see anything at all, though, did you Juliet?"

She'd been lying to Una their whole life. "I didn't. Did you, Ashes?"

"Nope, nothing." Ashley lit another clove, staring hard at Jenner, who didn't notice in the slightest. They got back into the car, Yorick going very close behind Jenner before jumping through the open door and onto the seat. Jenner slammed the trunk shut and climbed into the driver's seat. Yes, he did seem pleased.

"So was it everything you hoped for?" Jules asked. "Because it looked like a whole lot of nothing from my standpoint."

"Oh, I'd say it went quite well. We'll have to see how things progress in the days to come."

"You aren't getting us back out here," Ashley said with a crackle in her voice like a campfire and Jules thought finally, finally she's angry enough. "I'm more than a little pissed that you'd drop somebody into that, assuming it would be okay because you *assume* they're ignorant. It could've hurt Una. It could've hurt you, considering we don't know if you're allowed to be playing with the big boy toys."

"I won't be asking you to do that again," Jenner said, as though their objections were the epitome of tiresome.

"No, you won't. And I'd say you owe each of us a pretty weighty favor for using us as your 'conduits' to the other world without explanation or actual request," Jules said.

"I thought it was creepy and I didn't know you were going to be speaking another language," Una said. "What were you even saying?"

"They aren't words you say if you don't intend to use them," Jenner said, the best sense Jules ever heard him make.

"You said you would explain," Una said, and a whine crept into her voice that made Jules back against the head rest and close her eyes.

"No, I said it was impossible to explain and still get things done on time. There is a difference."

"No fair."

"Life isn't fair sometimes." Jenner glanced in the rearview mirror. "Right Jules?" Shocked, she met his eyes. Her anger flared, and then faded. He was deliberately baiting her, and for once, she wasn't going to play that game. She didn't want to play any games, especially not with Jenner.

"Nothing is fair sometimes," Jules said in as neutral a tone as she could muster. "And you aren't welcome in the apartment anymore if you don't explain. And apologize for taking advantage." He hadn't expected that.

"I don't understand what you two are mad about," Una said.

"I guess perhaps explanations are in order from all involved parties," Jenner said smugly, and Yorick growled deep in his chest. Jules put her hand on his neck, and he quieted but still grumbled under his breath.

Chapter Nineteen

Of course, when Jenner pulled up in front of the apartment, he left the engine running and just let them out. "But you were going to stay over," Una said, but her disappointment seemed like a cover for her relief.

"Maybe tomorrow," he said, and once all their doors were closed he drove away.

"Motherfucker," Ashley said.

"Let's just go inside," Jules said, Yorick leading the way.

Puck greeted them at the door, dancing up to Ashley in that rocking horse gait ferrets all seemed to have. She scooped him up and went into the kitchen to fill his bowl. When she came back, it was minus ferret but plus a bottle of wine and three glasses. Jules kicked off her shoes and settled into an easy chair, before accepting her glass. Una plopped onto the couch, pouty, and while she took the wine she didn't do much more than kind of sip at it a couple of times before putting it on the coffee table.

"Okay, straight talk," Ashley said. "What Jenner pulled tonight is not okay and will not happen again."

"Maybe we're making too big a deal out of it," Una said. "I mean, it's okay if he didn't stay over. I don't know why you two are so mad about it though."

"That's not what we're talking about," Jules said. How did she keep missing the point?

"Well what are you talking about? You didn't think Essex Road was kind of...I mean, it was spooky, it was like a haunted hayride, but in July. It was kind of fun, right?"

"Do you really think it was fun?" Ashley asked. Una hesitated. "Okay, you don't need to say it. But if something is happening to you and it's not fun and you're not enjoying it, say so. You absolutely always have the right to say no."

"Well, except for paying taxes. That kind of thing."

"Shut up Jules."

"You're making it sound like—"

"I know what I'm making it sound like. Una, you remember what we talked about that morning? And you asked if there were any books you could get from school so you could learn more?"

Una shrugged. "Kind of." Ashley and Jules exchanged another glance, and Jules put her glass down.

"We said that you wanted to be here, and be our third? That the three of us could be good and strong together, and we'd teach you what we knew? We even got you a couple of tarot decks."

"Oh neat!" Una was trying to do more than just listen politely, Jules could tell, but she wasn't connecting. How could she not remember? What had Jenner done?

Jules scooted to the edge of her seat. "Listen, okay? Even just talking about tonight, nothing else, there's some shit out there, stuff you want to protect yourself against, not invite in. So not only did he keep us deliberately out of the loop, which is shitty on its own, Jenner looked an awful lot like he was inviting something in."

"Wait, you two saw something out there? Like, more than Jenner with his rope and some candles?"

"Ghosts," Ashley said.

"And something else that even the ghosts stayed away from," Jules said.

"You're making fun of me," Una said, trying not to cry, her chin crumpling like paper.

"We're not." Ashley sat next to Una on the couch, hugged her. "Look, we wanted to invite you in, even before Jenner showed up. He just sped up the timeline. You already have the tattoo, that's a first step. We match, like you said." She held out her right hand, with the brimstone tattoo, and Una sniffled and held hers out too.

"Plus, like I said, we got you some tarot decks. A person's first deck should be a gift. Ashes and I just couldn't settle on which of the three was the best one to give you." Jules went to the cabinet where they'd stashed the decks, lined the boxes up on the coffee table next to Una's wine. Yorick followed in her shadow, casting glances at the door.

"So what now?" Una asked, looking at the boxes but making no move to touch them.

"Now we try and teach you enough to protect you, make sure we're all going to be okay," Ashley said.

"Protect me? What, from Jenner?"

Yes, from Jenner, Jules wanted to yell. She took a deep, careful breath. "He seems to be reckless, at least with our safety, and I don't think he knows as much as he wants us to think he knows."

"He promised he wouldn't hurt us," Una said.

"He also promised an explanation," Ashes said. Una quirked her lips unhappily. They sat in silence for a while.

"I need to think about it," Una said finally. "Let me sleep on it."

"Makes sense," Ashley said, giving Jules a warning look.

"It does. Choice and consent are important here. We're not trying to trick you, and we're not going to force you into doing something because we think it's for your own good," Jules said.

"I understand," Una said, and managed to mostly produce one of her sunny smiles. "Goodnight."

"Goodnight." She doesn't understand a damn thing, Jules thought.

They waited awhile, sipping their wine, listening to Una move around in her room, turn the fan on, and finally silence in the apartment.

"Well that went over like a lead balloon," she said finally.

"I didn't think it was so bad," Ashley said. "Weird maybe."

"You're too much of an optimist, that was really bad. Why didn't she remember anything we told her before? She just felt like she had to defend him."

"Well, yeah, of course she did," Ashley said. "But I don't know why she wouldn't remember. She didn't remember at all."

"Yeah." Jules checked her phone; somehow it was two in the morning. "He did something. He had to have done something."

"God this is so shitty." Ashley finished her wine. "What do we do?"

"I don't know. We waited around too long I guess. Now it's damage control instead of preventative measures. Though really, now would be a really great time for MaryAnne to come back."

"It would." Ashley got up. "I'm supposed to work tomorrow, I need to go to bed. Unless...?"

"I don't think there's anything we can do tonight. We're both tired and freaked, it'll be better after we've slept. We can do better tomorrow."

"You're probably right." Ashley kissed the top of her head and went to bed.

Jules took the glasses and bottle to the kitchen. There wasn't enough wine left that it was worth putting away, and she drank the rest right from the bottle. She licked her teeth when she was done, dropped the bottle in the recycling bin. Yorick came and stood just beyond the bead curtain, and she went and took his head in her hands. "You are the best dog," she said to him, their noses almost touching. He wagged his nub slightly, licked her face. "Good boy. Let's go to bed."

She'd just gotten changed when there was a light knock at her door. "It's me," Una said.

"Come in."

"I'm sorry I got mad at you guys." Una stood awkwardly on the threshold. Her eyes were puffy, as though she'd been asleep already and woke up with an apologetic directive. Or she'd been crying.

"It's okay. There were only a couple ways that was going to go," Jules said. "We care about you and we want things to be okay."

"And I get that. It's just...Jenner and I aren't really boyfriend-girlfriend yet, but he's the first guy I've been able to really go out with, you know? And I want him to get along with you and Ashley, and I don't want him to be the wrong choice."

"Una, the first guy you go out with isn't necessarily going to be the guy you spend the rest of your life with," Jules said.

"I know that. But it doesn't feel like I'm just having fun with Jenner, you know? It feels like it could be a real relationship. And the couple times he's stayed over, he's been a gentleman. Kissed me a little, and we cuddled, and that's it. So far."

"Well that's good," Jules said. She couldn't help but look at Una's lips, only sort of listening, and Una seemed to notice. She bit her lower lip and blushed a little.

"I don't really know what I'd do if he wasn't a gentleman," she said.

"Tell him to stop and that should be it," Jules said. "If not, pretend he's a shark and stick your thumbs in his eyes."

"Juliet!" Una actually put her hand over her mouth. Ashley was probably already asleep. "Have you ever..."

"No, I've never had to physically fight off somebody's advances." Jules thought about John for a moment. "You didn't mind it when I..."

"When you kissed me? No, I didn't." Una blushed more. "Maybe that's why Jenner and I haven't gone further. I don't know if he's right for me. I don't know if you're right for me. I'm just confused."

"You've got plenty of time to decide," Jules said, and leaned in to kiss Una, who stiffened a little bit, then relaxed and was kissing her back. There was a certain comfort in being with a woman, perhaps because of the familiarity of parts. Girls knew what to do with nipples. Girls knew how to take their time and be patient.

Jules lay Una down on her bed and kissed up her thighs, softly, pulling the hem of the pink flowery nightgown up as she went. Una pressed the back of her hand to her mouth, back arching, smothering her own soft little cries. Una all but sobbed when Jules pulled her underwear aside and kissed her sweetness there. "Shh," Jules murmured against her. Una reached down and pushed her fingers into Jules' short hair, her body a live wire, and Jules kept going. When she sighed and relaxed, Jules sat up again, pulled the nightgown down and patting Una's legs. "Now go to bed," she said.

Una sat up, hair sweetly mussed, and looked at her. "But—"

"Nope. Go on. Goodnight." Jules got up and went into her bathroom, closed the door. Yorick whined softly, and Una said something too softly for Jules to hear. Then the bed creaked as she got up, and she gently closed the door after her. Jules opened the medicine cabinet, looked at her pills. She felt the most clear-headed she had in weeks, months. Not even a headache.

Back in the bedroom, she locked the door, and got out her iPad and headphones. YouTube told her everything she could have wanted about cleaning the derringer, checking the firing pin, everything. Once she got it apart, though, it looked pristine to her. She wiped the parts off anyway, took five times as long putting everything back together. She slipped the derringer back into its cunning little case, put it in the bottom of her purse. She could get new bullets. She could figure it out. The gun was a gift, a solution to her problem.

Chapter Twenty

They made quite the tableau around the breakfast table the next morning. Una stealing the occasional blushing glance at Jules, who was basically slumped into her coffee trying to see the world around the static in her vision. Goddamn red wine anyway. Ashley noticed the glances, and the empty bottle in the recycle bin, and gave Jules the standardly accepted 'I can't fucking believe you' look over her own coffee, but said nothing.

"Ashes, can you give me a ride to the pharmacy on your way to work?" she asked.

"And take you home too? I'm sorry, I'm late already."

"We could call John," Una said helpfully.

"I wouldn't want to bother your sainted brother," Jules said. Morning after Una and John too, she didn't know if she could stand it.

"No, you wouldn't, but Dad wanted me to come home this week anyway and I'm sure your mom would be happy to see you. It would be a nice surprise for her! She works so hard!"

"Well exactly, she's always working. She might as well see me behind glass, at a remove from which she could continue to make her business calls."

"She spent a lot of time with you in the hospital," Una said in a small voice. "We thought we were going to lose you."

I didn't know that, Jules thought. Morning revelations were not her style, or preference. "It's harder than that to get rid of me, apparently," Jules said, and she closed her eyes so she could stand to finish her coffee. So she didn't have to see Una's crestfallen glance. "Okay then, call John."

"You kids have fun!" Ashley finished her coffee, dumped the mug in the sink, and was out the door.

Una walked off to call her brother and Jules sat stroking Yorick's head. She should organize her thoughts. She should try to make a plan. The problem was she couldn't write anything down, be so amateur as to leave a paper trail. She should stop being so indecisive. She already knew, in her heart of hearts, that Hector killed her dad. She wasn't preparing a trial by jury. She should just—

She almost jumped out of her skin when a hand touched her shoulder, and Yorick looked up at her. "Sorry, what?" Una was staring at her.

"I said John would be here soon. He was already out, running an errand."

How convenient. Jules loved and hated cell phones. Sometimes they didn't give you enough time. "I'd better get dressed then," Jules said, pushing away from the table, counting on Una to be too timid to bring up last night even as she, on impulse, leaned in and kissed her on the cheek before locking herself in her room.

John was in the living room and talking to Una before Jules could do much more than pull on a sundress and lace her sneakers. She dropped the pill bottle of bullets into her purse, did an editorial pass with some deodorant and dry shampoo, and winged some eyeliner. She stared at herself in the mirror, too pale, too hollow eyed. Too tattooed. Good enough.

They got in the car, Una both talkative and reticent, occasionally blushing. John didn't seem to notice, or he put it away for later. Don't mention Jenner, Jules thought, buckling the dog in. At least John had the sense not to talk about the dog.

"Where's your prescription?" he asked.

"The pharmacy by the estate."

"Not too convenient for you."

"I guess not. But I don't have a car right now anyway." Did they tell her not to drive? They must have. She'd have to bring it up; being rich enough to be driven around everywhere didn't mean she wanted to be driven around anywhere. Especially not when maybe kind of planning a murder. Apple seeds. What did they mean? Could they mean anything other than poison? They could mean a lot of things. She looked out the window for a while, John and Una engaged in brother-sister talk. The traffic was stop and go, a lot of New York plates around. "What day is it?" she asked.

"Thursday," John said. There was something to be said for John's deadpan; it was for his own peace of mind that he didn't ask why she wanted to know.

"Fireworks, right?" Una asked, twisting around a little. "Is that okay?"

"It's not for like, eight hours, it'll be fine."

"Why would fireworks be a problem? Oh, you think Juliet is a mere mortal, bothered by trivial celebrations."

"John!" Una's tone could scrape glass, and Jules winced. Yorick put his head on her lap and grumbled. "Sorry," Una said, much more quietly.

"It's okay," Jules said. "Besides, John and I poke fun at each other all the time. It's all part of our courtship isn't it?"

"Whatever you say, Miss Duncan," he said, the picture of decorum.

The pharmacy had a drive through, and the transaction was over almost before it had started, the white bag in Jules' hands, top folded over and stapled with the drug info sheet. She hadn't thought to bring a bottle of water, and debated how much of a junkie she'd seem if she dry-swallowed one now. Potentially tattling eyes were everywhere. "Want anything from McDonald's?" John asked, saving her either accidentally or on purpose as he turned into the drive through. "Some of the guys asked for chicken nuggets."

"A frozen coffee thing." The front seat dutifully made no comment when she finally took her pills. What a relief, they knew it would be redundant to ask how she felt.

Once on the estate, she turned Yorick loose. She trusted his judgement more than her own, if she troubled to think about her own. "Where's Gladys going to be?" she asked John. Mr. Poling appeared, in his typical manner, and gestured to Una, who gave them a pleading look that Jules carefully ignored before she went with him.

"Business meeting with Japan, maybe," John said, gathering up the armful of fast food bags.

"And what are you up to? After McNugget delivery." Jules fell into step with him, to the security wing.

"Security duty, of course. You're on premises."

"I can't tell if your father wants us to hate each other, or wants us to marry each other."

"That makes two of us." At the door, John started to put the bags down to enter the key code, but Jules entered hers. "I didn't know you had a code."

"I'm an owner, of course I do," she said. "I'll behave. Cross my heart."

"I noticed the necklace. Turned over a new leaf?"

"Oh, it's old religion," she said, keeping the door open with her toe until he was inside. She'd slip off to the armory, get two rounds. YouTube seemed to think her derringer was a .41, she had no way to know if it was right or not until she was jamming the bullets into it. She had a feeling it would be right. Like things were clicking methodically into place, aligning neatly like railroad ties. When asked, because of course he would ask, she'd tell Mr. Poling that she wanted them made into earrings but then couldn't find somebody who would actually do it. Something like that. Maybe she'd never need them at all. Maybe a better story was that after what happened, she felt like she needed a gun to protect herself. No, that would open her to too much scrutiny, too much of a process. She was already on the path.

"Look, just don't fuck anything up," John said, as he went to the lounge.

"Hush now, don't talk to me like that where the kids can hear," she said, and continued down the hall. She left her coffee thing somewhere. The car? The vestibule? The armory was also key coded, and also had a security member in it, who was reading something on her phone. She dropped the phone on the table as Jules came in, though, and got to her feet.

"Miss Duncan!" she said. "We don't see you here very often."

I wish you hadn't seen me at all, Jules thought. "I'm sorry to intrude," Jules said, fumbling a little. She tried very hard to know the names of everybody who worked on the estate. She scanned the wall for where the ammo was kept, saw the neatly stacked boxes behind locked glass doors. If she killed Hector with a gun, they'd know. Fuck it. "I hope I'm not bothering you too much, Shirley."

"Nah, you're fine. But what I can do for you?"

"It's kind of weird," Jules said, and waited.

Shirley thought about it briefly, Jules could see the gears turning, and then said, "Tell me and we'll see."

"I need two .41 rounds," she said.

"I didn't know you were a shooter."

"I'm not. But..." Then inspiration struck. "I want to have a set of cufflinks made for John, but I really don't want anybody to know. I just wanted to thank him, you know?" The staff would know, or suspect, she and John had a thing. The staff would know that he was the one who got to her first, that day.

Shirley waited long enough that Jules thought maybe she should just leave, and then she smiled. "Yeah, give me a second, I'll see what

I can do for you" Shirley went and unlocked the doors to the ammunition and rummaged around. "John's a good guy," she said conversationally. Carefully not looking at Jules. "And Una's a sweet kid."

"Mr. Poling is kind of hard on them," Jules said. So Shirley'd seen some things on the cameras, she thought.

"Well, he has expectations, every parent does. And they meet them most of the time too, that's the great thing. Here you go."

"Thanks." The brass warmed in Jules' hand, and she smiled. They seemed like the same thing as what she pulled out of the derringer. "Thanks a bunch, Shirley."

"Oh, who am I to get in the way of kids in love? Cufflinks. Be nice if my husband got me earrings once in a while." Shirley laughed and went back to her phone as Jules slipped out.

By some miracle, her mother was in the home office and wasn't on the phone. Gladys looked up from her computer screen, coffee halfway to her lips, and she gave a little start and smiled. "Juliet! What a nice surprise."

"Hi Mom." She sat in one of the wooden and leather chairs across the glossy desk expanse from her mother. "How goes the empire?"

"Swimmingly. Nothing earth shattering has happened lately which, believe it or not, is a good thing."

"I believe it." Her mother's office was in the corner of the house furthest from the orchard, closest to the bridge. Did she hear any of the gunshots? Jules thought that was something she'd never ask. Gladys had a golden apple paperweight that Julian gave her the Christmas after Jules was born, and Jules couldn't decide if she was relieved or disappointed that it didn't have 'to the fairest' engraved in it.

"What's new on your end?" Gladys seemed inclined to give her daughter her full attention, another rarity.

"Not a whole lot. Well, one thing, but you can't tell anybody."

"I solemnly swear."

"Una has a boyfriend. Kind of."

"Juliet, you're kidding!"

"Nope. He has a ponytail and tattoos and thinks he's quite the learned man."

"Oh, Mr. Poling would have kittens."

"He really would. It's been torture keeping it to ourselves."

"So even John doesn't know?" Gladys sipped her coffee, one eye on her computer monitor for a moment before returning her attention to Jules.

"Even John doesn't know. Unless he's been spying on us like a creep, but he's not that good a liar."

"Is that why she moved in with you and Ashley?"

"One reason. It really is easier for her to get to school this way. And she's doing summer classes. Well. At least one."

"That girl." Gladys shook her head.

"I know, right? But she's nice to have around. The three of us get along well." Which wasn't untrue. And it was definitely the kind of thing Gladys wanted to hear.

Gladys indeed seemed about to say something, perhaps express praise or relief, and then her phone rang and her eyes dropped to the screen. "I'm sorry, darling, I have to get this. I'm so glad you came."

"It's okay. I'll see you later." Jules was almost out the door before Gladys answered the call.

Chapter Twenty One

S he went to her room long enough to load the derringer. It was deeply satisfying for everything to click into place, like it was meant to be. Like she'd done it before. There were no engravings on the small gun, nothing to indicate who'd owned it before. Just that curl of map her father had burned. Just the Bible, which she hadn't really perused yet. Later. There would be time. She had a couple of vials of salt in her bedroom desk drawer, and dropped one into her purse. A slapdash protective circle would be better than nothing at all. She had the cross necklace for the bloodletting, if it was even necessary. Her father had shed enough blood in the orchard as it was, they both had. The ground had soaked it in, in addition to the bench, perhaps drawn some Other which now lurked there.

She slipped out to the orchard, through her door this time, not the window. Yorick ran ahead a bit, came back, ran ahead, tips of his ears flapping in the sunlight. If she estimated right, John was just now circulating past Gladys' office looking for her. Not much time. She could only hope Una wasn't unloading into Mr. Poling's ears the occult escapades they'd had, but no, Una would have to tattle on herself with regards to Jenner in order to achieve such a feat.

Sunlight sparkled off the water, and Jules didn't at first realize there was already somebody in the orchard. Yorick had run off briefly with one of the other dogs, and his tags hadn't warned the person there either. A tall man, standing at her father's bench...it was Hector. The sun was beating down, the top of her head on fire, her temples and base of her skull throbbing, and Jules would've sworn on the

Bible in her purse that she felt her pupils constrict. And that whisper
had started in her head of course, her head or her ear or her soul: *it
was Hector.*

Could she believe it? It seemed so easy, so possible, so true. But
did she really try to investigate? Had a couple of combative meals
with the happy couple. Tried to get on with her life, the way people
tried to do, were supposed to do, when there was a death of a loved
one. Was it enough?

It was Hector.

But if the voice was her father. If it was Hector. She might never
again have such a golden opportunity. Unawares. At the scene of his
crime. Wasn't that what they said murderers always did? Fucking stupid, if you asked Jules. Nobody asked Jules. She'd never even met the
police investigating the shootings. No, she had. Not long after she
woke up. They listened to her story and assessed she had nothing
to tell them, which was true. And now was somewhat not true, but
what could she say? "I called my dead father on his old rotary phone.
I can't find his cell or I would've used that."

It was Hector.

She had a gun in her purse, two fresh bullets in it. It was a tiny
gun, probably it wouldn't make very much noise at all. Maybe not
even enough to carry to the house. Jules wished she could hear what
he was saying, wished she knew what he was doing, standing over the
stain of her father's blood, at her father's bench, in her father's orchard.

Was he sorry?

She'd worked herself nearly into a trance, slipped her hand into
her purse and undone the snap on the derringer's case. It could probably properly be called a holster, but she didn't have a belt to hang it
on. She wondered how the gunman felt, the progression of his day.
Cleaning his rifle, loading it. Getting to his vantage. Had he worn
sunscreen? How long had he been there? Julian Duncan sitting on

his bench, trusty hound by his side, staring out over the water. Julian perhaps little more than a silhouette, turning as Jules came up the path. One shot, run the bolt to eject the shell. Julian slumped over on the bench but didn't slip onto the ground. Had the spray of blood caught the sun, made a rainbow? Could blood do that? Then Jules came into sight, the dog running to meet her to warn her off, but something, maybe she was too fast, maybe wind kicked up, maybe whatever silencer he'd rigged threw off the shot, and it had hit the bench next to Julian rather than hitting Jules for another kill.

Hector.

Or.

Hector. It was Hector.

The second shot was to make sure Julian Duncan was actually dead. Jules wasn't supposed to be there, wasn't one of the targets.

Or.

Hector it was Hector kill Hector he killed me it was Hector

Though she favored her father in demeanor, Jules favored Gladys in appearance. What had she worn that day? Did the gunman really just want to kill Gladys and Julian, leaving grief-stricken Jules in charge of a corporate empire she couldn't handle?

HectoritwasHectorMURDERitwasHector

was Hector it was Hector it was Hector

She pulled the derringer from her purse, took aim at Hector through the reflected sun-sparkles, the throbbing pressure of her skull, she could feel her heartbeat in the base of her throat, as though she'd swallowed somebody else's heart and had two. Hector still hadn't turned.

Then an explosion came from the sky, and all the dogs on the estate started howling and barking. Jules dropped onto the path, shoving the gun back into her purse, and could not see how Hector reacted. What was that? She looked at the sky, which had been cloudless, and saw the near-colorless starfish of a spent fireworks cloud dissipating. A test fire. Her heart shuddered and she pressed the heels of her hands in her eyes, because the sparkles she made that way didn't hurt more, anyway, and her mouth was so dry it was like she'd never had liquid before in her life. She had to get up before Hector came down the path and found her, before anybody found her, but her legs wouldn't listen, she couldn't get herself up, and Yorick was there beside here now, and he nosed and crawled under her right arm and stood, boosting her partway. She leaned her hands on his shoulders and stood the rest of the way, swaying, uncertain.

Yorick moved them away from the orchard, to the old weeping willow tree on the border of where the grass petered out into sand and went down to the water. She wavered, leaning on him still, and he stopped and Jules sank to her knees, and then sat with her back against the tree. Yorick leaned in and sniffed her face intently without touching her, then lay down against her hip with a sigh, occasionally rolling his head back to look at her. Jules put her hand to her face; she'd bitten through her lip. Three times I've bled in that orchard, she thought. It had a significance, though she was too weary, her head was filled with jagged glass, and the breeze off the water was nice.

After a while, she felt all right enough to stand up slowly, and she did, hand against the rough gray-scaled bark of the tree, the whisper of leaf whipped branches all around her like rain. She left the shelter of the tree and walked off the grass, to the water's edge, sand wetly giving beneath the soles of her sneakers, sucking the waffled Converse pattern as she lifted each foot for the next step. The tide was out and the shallow water clear, with an edge of foam. Tiny translucent crabs scuttle swam along the bottom, and one horseshoe crab trundled its way past on unknowable business. They used to put a mesh trap down here for bait fish, Jules thought. They called them killies, whether that was the actual fish name or just a colloquialism, she didn't care to look up. Some childhood things could be left unexplored, just accepted in the golden summer haze from which they emerged.

Another glint of white caught her eye, impossibly small, and she almost ignored it. There were so many flecks in her vision, but then she bent and sank her hand into the silky cool wet, dipped her fingertips into the water-heavy sand, and came up with a shark tooth, unbroken by its journey through the waves and rocks, the edges still sharp. Jules held it cradled there in her palm, a few grains of sand still sticking wetly to it, and turned when she thought she heard her name. John stood there on the dry land, and Yorick was halfway between them. She hadn't realized how far she'd walked into the water, but the hem of her dress was dragging from the weight of skimming the surface. She knew now, she went into the salt water for protection. She didn't hear any voice, standing here.

"What are you doing?" John asked, gesturing impatiently. She almost just stayed there out of spite, the sun pounding the top of her head, toasting the tops of her shoulders.

"I found a shark tooth." She sloshed back to shore and held her hand out to him. He gave it a cursory glance.

He peered into her face, though not kissing close. "Are you bleeding?"

"Not anymore." She rubbed at her lip and chin with the base of her thumb. "I'll go wash up."

"You're going to want to change."

"Change for what?"

"Dinner. Family dinner, you and Mrs. Duncan and Hector. Additionally, my father, sister, and I have been invited." Gladys really was thrilled she came to visit.

"Oh good, family dinner. Hold this." Jules dropped the tooth into his hand and bent to unlace her sneakers.

"And we'll take the dog to Mr. Crab for yet another bath. He'll reek after being in the water at low tide. I don't know what you were thinking."

"I don't know why you think it's such a big deal," Jules said, wiggling her toes in the sand. She knotted her shoelaces together and took her shark tooth back.

"It's a big deal for me because it's on my head if you faint and drown yourself."

"Oh you'd be happy to be rid of me, don't kid," she said. "Yorick, Kennel." He looked at her for a moment, looked at John, and then turned and bounded off.

"I'm sure Mr. Crab will be delighted," John said dryly. "Did you fall again?"

"No."

"Just don't keep it from your doctor if you do, okay? And take your medicine."

"I do take my medicine. If you'll recall, we got a refill this—"

"Of painkillers. You have other things you're supposed to take." John held the door for her as she wiped her sandy feet on the woven rope door mat.

"They give out fewer painkillers at a time. Lower chance of abuse or something. Or not enough to kill me if I take them all." She paused a moment, saw his face. "Oh, don't look at me like that. I'm not going to kill myself."

"I wasn't aware I'd looked at you in any particular way."

"Oh, nothing that would hold up in court. Just the littlest hint that perhaps you actually care about me."

"Of course I care about you," he said, face solemn as a statue's.

"Look, for once I'm not trying to trick you. I was just saying." Her keys fell from her numb finger, both forearms ached, burned like liquid fire. She knocked her shoulder into her room door, then clutched the frame as the whole world did a long slow rotation, like when they slowed down the Ferris Wheel and were letting the people at the bottom off, but she was nowhere near the bottom and just swaying up there in the wind. There was light in her eyes again, in the dark hallway, and then she saw faces in the lights and saw the ghosts. Was one of them her father? Her sad, disappointed, father. Shit. John picked up her keys. "Thank you," she said.

"You're welcome." He opened the door and guided her to the bed. People talked about money burning a hole in one's pocket and right now, though, the derringer felt like it was white hot in her purse, yearning to be used on Hector, a blazing flag for anybody who looked at her. How did John not know she had it? He unwrapped the shoelaces from her fingers and went into the bathroom; the sneakers thunked into her tub.

Jules crawled onto her bed and closed her eyes, Hector standing at the blood stained bench hanging in her vision. "I don't know if I can do this," she said as he came back.

"Do what?"

"Dinner." Hector, alive, while her father was dead. Gladys' smiling face, the emerald on her finger. Hector. Una blushing across the table. Hector. Mr. Poling. John. Secrets. Hector. Jules gritted her teeth; she was starting to shake.

"What should I tell your mother?" he asked.

"I don't know. Tell her I don't feel good. My head. That should be enough. I'm going to just lie down for a while, come get me when Una's ready to leave, though, I don't want to stay here." Dimly, she felt John come and pull her purse off her arm, heard him set it on her dresser. It did seemed to take a few minutes before he left the room, and she wondered if he was standing there looking at her. Then her door clicked softly closed.

Chapter Twenty Two

At some point Yorick climbed into bed with her and she snug-gled with him in whatever strange haze had fallen over her, not bothering to worry about how he got through the door, inhaling his fresh-washed doggie smell. An indeterminate time after, John came and with unaccustomed gentleness shook her awake. She'd some-what expected Una, or Gladys. She felt wrung out, and dazedly picked up her heavy purse.

"What's in that, anyway?" John asked. "Rocks?"

"Sometimes," she said. Una already sat in the back seat of the car, a tinfoil swan in her lap. "Leftovers?" Jules asked as she got in the front seat.

"Of course," Una said. "Are you okay? John said you just needed sleep and wouldn't let me come check on you."

"He was right. I just had a headache, had to ride it out in a nice dark room. No worries."

"Your mother took it gracefully," John said, reaching across Jules to buckle her seatbelt, closing her door. She had the impulse to kiss his neck, right under his jaw, or maybe nibble him, just a little, but couldn't gather the energy. He smelled so good.

"Hector was surprised. He didn't even know we were here," Una offered.

"It's almost like I wasn't," Jules said. What did she do with her shark tooth? "I'm like the wind."

"Sure you are," John said.

She rested her forehead against the cool glass as they drove back to Asbury Park. Jenner's gangster car was parked out front, and he was not waiting inside it. Jules glanced up at the apartment windows; either candles were burning, or he went up there to Mrs. Danvers the place. She really just wanted to sleep. She really just wanted to do a tarot reading over what had happened and not happened in the orchard and try to make sense of it. But no, Jenner was there. And Jenner owed them an explanation.

"Whose car is that?" John asked, just when Jules assumed he was going to ignore it.

"Somebody's boyfriend in the building," Una said, and Jules was impressed. Technically not a lie at all.

"Pretty good shape for its age." He partly turned to Jules. "Do you need help getting upstairs?"

"I'm okay." She couldn't not say it. But she thought she could get up the stairs. She half hoped John would insist, come up anyway and roust Jenner, but then that would rob her of the satisfaction of doing it herself. Maybe Ashley already killed him, and he was cooling in the bathtub while Ashes smoked and waited for Jules' return.

"Una, call me tomorrow," John said.

Una hesitated a half second. "Okay."

He stayed at the curb, engine idling, until the heavy front door closed behind them, Una waving through the dark glass. Climbing the stairs, Jules stepped over a cat that may or may not have been there; she didn't remember seeing a cat in the building before, and Yorick didn't react to it. The married couple across the hall from them were cooking dinner, something with red sauce. They had that every Wednesday. No, Thursday. They listened to classical music on the radio all the time, that couple, on a volume carefully selected to make sure you knew, but not loud enough to complain about. She and Ashley joked that they even drank their Pepsi from the cut crystal. Una got to the apartment before her, got the door open.

"You look like shit," Ashley observed.

"Thanks." Jules unleashed Yorick, who went to the kitchen and started loudly lapping his water.

"I'll make coffee."

It was either a great idea or the worst idea. "Put Kahlua in mine," Jules said, as Una went to get changed. They all had estate clothes and public clothes. She remembered that she left her wet sneakers in the tub in her room, and peered curiously at the black flip flops she wore with no memory of having put them on. Yorick came and slumped at her feet with a sigh, his nose against her toes. She didn't see Puck, but Ashes had been keeping him away from Jenner.

"I brought acid for us to do tonight, but if you aren't feeling one hundred percent, I don't want you to push it," Jenner said. Jules clutched her steaming hot coffee cup in both hands without feeling it, smelled the bittersweet steam piling up overtop of it.

"Maybe it'll help," she said.

"Help what?" Jenner asked. "I'm unaware of your particular condition."

Bullshit, Jules thought. Google her name and articles all about it come up. The ambulance that took her to the hospital, all the emergency vehicles bottlenecked at the bridge to the estate, coast guard boats in the inlet. He fucking knew. "Oh, I took a bullet to the brain at the end of last summer," she said, affecting as breezy a tone as she could muster. "Bullet fragment, I guess you'd say." She sipped her coffee. The clock ticked, but they didn't have a ticking clock. Ashley lit another cigarette.

"Well," Jenner coughed, looked to Una, who had come to the living room and then frozen, like a deer at the edge of a clearing. "Why don't you get Jules a glass of ice water as well."

"I'm going to have to pee like you wouldn't believe in like an hour," Jules said. "Or sooner."

"It'll be okay."

"I'm not sure it will. You owed us an explanation."

"I did," he said, nodding calmly.

Ashley sat next to her on the couch. "You don't have to do this, obviously."

"It's cool, Ashes. Anyway, haven't they used LSD for therapy?" What did he tell Ashley, Jules wondered, that she let him in and agreed to this?

"Okay, we're going to do it a little differently this time. More like guided meditation. You three are going to take the LSD and I'm going to talk you through the dream sequence. In theory."

"This is your explanation?"

"It actually used to be a very common approach to acid usage, if—"

"That's not the explanation I mean," Jules said.

His jaw tightened and he blinked slowly. "Yes."

Jules set her coffee cup down and picked up the water. There were a couple of ice cubes circulating in it, knocking against the sides, clink clink. Little things seemed too loud and bigger things, like a motorcycle going by out front, seemed too quiet. Maybe she shouldn't do this after all. Fuck it.

"There aren't any guarantees, when you drop acid, what will happen. But we have a link established already, however tenuous, and we'll build on that. What music do you want?"

"Bruce Springsteen," Ashley said.

"Which one?"

"Born to Run," Jules said. "What else are you going to do? For our tenuous link?" She knew things that could be done. Ashley did too. She also thought that their protections would keep that link right where it was. For them. Oh but Una.

"Nothing too elaborate. This is relaxed, just relax. We're in an exploration phase."

"That sounds pretty creepy," Ashley said, stubbing out her cigarette.

"Stop teasing him," Una said, but with that weird giggle in her voice. The Una's taken leave of her senses around her *boyfriend* giggle. What did he do to her? And how?

"Sorry."

Jules drank her water and watched Jenner select the album and put it on the turntable, but he didn't lift the needle just yet. He'd left a box of chalk on their table, and selected a piece. He'd almost touched the wall with it and then paused and turned to Jules and Ashley, both staring at him. "Is this all right?" he asked, stilted, but he'd stopped himself for once.

"Why the circles?" Jules asked. "Expecting trouble?"

"Insurance. Spiritual activity has the potential to draw unwanted attention," Jenner said.

"What kind of unwanted attention?" Una asked.

"Demons," Jules deadpanned.

"And things, yes. I think that people got in the habit of referring to things they did not understand as demons."

"So you're saying ghosts and demons and Others are just different names for Things That Are Not Human?"

"In a manner of speaking, though that's very simplistic."

"Simplistic is how you've been running things," Ashley interposed.

"I can never tell if the three of you are fighting or not," Una said.

"Not at the moment," Jules said. "Though Jenner may have been better served asking if we had our own protections in place, before just deciding to go ahead and do his own."

"I apologize for infringing," he said. "I'm not used to dealing with people in the know."

"This isn't inspiring much confidence," Ashley said.

"It sounds more like you go around taking advantage of people," Jules added.

"I'm so pleased with your high opinion of me," Jenner said, setting down the chalk.

"So Jenner isn't going to use the chalk?" Una asked.

"He is not," Jules said. "Bathroom break." She made it out of the couch and across the living room without wavering or stumbling over something that wasn't there. She just sat for a few minutes with her head in her hands. Dropping acid with Jenner as their 'spirit guide' wasn't a reasonable thing to do, but dropping acid and having a spiritual journey with the experience she already had this afternoon had a strong potential to be enlightening. "All right, let's get this show on the road," she said, returning to the living room. She looked at Ashley. "You already took yours."

"I did, I needed to get it over with. Una waited for you, though."

"Well it's good to know who my real friends are." Jenner held out the Altoids tin, and Jules grabbed two tabs of acid. She put one on her tongue and kissed Una; Their tongues touched, and the tab transferred. Una pulled back, slowly, and Jules took her own tab. Jenner dropped the needle on the record. The piano and harmonica hit for "Thunder Road" and Jules lay back and closed her eyes.

There were a few moments of just music, time for the drug to circulate, time for them to relax and settle in to their respective spots. And then Jenner talked. For his sinister faults, Jenner had a great speaking voice, one that begged to tell stories, and he was telling one. Even when she concentrated, Jules didn't know what he was saying, not the words. She heard the timbre of this voice, the rise and fall, the pauses when he took a breath. It was like somebody's hands were held protectively over her ears, though she knew hers were folded on her belly.

Una said something and laughed, and Jenner laughed with her. Jules slipped into the sort of state she reached for when she was actually reading Tarot and not just playing around. Jules opened her eyes, in her dream or in her third eye. She was on her back on their broken down old couch; she was standing at the arched door to the heating plant, behind the carousel building. The carousel ride itself was long gone, packed up whole cloth and taken away to an amusement park down south somewhere. Jules had actually never approached the heating plant directly, and didn't know if it really had big greened bronze doors with a medusa on them. Did the carousel have big greened bronze doors with a medusa on them? No idea. But the medusa stared at her balefully, and she pushed the door open. It didn't even creak as it swung away from her, and the blackness before her was a warm mouth, concrete floor leading immediately into shadow and darkness.

Because Jules did not know where else to go, she took a step inside, and then another. The sound of the ocean was at her back, but also echoed up through the heating plant, and she knew there were tunnels, tunnels under the boardwalk so the plant heated the Casino and the carousel, all the way up to Convention Hall too and more, she didn't know. But there were tunnels and the ocean pounded and roared above them and through them like an open throat.

And there were ghosts there. Pale hands and faces came to her from the darkness, and she was frozen at first, chilled through her throat and spine and belly to be confronted by them, but they were kind to her, and took her cold hands in their cold hands, and led her down into the steam and darkness. She could see the walls sometimes, and they were bare concrete sometimes, others painted. The paintings were of mermaids and winged seahorses and the ocean always the ocean. There were playing cards and apples and darkness. Jules tried to look behind her once, but the way had closed, and there was only darkness. She couldn't even say how the dark behind her was less welcoming than the dark in front, or how the dark in front asked her to keep coming through it, but it was how she felt, and it was how the ghosts were acting. She didn't have any reason not to trust the ghosts.

She turned to one, to ask it about Jenner, or even about Hector and her father, because of course ghosts would know. But they were unable to speak, the ghosts, and only shook their heads at her and patted her bare arms with their icy fingers. She stumbled on the steps, when had she started walking down steps? It had been a slope at first. But she couldn't catch herself, her balance had been crap since she'd been shot, accidentally or not, what a notion, and she landed on her hands and knees at a turn in the tunnel, steam pushing past her, not hot enough to burn, an exhalation. There were pipes bolted to the walls. Her hands and knees ached, throbbed, and she brushed little pebbles from her skin. Just scraped, not really too bad, some blood bubbled up. The ghosts circled closer, and where they touched her broken skin, they grew a little more substantial, less like exhaled smoke and a little more colored in.

They pushed her forward.

There were other tunnels off the one Jules walked, and when she peered down those passageways, the ghosts pushed her again. The pounding ocean was like her pounding heart, though she heard music too. Carousel music, and then band music. So many bars had bands in them of an evening, accidentally or on purpose. The Jersey Shore Sound used to be a Thing.

A couple of times, somebody else walked past her in the tunnel. She couldn't see anybody's faces, and their clothes didn't make sense either. People must work in the tunnels for maintenance, she thought. Or were these more ghosts? Or more Others? She didn't sense a darkness anywhere near her, not like that night on Essex Road. Maybe it was just luck. Or maybe it was by Una, the most vulnerable of their group.

Jules tried to look for Una. Una, who just thought she had a cool neat boyfriend and didn't see the same things Jules did despite what she'd been told. She tried to look for Ashley, her partner in crime, her other magical half, or at least another piece in her magical puzzle. One of the turns had another bronze door right at the end of it, a cool white light shining down on the handle. Jules ran for it and pushed it open, the ocean growing louder and louder, the cries of gulls frantic in her ears. The door opened onto the beach in front of Convention Hall, in between the building and the ocean. The sand was heavy, wet, stormed-upon sand, and when Jules looked out onto the water, she saw an old steam boat foundering there, smoke rising from its decks. It was people whose cries she heard, not seagulls at all. How weird and horrible, to be stuck on a burning ship so close to shore.

People on the top deck of the Morro Castle looked like they were jumping off, or flying away, and Jules stood and wiggled her toes in the sand and watched them. She knew enough to realize she could change nothing about the scenes she was shown. Ghosts could be of events as well, not just people. Some seemed very upset, but a lot of them seemed unconcerned as well. The smoke looked a lot like the ship was just overflowing with steam. But it glowed too, like a miniature sandbar sunrise.

She heard a voice in her ear, but it seemed so far away, and she turned away from the ocean and walked up the beach. She remembered reading that when sea turtles hatched in built up areas, they got confused and went further inland instead of to the ocean, because of the lights. All the lights confused them. Jules could understand where the baby sea turtles were coming from; who was to say the moon was more important than street lights? They didn't have that kind of a living lexicon. There was no moon, not that she could see, and the boardwalk lights drew her. Convention Hall was lit up too, and Madame Marie's. The fortune telling stand was open, and there wasn't a line, so Jules walked right in off the beach, sand still clinging to her skin.

A woman sat behind a lace covered table, though Jules couldn't say whether she thought it was Madame Marie or not. The woman was dark haired and dark eyed, and had a pack of cards. "I don't know what a fortune costs," Jules admitted.

"What do you have?" the woman asked, shuffling the cards in her long fingered hands. Her nails were painted a deep wine red, fingers tattooed with blue-faded alchemical symbols, and flowers grew up her arms from her wrists. A bracelet of green eyes hung from her left wrist, a rosary on her right.

Jules dug in the pockets of her cutoff shorts. A piece of blue beach glass. A ticket stub for the Carousel and another for Rocky Horror. A guitar pick. A silver dollar. The shark tooth. The woman reached out and plucked the shark tooth and the silver dollar from Jules' proffered palm. "Is that enough?" Jules asked.

"It's enough."

Jules sat in the chair opposite the woman. The lace on the table seemed like doilies, or curtains, sewn together, hem to hem, to make a tablecloth long enough to drag on the floor and partway across the room, like ivy overtaking a brick building. Shelves lined the walls, and they were full of jars, some empty, some liquid filled, and some had things in the liquid. Jules noticed an eye, and a shark, and a tangle of throbbing vegetation, before she returned her attention to the fortune teller. The room smelled warm, like cloves and patchouli, and the cool ocean air blew in once in a while and stirred their loose hair.

"What will you tell me?"

"What do you want to know?" The fortune teller stopped shuffling and started laying the cards out. She stopped at ten, the Celtic Cross spread.

"Who killed my father. What Jenner wants. If Una is safe. And Ashley."

"That's a lot of things."

"Is it too much?"

"It might not be enough." The fortune teller laid her finger on the cards in the center. "These two are the heart of the matter. The Hanged Man. The Fool. This is you and one of your friends, and your friendship."

"Who's who?"

"I don't know you. I'm only reading the cards." She tapped the top card and the bottom card. "This is the deeper wisdom, the real matter. The top, this is how things appear to be." The Devil and The Magician.

Jenner, she thought. Or Hector? Could she still not tell, even in this dreamtime?

The fortune teller laid a hand on the cards opposite each other. To her left, Jules' right, was the Eight of Wands reversed. To her right, Jules' left, was the Nine of Swords. "You've come to a point where maybe you should make a decision, but perhaps you feel like you don't have enough information. Maybe you're unhappy with the source? And this—"

"The nightmare card," Jules said.

"Yes. You're moving towards a very dark time indeed."

"I'm not sure how it can get much darker."

"You'll regret saying that." The fortune teller moved to the bottom of the staff. "The Two of Swords, in the position that most clearly represents you, the subject of this reading. You are blindfolded, though not defenseless. You are unsure of your situation. You are avoiding quite a lot. But you can be in control, if you so choose. The Nine of Wands indicates you have hidden enemies, or a hidden enemy, somebody who has fought and won many battles." She moved to the top card. "This card, the Five of Cups reversed, plays against The Devil. This is the future, not tomorrow, not next week, but maybe weeks, maybe a month. Maybe a year. It's acceptance, and the appreciation of lessons learned. The Devil, though, is the adversity to be faced now."

"You skipped one." Jules pointed. It was the Hermit.

"That's your wild card," the fortune teller said. "It's being alone, but it's also guidance, perhaps inner guidance, perhaps outer."

"Isn't that the card that's supposed to tie everything up and put it in perspective?" Jules looked at the spread. Jenner was the devil. Hector was the devil? Jenner summoned devils? Hector killed her father, or paid the person who did? Jenner wanted to control a devil. Either all the pieces were here or they weren't.

"I suppose that's for you to decide."

"I wish this was more clear."

"If wishes were horses then beggars could ride."

"I don't know what that means. Oh wait, I do know what that means." Jules stood up. The sand on her feet had dried and mostly brushed off onto the concrete floor. She caught sight of herself in a mirror on the wall, the inside of this place didn't make any kind of sense, and on her normally bare left shoulder there was a tattoo she couldn't quite make out. She looked down; it was of a rose with angel wings wrapped around it, and a banner that said "We all fall down." She looked back up, and Madame Marie's had disappeared or she wasn't there anymore. She was standing in the middle of Ocean Avenue, and there were no people, no cars. Sand had blown across the road and the street lights were out. The moon was a frowning crescent through the roofless casino, though there had been no moon before, and a tall dark figure approached her from the other end of the street. Hector or Jenner? None of the shadows had faces. All of the shadows had faces.

A hand closed on her arm, and Jules jerked upright. "Jesus Christ, Jules, you almost hit me."

"Ashley?"

"Yeah. Are you going to sleep on the couch all night or what?" Ashley's curls were somewhat flattened, and she was in a big concert t-shirt, the kind they used to throw off the stage for free.

"I wasn't sleeping." Jules looked around.

"Shit, you were still tripping?" Ashley asked.

The candles were gone, the chalk was gone. "Where's Jenner?"

"He left hours ago. Una went to bed." Ashley sat on the edge of the couch. "How was it?"

"Edging into dark woods bullshit. Though perhaps enlightening."

"Me too. We need to figure out what the fuck to do about him."

"Like I've been saying. How did Una seem?"

Ashley shook her head and lit a cigarette. "A little shell-shocked."

"I thought it was bedtime." Jules took a cigarette for herself and lit it, settled into her corner of the couch with her feet tucked underneath her. Yorick lifted his head and looked at her, sniffing audibly.

"It was, when you were still out. I'm awake now, though."

"Me too, I think." They smoked in silence for a little while.

"What are we going to do about Jenner?"

"I don't really know. Puts it into perspective just how on our own we are, right?" Jules laughed softly. "We could just kill him and throw him in the ocean."

"That's dark, even for you."

"Dark trip, dark thoughts."

"True enough." Puck chittered in the darkness somewhere, and then his pale shadowy self came across the floor and up onto the couch. He reminded Jules of the ghosts, and she looked around. None, at the moment. No ticking clock either.

Chapter Twenty Three

When they sat down the next morning, they would've liked to include Una, but she was gone already when they got up. There was French toast in the oven on 'warm' with a note on the kitchen table that she was having lunch with John and going out with Jenner in the evening.

"Well isn't that something," Jules said. Ashley pulled the cookie sheet of toast from the oven and set out plates.

"Awfully nice of her."

"Wonder what she saw?"

"Probably something Care Bear and perfectly safe just like last time."

"Shit, we didn't do this last time, did we?"

"We did. The ghosts, remember?"

"Oh yeah." Jules drank her coffee, pretended not to notice the concern in Ashley's face and voice. So fucking what, she forgot things sometimes. She could be dead instead. It was an okay trade. "So I walked through the steam tunnels and then got a tarot reading at Madame Marie's after watching the Morro Castle sink. And I'm still not sure if it was Hector. I'm very sure Jenner is a big problem, but I'm not sure if he's related to my problem or his own thing. It might be both. You?"

"I was at Sandy Hook, at the concrete bunkers and stuff? It was all grown over, though, practically woods with the buildings sticking out of it at weird angles. It was pitch black but sunrise, except sunrise was in the wrong direction, and not sunrise at all, because it was the Minuteman missile they used to have there launching." Ashley paused, looking into the swirling surface of her freshly stirred coffee. "Faces in the woods," she said finally. "Lots of faces in the shadows, watching me. I looked for you, and Una, but didn't see either of you. Didn't see anybody. And then the ocean came up and took it all, as the bomb flew away."

"Well Jesus."

"Right?"

They drank their coffee, ate their French toast. Jules scrolled through the news on her phone, not for any particular reason, just to see possibilities that she declined to interact with. She hoped she would, hoped she wouldn't, see any news about her dad. About the shooting. About the police investigating or not investigating. Anything. Nothing. She didn't want to know, actually.

"Do you feel awful?" she asked once she hit bottom on her coffee. Ashley nodded.

"Yup."

"Do you feel like he explained anything like he was supposed to?"

"Nope."

"So what do we do?" It was hard to break up with somebody else's boyfriend, if you cared about that somebody else still being happy with you. Did she? It was better to have Una in their apartment than just at Jenner's mercy, though they hadn't really kept him from her either. They'd tried. Kind of. He just ignored any attempts at decency. He just needed warm bodies and used them towards his own purposes, pulling Una deeper and deeper while telling her nothing. He was going to abandon her, Jules felt it suddenly, her eyes going magnetically to Ashley's.

"Are you thinking what I'm thinking?" they both said, both laughed tensely.

"Okay. He's awful, you knew it all along. Thank you for never saying I told you so, you are the best friend a girl could want."

"Thank you," Jules said. "He's not a vampire, though. We can't just uninvite him and expect that to work."

"No. But. He did some kind of forgetfulness thing to Una. What if we...tried to reflect it?"

"Would that work, after so much time?"

"Wouldn't hurt to try then, right?" Ashley grinned that I-dare-you grin that they used to wear so often, when they snuck out, when they borrowed a car without licenses, when they got somebody to buy them booze, when they got their first piercings, and tattoos.

"Guess not," Jules said, and then her phone rang mid-scroll; she flinched, fingers dragging across her mother's name. "Fuck," she said.

"I think you just—"

"Juliet? Juliet, I can't hear you!" Gladys' voice, strident and tinny, issued forth. Jules covered the phone with her hand.

"I wasn't ready for this," she whispered to Ashley, who smiled sympathetically, shrugged.

"She's just checking in, go take it."

"Sorry Mother," she said, stumbling out of her chair and pushing through the beads to go to her room. Those fucking beads, clack-clattering and grabbing at her hair. She stopped, grabbed a handful of them, and yanked. It came partway loose from the thumbtacks above the doorjamb, and one of the strands broke, pattering beads to the floor. Ashley brayed laughter and Jules stomped off to her room. Fuck the neighbors.

"Juliet what was that?"

"A bead curtain incident."

"A what?"

"Nevermind, what's up?" She shut the door and flopped on the bed before she realized Yorick hadn't followed her fast enough. Maybe he'd been confused by the beads. It was fine.

"I wanted to talk to you about Hector," Gladys said. "I'd hoped to tell you this over dinner last night, rather than over the phone, but you were indisposed."

"I was," Jules said. If she was a dog, she thought, the hair on her neck would be standing up. She almost shot Hector yesterday. She could've just shot Jenner, why didn't she think of it? Oh. She didn't want to go to jail. Was she rich enough that she could get out of that? Maybe. Maybe if it was Jenner, probably not if she killed Hector. "Wait tell me what."

A pause, like the pause when she called her dad. Was there a crackle on the line? There was no line, they were both on cell phones. "Hector and I eloped," Gladys said, the joy in her voice a knife in Jules' heart.

"You what," she whispered, or shouted.

"Well, the questions you were asking about the wedding reminded me of just how *tiresome* wedding planning is, and how I already did that with your father," she stumbled over those words, a little, at least, "and I just didn't want to go through that again. And the police captain in charge of the case got in contact with us and said that we were cleared of any suspicion and so we just went to the courthouse and got married! Mr. Poling and one of the secretaries there were our witnesses." Jules couldn't say anything, could only breathe. Her head was filled with the roar of the ocean, or maybe the gathering rage of her father's ghost. She waited too long. He *told* her and she waited too long. "I was going to tell you in my office but then the phone rang and—"

"Is that the only reason why you waited?" she choked out finally. She hated herself, for not noticing a wedding band on her mother's finger. She hated her mother more, for doing this.

"Pardon?"

"The police investigation. Is that the only reason you waited, to marry Hector?"

"Oh well no, there was more to it than that but—"

"Is that why you kept Hector around all this time, so you had a backup in case something happened to Dad?"

"*Juliet.*" She'd never heard her mother sound like that, and it hurt but it was satisfying too. Like finally she'd broken through the polished shell and was dealing with the real Gladys for the first time in years.

"I'm just trying to understand, Mom. How *could* you? Somebody *killed Dad* and now, well, the police say it wasn't either of you so you might as well make it official. How long did you wait? Like, modernly, I mean, I know you were fucking in college too. Were you cheating on Dad? With Hector?" She was definitely yelling and Ashley was knocking on her door and saying something and Yorick was barking and the phone was getting really hot.

"Juliet I am your mother and you will not talk to me like that." Gladys was crying, or almost crying.

"That's right, you're my mother, and I needed you to *act like it,*" and her final words were in her father's voice and there was such a pressure in the room, in her head, and then a sound like a balloon popping as her phone caught fire in her hand, and the sound of the door splintering as Yorick broke through snarling, and she fell to her knees as Ashley grabbed her wrist and used her momentum to fling the phone away towards the bathroom, where it clanged into or against the cast-iron tub.

And then everything was quiet. Just her breathing, and Ashley's breathing, and Yorick's panting. Splinters falling to the floor. The pinging of hot metal. The chemical smell of burned battery.

"Jules what the fuck?"

"Mom got married."

"And that made your phone explode." Ashley's eyebrows were raised so far, they seemed to be trying to reach orbit.

"My dad made my phone explode."

"Your dad..." Ashley trailed off, walked to the bathroom to check on things, came back. Yorick snuffled around the perimeter of the room, left, came back, bumped his head into Jules' shoulder. "Well it doesn't look like we're going to burn the house down anyway."

"Okay." Jules wondered if her hand should hurt and looked at it, but things seemed okay. She crawled the couple feet to the bed and got up on it, and once she was there, surrounded by the carved symbols, her head was quiet again.

"Are you okay?"

"No." It was such a relief and no help at all to not have to lie.

"Are you not okay in a way I can help with?"

"I don't think so." She thought about it. "Not right now. I think I just have to process."

Ashley nodded somberly. "Maybe wallow a little."

"Maybe." She wanted Ashley to leave and was afraid Ashley was going to leave and didn't know what she wanted after all.

"Move over, you dope," Ashley said, and she realized she was crying. She moved over, and lay down, and Ashley stroked her head, and rubbed her back, while she sobbed herself hot and hollow and dry. After that they just stayed there spooned together, Jules' skin feeling stretched too tight on her bones, unable to find any of her thoughts, other than the echo of her father's ghost, other than her mother's happiness that she was so swift to wound. She took too long. If she'd shot Hector yesterday, in that same place, her mother would have been twice widowed, once again under suspicion. If she'd shot Hector yesterday, maybe she'd have some peace already. She took too long. She finally drifted into a fitful and uneasy sleep, Ashley her calm anchor.

Chapter Twenty Four

D ays passed, some with Ashley leaving to work, some not. Una came and left like a shadow; Jules was mad at her, a little, for knowing that Gladys got married and not saying anything. But being mad at Una wasn't something that ever *lasted*, they knew that from childhood. Still, Una stayed away.

Jules felt like a raw nerve; she felt like she knew when every single person entered and left their building, like she had some cosmic sense of their life energy. Sometimes the ghosts stood in a ring around her bed and sometimes they didn't. She didn't see her father's face among them, but she heard his voice sometimes, at a distance, like he was at one end of the hall and she the other. At one end of the huge dining room table and she the other. As if she was living and he was dead. Every time she remembered that, the pain flared anew.

Her floor creaked and somebody sat on her bed. Yorick didn't even move to acknowledge them, and they didn't say anything, but after a moment, she smelled John's cologne and without opening her eyes, asked "What do you want?"

"What's wrong with my sister?"

"How the fuck should I know? Did she get a B or something?"

"She's stopped going to her classes."

That made Jules open her eyes. "Oh really?"

"She hasn't gone for about a week now." He looked into her eyes, seemed to really see her. How often did he do that? How often did anybody but Ashley do that? "You look like hell."

"I feel like hell." Or, she didn't feel like anything. Which was. Perhaps concerning. She couldn't make herself care right now. She sat up and still felt nothing. When was the last time she took any meds? She found cigarettes on her bedside table but no lighter and sat there, stymied.

"Is it related to what's happening with Una?"

"I hardly think Una is upset that Gladys and Hector eloped."

"She cried at the news, but that girly happy kind of crying." John watched her looking around but made no move to help.

"Of course."

"What happened to your door?"

"Yorick." The dog moved his head to her knee and she ran her hand up his nose, held one of his upright ears for a moment. She saw the look on John's face and was too exhausted for much of a lie. "It was when my phone exploded."

To John's credit, his facial expression didn't change. "Your phone. Exploded."

"I think it's still in the tub? It was an old door."

He got up and walked to the bathroom, presumably poked the phone, came back. "Juliet, why did your phone explode?"

"How am I supposed to know?" She stroked her hand across Yorick's head, ran his velvet ears through her fingers.

"When did that happen?"

"The day Gladys told me about her marital status." Her head was buzzing again and it could've been from any number of things. It was better because she was still on the bed, she thought. Even so, she could feel her father's disappointment. His weary, deep-seated rage. "I was on the phone with her actually. Great timing right?" She laughed and knew it sounded all wrong.

John was still staring at her oddly. "Una needs some kind of help, if you wouldn't mind stopping whatever this is for five minutes to have a look at the people around you."

"Oh what a good idea, John, I could just...snap out of it! Shit, why didn't I think of that?" She put on her Juliet Duncan doing picture for the newspapers smile and climbed out of bed to stand with the most perfect posture and shake his hand. Yorick watched with interest. "I'm healed, you're a genius!"

"Stop it." He jerked his fingers out of her grip. "Look, I know I'm an asshole but everything isn't about you."

"It isn't?" She let her smile turn into a bared-tooth grimace.

"Jules..." her name a sigh, he sounded as tired as she felt.

"Fine. Una has some scumbag of a boyfriend and we told her, and him, that he isn't welcome here anymore. I'm not sure if he stayed in touch long after that, you'll have to ask Ashley."

"A boyfriend? Una's acting like this over a boyfriend? I thought you'd let her get into drugs or something."

"I didn't let her do anything," Jules muttered. This was very weird in a way she couldn't quite pinpoint. "She's acting like what?"

"Well she stopped going to her classes. Didn't withdraw, or talk to the professors or anything. And when I call her, or Dad, she answers but she's not herself." She rolled her eyes and he tried again. "She's wandery. Spaced out. She seems disconnected from the conversation and it doesn't end up going anywhere. And she doesn't really say anything."

"That does actually sound like drugs," Jules said, confused, uncertain. They didn't smoke *that* much pot, unless Una decided to dedicate herself to blazing everything she could get her hands on. They only dropped acid those two times since she came to live with them. Though the second time, the dark-woods time...if Una's was worse than hers or Ashley's. "What?"

"Well first I said really funny, doing an impression of Una's detachment but you were really gone there." She was sitting on the edge of the bed again, somehow. He held her wrist, lightly, like he was taking her pulse, or like he didn't know how else to touch her.

"I'm sorry." She was sorry for so many things. She probably really did owe John an apology. "I'll try to catch her tonight, talk to her, see what's going on."

"Thank you," he said, and he seemed to mean it. "Ashley said she was going to be back in an hour or two, do you want me to wait?"

She did, and she hated herself for it. "Better not. If you're still here when Una comes back she'll just clam up."

"You're probably right," he said, and he finally let go of her wrist. Her skin tingled where his fingertips were. "You should eat something. Get out for some fresh air. You look like your own ghost." Again. He didn't say it, but she clearly heard him think it.

"I'll take that under advisement," she said. "I'll call you if I find anything out."

"No you won't," he said, and at first she misunderstood. Thought he meant she wouldn't discover anything, wouldn't call him. Then he nodded towards the bathroom. Oh. She couldn't call him.

"That wasn't the last cell phone in the world. Ashley has one. Your sister has one. I could just buy another one."

"You could at that, Miss Duncan." And he left.

She went into the bathroom, because a shower seemed like a good place to start, and then she just stared at the charred husk of her phone, feeling utterly bereft. She got the last text from her dad on that phone. The last living phone call she had with him was on that phone. And now it was just a puddle of slag in her ancient tub. She couldn't begin to decide what to do with it, went and used the other shower instead. You can't just throw phones away.

The apartment's landline was ringing when she got out, and she yanked on a robe and went to answer it, the silk immediately clinging to every surface of her skin. "I got a pizza here for Juliet Duncan?"

"I didn't order—"

"He said you'd say that. He said to say you're welcome?" Delivery people must see a lot of weird shit, Jules thought.

"I'll be right down," she said. She found her purse, her wallet full of twenties, no smaller bills. Fuck it. "I'll be right back," she told Yorick.

The pizza dude on the front porch looked like he must still be in high school. "Here you go," he said, face flushing bright red, and she thought that maybe a different robe would've been a better idea.

"Thanks, here," she said, awkwardly shoving the twenty at him, and let the door fall heavily shut behind her.

The pizza did smell good. Upstairs, she took the time to dry off and get dressed before opening the box. White pie, in her top five. She would be flattered that John knew that, but it was probably in her dossier. Was he being thoughtful, or a good employee? It was rare that John had her guessing.

Yorick circled hopefully, and she dropped a slice of pizza in his bowl. He was a good dog.

Chapter Twenty Five

When Una came back that night, Jules felt reasonably alert, reasonably focused. Had a sick, solid feeling in the pit of her stomach that she was fucking a whole bunch of this up. Her dad told her about Hector. They should've driven Jenner off long before now. Her dad wasn't her fault but Una was supposed to be safe with her. She was supposed to be keeping an eye out for Una and instead she was so depressed and messed up and also curious and into magic that she didn't follow through.

"Juliet!" Una said when she came through the door and flipped on the light, clearly surprised. Clearly not expecting her to be on the couch, waiting.

"In the flesh," she said, tired again already but wired. Una looked like she'd been crying, her eyes a little puffy, a little glassy. "Want some pizza?"

"No, I ate at school."

"No you didn't." Jules meant to handle it more smoothly than that but her veneer was worn very thin. Una pressed her lips together into a line, a very Mr. Poling like look of displeasure, and picked up Jules' cigarettes off the coffee table. As she took one, Jules leaned forward. "Did you get another tattoo?"

Una fumbled lighting the cigarette, got it right the second time. How long had she looked so pale? When was the last time Jules saw her? "I thought it might make me feel better," she said in a small voice, setting the lighter down gently before holding out her wrist for inspection. A witch's knot, not quite the same one Jules had, but similar. Protective. Comforting, Jules always thought, until she'd received wounds far too mortal to assume any manner of comfort might work ever again.

"I like it," Jules said. "Did you go alone?"

A further shadow on Una's face. "I did," she said. She dragged on the cigarette, coughed, did it again, hugging herself with her other arm. Jules wasn't sure that she knew she was doing it. "Jenner hasn't been around."

"I'm surprised," Jules said, truthfully. She would've thought Jenner still had something to pursue, still had something to wring out of this situation. Or their pushback was starting to be too much, feeble though it had been. God damn it, she was uselessly mad about that.

Una stole a glance at her, to see if she was making fun, then reached over and stubbed out her cigarette. "He said something about his seeking taking him elsewhere. He said he'd call." It was the most bitter she'd sounded in her entire life, Jules was sure. It would've been funny, if this was a normal situation. Not drug and magic fueled.

"I'm sorry."

"I guess he got what he wanted," Una said and Jules froze a little inside.

"Una, did he—"

"No. No it wasn't like that. I wanted to." She sank down on the couch. "It was special, rose petals and lit candles special. I know you didn't like him Jules but I did. A lot."

"I know you did," Jules said, still feeling sick and frozen. Una liked Jenner, or thought she did. The way Una'd forgotten what she and Ashley told her, Jules wasn't sure of how much sway Jenner had over her thoughts and feelings, even for that small amount of time. It was enough time, obviously. Her first freedom, her first boyfriend, her first—Jules leaned over and hugged Una, who crumpled into her immediately. She cried, shaking, and it took Jules a while to realize that the shaking was separate, like she was cold. Jules pulled back a little and Una was covered in goosebumps. "Do you want a blanket?"

"No. I don't like how it feels on my skin." She shook Jules off, got up and paced around a little. Puck appeared in the doorway to Ashley's room, watched them for a little while with his beady eyes, retreated again. "Do you see them too?" she asked abruptly, gesturing at the dark corner, where two ghosts stood.

"Yeah, I do."

"I never did until the other night? Have they been there long?" Jules shrugged. "What's worse is they're not just looking at me. They're trying to talk to me but I don't speak whatever language they're using. But I can still understand it sometimes."

"That doesn't make any sense." Jules was almost starting to get the shivers herself.

"No, it doesn't."

"I don't know what to do for you, Una." She wondered if Jenner did something on purpose, the last time they dropped acid. Called something somehow, attached it to Una. Did something to Una. She didn't see ghosts until then. And Jules hadn't seen them before Jenner. What did he *do*? And where was Ashley? "Will you try something, though? Will you take one of the rosaries out of the cup on the shelf?"

"Okay. Why?" Una crossed the room like it was the tilting deck of a ship, and Jules watched her go, chewing on her thumbnail. The beads clacked quietly against each other, blue plastic faceted to look like sapphires or blue diamonds maybe, silver colored cross and centerpiece.

"I just thought of something. Put it on like a necklace."

Una wrinkled her nose. "You don't wear a rosary as a necklace."

It was funny, but bad-funny. "We both know that but humor me."

"Okay." Una stood there, looking at Jules with her big blue eyes like she was going to do something. Pull coins from behind her ears or make Yorick bark doves or something. "Now what?"

"Do you feel any different?"

Una closed her eyes for a second, rocking back and forth a little on her feet, toes, heels, toes, heels, rubbing the cross between her fingers and thumb. "No," she said, opening her eyes again. "Maybe? No."

"Nevermind then."

"I haven't felt normal since the last time we did acid."

"That's been...a while." Jules wasn't sure of how long, she'd had her own difficulties. Selfish, or part of her own bad decision-making? Or not making decisions at all. "That's been way too long, you should go to the doctor."

"And tell them I did drugs?" Una's voice raised.

"It's okay, they have to help you. They won't like, call the cops." Jules didn't think. But also, could there possibly be a not-magic reason Una might still be fucked up however many days later? She didn't think so. She needed Ashley here. They needed MaryAnne.

"I want to see the moon," Una said suddenly.

"We can just turn the lights out and—"

"No, not through the window. Let's go up on the beach."

"Okay. Text Ashley that we're going though. Please." Jules felt like she should say no, couldn't think of a reason good enough to say no.

Una shrugged, digging in her purse. "Why, where's your phone?"

"Battery blew up."

Una's eyes went wide. "Oh wow, Juliet. That's really scary." Her phone buzzed and she looked at it. "Ashley says she's working until one."

"Okay." Jules didn't know what time it was. Didn't know how long it had been dark before Una came in. "You're sure you want to do this?"

"Take a walk? Yes I want to take a walk." Una's laugh sounded tinny, hollow.

They locked up and went out the fire escape door, so they wouldn't have to go through the dark entryway, past all those pale faces in the corners. Una took off the rosary and left it on the kitchen table as they walked through; Jules watched her do it, and then figured there was no point and let it go. It didn't seem to do anything anyway. Maybe she was thinking too literally.

They walked up to the beach, and then up and down the boardwalk. The ocean sounds seemed to help Una chill out a little, and eventually they sat on one of the benches and watched the cars go by, listened to the near-distant murmur of people waiting in line to get into the bars. The huge full moon hovered low on the horizon, so stern, so pale. Jules kept trying to start conversation, talk about anything at all, but Una wasn't listening. Her eyes roamed across the few passing faces on the boardwalk, and traced the roofs of buildings. She twisted the edges of her hair and nibbled at her nails and bounced her feet. "You okay? What should we do now?" What time was it? How long before Ashley came to find them?

"I just want to look at the moon," Una said, her voice strained, and she so rarely said she wanted anything that Jules didn't argue. The air grew damp and heavy, the waves more grumbly, and the moon wheeled out into the heavens above them, flanked by glittering stars. Una stared up at the sky for a while, loose hair stirred by the ocean breeze. She didn't have goosebumps anymore, wasn't shivering and fidgeting either.

"Do you want to go back?" Jules asked, once she realized they were the only ones on the boardwalk and had been for a while. None of the places nearby were lit up.

"No." Una stood up, grabbed Jules' hand. "Let's go out on the jetty!" She pulled her across to the stairs and down on the sand before Jules could protest, or take off her sneakers, and they stumbled to the big black rocks, so much like the rocks that built up the edges of the estate to prevent erosion, flat on the top, sharp-angled.

"Una, the tide is coming in pretty high," Jules said, eyeing the slick rocks glinting in the moonlight, the dark, white-wreathed waves seething up around the edges.

"I thought you weren't afraid of anything, Juliet. You always act like you're not afraid of anything. I'm afraid of so much." Una kept pulling her, and she kept following. What was she going to do, leave her here? No matter what John thought of her, she was better than that. She had to be better than that, she should've taken more responsibility for Una. She wasn't used to the taste of regret, cloying in the back of her throat with tears, with the spray of waves. She slipped more than once on the rocks, and Una slipped more than once, stumbling, catching themselves, sneakers sodden and laces flapping, walking out almost to the end, the waves surging up, the moon shining down. There were puddled dips in the rocks, slick and seaweed-furred, either containing little white crabs or reflecting the moon and stars, or both. Then Una dropped her hand, jumped up onto one of the rocks that jutted further than the others, arms flung out. "Do you remember when I asked Jenner if he knew how to fly?"

"Una, come down from there. Yes I remember, and I called him a liar when he said it might be possible."

Una turned to face her, arms still out. She was smiling now, what seemed like a good happy Una smile, except for the moon glinting off her too-shiny eyes, the tears running down her face. "He did lie. He didn't know."

"Come on. We can talk about this at the apartment, we're both all wet." Jules held out her hands, like Una would Dirty Dancing jump to her, or like Jules could hand her down like a lord and lady alighting from a carriage.

"He didn't know but I do. He thought I didn't know anything but I know."

Shit, Jules thought. No no no no. "Una right now is not the right time to show me you can fly. Show me at home, okay?" She stepped closer, carefully, as another big wave whumped against the rocks, slapping them with so much water it took her breath away. Una stumbled, and Jules thought she would come down. Thought it would be okay.

"I'll be fine. I saw the shadow of the moon." And she started to turn in place, maybe to diving board leap and show her, no the air catches me, but her foot slipped and her hands flapped like startled birds, and Jules jumped for her even though she was too far away, she had to be, and their hands slapped together, Jules catching, grabbing, Una slipping, both of them falling, Una over the edge, Jules right at the brink, rock and mussels biting into her knees, everything in her left arm wrenching and stretching and groaning and straining like a wet rope against a ship's rail and then Una's weight was too much and she pulled free and fell, Jules slip falling after her. Una did not scream, Jules did, so loud she felt something catch and twist and tear in her throat, even as a wave slapped her in the face and her mouth filled with cold salt water.

She was too close to the rocks, the waves threatened to smash her to pieces against them, and first she kicked off from there, swam a few floundering strokes away, her dress wrapping around her legs, turning her into an unwilling mermaid. She tried to see and listen if Una surfaced, looking for her bright hair in the moonlight, looking for her white dress, but it was just the waves and the darkness, cold and salt. For all her inadvisable experiences, she'd never swam in her sneakers before, and spent a few tiring and probably wasted moments yanking at the laces and kicking them off. Still no Una. Her throat stung and her eyes stung and she saw pale hands reaching up but it was ghosts, not Una, so many ghosts, so many pale hands and she muttered a phrase she remembered from one of their old dusty books, something that might've just been a nursery rhyme once upon a time but weren't so many nursery rhymes cautionary tales? The hands shrank away from her.

The current pulled her towards the rocks, tried to pull her under and she was already so tired. Then a sputtering, a thrashing, Una, further out but there, struggling and crying out, and Jules swam to her, tried to call to her, but her voice wouldn't come, wouldn't carry, cramping up in her throat. She caught Una under the arms and a wave slapped down on them, another, another, and she knew what she was supposed to do, she knew how she was supposed to handle this, but she was choking and Una was flailing and they struggled against each other. She gasped as Una's panic forced her under, tried to cough, inhaled more water, fought to break the surface. Maybe if she died, Una would live, and it would reset some cosmic balance. And she wouldn't have to worry about anything anymore.

Somebody put their arm around her from behind, under her arms, and got her head above water. She didn't lose her grip on Una that time, and her head popped up too. Jules tried to fight them at first, coughing, choking, Una's panic feeding her own, then reminded herself no, stop that. Drowning people drown their rescuers like that. Una had gone very still, wasn't fighting her anymore. Jules couldn't even turn her head to look but she knew, suddenly she absolutely certainly knew, that it was her dad. She kept her grip on Una, somehow, her left arm burning from fingertips to shoulder, and they were away from the jetty, they were almost to shore, and then they were in the surf and as Jules tried to get her feet under her, her father's ghost swung her into his arms, Una falling limp to the wet sand.

She looked into his face in the moonlight, his same face, calm, concerned, caring. Laugh lines crinkled in the corners of his eyes, his dark hair just starting to gray at the temples. Her new collection of six or eight gray hairs were growing in just the same way. She could see the ocean and Convention Hall right through him, and was so glad that his ghost was intact and she didn't have to see the ruin of his skull as she had so briefly on that day. He set her down in the dry sand, just out of reach of the waves, and looked at her a moment. He touched her hair, and then there was only Jules, and the moonlight, and the ocean. Una lying still in the foamed-up surf. She struggled to her feet with a single dry sob, which made her cough, which hurt her throat worse.

She grabbed Una under the arms and dragged her as far up the beach as she could manage, coughing and tasting blood, though she was probably imagining it. It was probably just an ocean's worth of salt. She couldn't remember what you were supposed to do, and dropped or fell to her knees and tried to listen for breathing, but could only hear the ocean's roar. Fumbled at Una's neck and wrist for a pulse, but she was shaking so much herself that she couldn't tell, didn't want to hurt her. Was that the moonlight she saw, or was it Una's silvery ghost standing just beside them, hands out like she couldn't get her balance, fingers splayed? Was that Una's ghost, deciding should I stay or should I go?

And then a stranger was there, somebody she'd never seen before, saying "I heard a scream, is she okay? I know CPR!" and Jules crawling out of the way in the sand and letting a guy who smelled like beer and sweat and whiskey but sounded clear-headed do all the things she'd just done, but right. Breathing for Una, doing chest compressions, and Jules sat and dripped and waited for her to be dead or alive, and it seemed like she could feel every vein in her body every time it throbbed. She watched Una's ghost. What would the beach look like, to a dead girl? The same, but through a glass darkly?

Another person came from nowhere and tried to talk to her but she was just hearing white noise and so much of her just ached and she watched Una's ghost fall apart like a rainfall of glitter and then Una, pale as the sand, feebly coughed water, her whole body jerking with the effort of it, and there were red and blue lights melding into purple on the sand and the waves, chasing the moonlight away and finally somehow Ashley was there, hugging her tight. A paramedic put a scratchy blanket around her shoulders and she tried to laugh, tried to say it's summertime I don't need this, but she clutched it to her instead, or tried, her left hand and arm didn't want to listen to her at all, like it had kept up appearances during the crisis but now all bets were off.

Una was on a stretcher now, with her own blanket, a paramedic leaned over with a little flashlight. Jules was staring, focused only on Una even though she couldn't see anything through all the people, through the gathered ghosts, couldn't tell what was going on, and Ashley nudged her, sending fire to her fingertips. She croaked a cry of pain, and now her mouth tasted more like pennies than like salt, and she wondered for a minute if, when she tried to talk, she'd spit coins out. A paramedic came back to her, and she offered her arm dutifully. "We want to take you to the hospital to check you over," the paramedic said, and Jules nodded.

"Call my mom," she rasped at Ashley.

"I already did. Gladys and Mr. Poling will meet us there."

"I'm sorry," she said, for no good reason and for every reason.

"Don't be stupid," Ashley said, pressing her face against Jules'. "I'm sorry I wasn't there."

"Is Una—"

"Honey just stop talking."

Chapter Twenty Six

Ashley rode with her in the ambulance. The siren was not on. Nobody would tell her anything about Una, and it was shocking how much her throat hurt. She didn't know you could hurt your throat like that just by screaming under your own power. Or maybe her throat had already been damaged, when her dad yelled through her at Gladys. Not that she could tell a paramedic that. Ashley understood, though. Ashley spoke for her, and she actually dozed off when they were waiting in an exam room, Ashley's fingers laced through hers, no ocean sounds, no ocean smells, no ghosts she could see.

Gladys's high heels were loud like gunshots on the hospital linoleum and she woke with a start and then a groan. Ashley put a hand on her shoulder and she felt immediately calmer. "You're going to need x-rays," Gladys said brusquely. "Could you be pregnant?"

"No," Jules said, or tried to say, and then just shook her head.

Gladys, to her credit, did not say 'thank God', she just nodded. "You're going to have to explain what you were doing out there. Were you girls drinking? Doing other things?"

Jules shook her head. "We just went for a walk," she said. Ashley pushed a loudly crinkling plastic bottle of water into her hands and she drank it slowly. It kind of made things feel better but it also hurt to swallow. "And then Una slipped. Is she okay?"

She thought her mother wasn't going to answer at first, was just going to stare at her critically and then click-clack off again. "I haven't seen Mr. Poling since we got here. I don't know."

"Was she—"

"Juliet I don't know." Gladys hesitated, then stepped in and hugged her stiffly. "I'm so sorry you went through that," she said, quietly. "When Ashley said there'd been an accident I was afraid I was going to actually lose you this time."

"I'm okay," she said, even though she was probably lying. How weird, to comfort a parent, not the other way around. What would her experience of Gladys have been, if she also hadn't been shot in the orchard that day? Would they be close, the way Ashley and Janie were close, that parent-child barrier breaking down with adulthood and shared grief? But there was no shared grief, and Jules thought anybody who talked about shared grief was lying. Grief was its own world, its own angry, rough beast that lived in dark corners and snapped without warning.

A doctor, or nurse, or somebody came in while they were like that and asked something that Jules didn't catch but Ashley answered, and they went away again. Her arm hurt in an increasing throb that circled from hand to elbow to shoulder and back down again. At least it was summer, they didn't have to worry about hypothermia, because her clothes and hair were dry by the time she was wheeled back for x-rays. The machine made a noise like a dialup modem, and though Jules couldn't say what noise she *thought* an x-ray machine would make, it was confusing.

"I don't want to be here," Jules said, once she was back in the exam room. Ashley wasn't there, but she didn't know what Ashley and her mother would have even talked about while she was gone. "Yorick is still in the apartment."

"I'll send a car for him," Gladys said. "You'll come home tonight."

"I don't—"

"Please, Juliet. Must you be so difficult? Even now?" Gladys just sounded so tired. Relatable.

"Sorry." Maybe she was, this time. Maybe she could've saved Gladys some heartache, or maybe it would have been even worse, if she hadn't taken so long about Hector. She put a hand to her neck; the chain and cross were still there. The warmth of her hand on her throat didn't help at all. She let it drop. "I want some stuff from the apartment."

"You have things at the estate. Or can't you have Ashley pack for you?"

I didn't tell Ashley about the gun, she thought. Was the gun really important, or was the gun a choice? The gun or the apple seeds. Violence or subtlety. Or she already chose, when she started to wear the cross. Option three, the wildcard. She shrugged. "It doesn't matter." Ashley came back before any hospital staff did, with more drinks from a vending machine, a few bagged snacks.

"I'm sorry, you probably don't want chips or anything," she said to Jules, putting the stuff down on the empty bed. "And I saw John in the hallway."

"That poor boy. How is he?"

"Okay, actually. They admitted Una, but they're optimistic." Ashley looked at Jules. "He wants to talk to you, of course."

Jules rolled her eyes. "Not here."

"That's what I told him."

Nothing ended up being broken in Jules' arm, but there were plenty of tendons and ligaments and things that she'd strained and stretched in ways that she ought not to have. They wrapped her up, and the compression helped, and gave her a sling, which was awful, and discharged her. Gladys shepherded them both to the waiting car and they sat three across in the back seat, Jules in the middle. She used to sit in the middle all the time when she was little, and her dad and Gladys took her somewhere. She loved it then. She hated it as an adult but this time, it felt comforting, her father's ghost still lingering. She had to tell Ashley.

The estate was a beacon as they pulled up, all the lights on, even as the sky lightened in the east. She couldn't imagine why they would have done that. Yorick came to greet her, sniffing her arm all over without touching, his back legs quivering from the effort of not jumping up. He knew something bad happened, but he didn't know how to fix it, but she was happy to lean on him. Despite her shock or trauma induced nap at the hospital, she was so tired. She was always so tired. Gladys and Ashley talked around her about sleeping arrangements and cots and she just couldn't follow and she was so thirsty. It was so weird to be here without John, without Mr. Poling hovering somewhere. Without Una.

"Let's get you to bed," Gladys said, and for once, Jules just went along with her. Gladys helped her get undressed and into a nightgown, and for once didn't seem to tsk over her tattoos. She also didn't seem to notice the little scars on Jules' hip and she was wearily grateful for that. At least she didn't have any fresh ones, nothing healing with a third-day scab. *I was doing it and then I stopped* was a fine enough defense if needed. Ashley was provided with a nightgown, and then some staff came in and assembled another bed for Ashley to use. *We could've just gone to a guest room,* Jules thought, but the thought slid away. Something bad happened and her mother was taking care of her and she could just let things happen for once. Her mother was taking care of her and it was going to—

Another knock at the door, but instead of staff again, it was Hector. He had a funny smile on his face, like he was proud but didn't know how things were going to go over, and he carried a tray full of milkshakes. "Oh, dear," Gladys said, but she was smiling too.

"Is this a midnight snack or breakfast? I don't really know," he said. "I brought strawberry for you, Juliet, and I didn't know what Ashley would want so I had them do one of everything."

"Thanks, Hector," Ashley said, hardly missing a beat. "Is the green one mint or pistachio?"

"I think it's chocolate chip mint," he said. Ashley took that one, and he held the tray to Gladys, who shook her head and looked at her watch.

"I've got a meeting in New York, I have to leave soon to catch the train," she said.

"Like it'll leave without you," Jules rasped. She did want a milkshake. She didn't want the strawberry one that was 'just for her.' "Actually, can I have chocolate?"

"Sure," he said, but she saw the shadow cross his face. Maybe he was just mad he'd have to wait for another one to be made. Or maybe that strawberry had a bunch of drain cleaner in it. She should've taken it and then accidentally spilled it, just to see the look on his face when it ate through the floor in front of everybody. She drank some of the milkshake and it was like the platonic ideal of a chocolate shake. She might have also been loopy from trauma and exhaustion. But also it felt great on her throat, even better than water. Of course they didn't give her anything at the hospital. They thought her existing prescription of pain pills was sufficient.

"Okay now Hector, we're going to let the girls get some rest, they had a terrible night. If you need anything, call me or text me. But you know—"

"Mom I know how the house works, it's okay."

Gladys started to say something, stopped, and hugged her instead. "I'll see you at dinner," she said, and left, ushering Hector along with her. He took the tray with the rest of the milkshakes, so no chemistry experiments for Jules.

"Do you want me to find a liquor cabinet so we can pour Bailey's in these, or do you want to enjoy as-is?" Ashley asked, sitting on her bed. Jules never thought about how big her room was, until a second bed was casually added and there was still plenty of walking around space.

"Bailey's is tempting," Jules said.

"Enough said. Be right back." Yorick watched Ashes leave but then settled again, and Jules rubbed her foot against his back. Her thoughts were adrift already, but her nerves were on fire, and she heard Ashley long before she came through the doorway. "Like on one hand I know I didn't have to sneak and on the other it was a point of personal pride," she said with a crooked grin, and Jules laughed and then flinched. "Sorry."

"It's okay, just give me my medicine, doc," she said, holding out her glass.

"Was it weird or nice that he brought us these?"

"I'm afraid he poisoned mine," Jules said and Ashley's eyes went to the glass. "No. The strawberry."

"I wondered why you went chocolate." Ashley poured and sipped and then poured a little more. "We can never leave here, all other milkshakes are wrecked for me."

"You say that every time," Jules said. She had to stop trying to talk so much.

"Well it's true." Ashley looked at her, then reached out and rescued the listing chocolate shake. More of it was gone than Jules remembered drinking, but she also felt numb at the edges now in the way that a quantity of Bailey's might provide, and her teeth were cold. "Come on, lie down now. Do you want me to cover you?"

"I don't know," she said. "No." Ashley helped her take the sling off, and then she took a minute to arrange herself and her arm into the least uncomfortable position. "Thank you."

"You're welcome. If I'd known it was that bad..."

"It's okay." We didn't know and it was almost too late, Jules thought. Maybe they were too late anyway. They wouldn't know until they could see Una.

She slept, and she did not dream, both blessings that she couldn't have begun to expect. Sleep just dragged her under the way the ocean's current tried, and she didn't even try to fight it. At some point she heard the sharp jangle of Yorick's tags, and footsteps, and thought dimly that Ashes woke up and was taking him out, but she slipped away again.

She woke up to pain in her left arm and cried out, then cried out again at the pain in her throat. John leaned over her, gripping her bandaged wrist in his hand. "What the fuck did you do?" he growled.

She tried to talk, couldn't, tried to wrench her wrist free and couldn't. She struggled with herself, with him, for a moment before she woke up enough to jam the knuckles of her right hand into his armpit. He let go of her, surprised, and stumbled back. She sat up, achingly awake. "I tried to stop her," she said with effort. Her throat felt worse, not better. "And when she fell I got her out of the water."

"You weren't drinking?" Jules shook her head. "You didn't give her any drugs?" She shook her head more emphatically. A light was dawning in John's face and if he hadn't hurt her on purpose like a bastard, Jules would've been able to take pleasure in his realization that, for once, she wasn't the bad guy. "You rescued her. Dad said that."

"I tried. We almost both drowned. The current..." She coughed, and looked around, got off the bed and pushed past him into the bathroom for water. "Somebody else gave her CPR. I couldn't remember."

He stood there looking at her. She'd spent so much time fucking with him, the struggle of whether to believe her was clear in his face. But she needed him to believe her, if only so he wouldn't hurt her again or more, so she wouldn't have to do something about it that would keep her from killing Hector, and maybe Jenner. She had to be careful not to get too much of a list; clearly, one was already a lot for her.

"What happened to your arm?"

"Tried to catch her. When we were still on the jetty. She slipped." Sure, Una was going to jump, but she didn't. Una didn't intend to hurt herself, Jules knew that for a fact. Una never wanted to hurt anybody.

"And your voice?"

"I screamed when we both fell." Just thinking about it made her tired all over again, the weight and pull of the water, the struggle to have control, the struggle to help Una. Her father's ghost. Her shoulders slumped and John guided her back to the bed, almost tenderly, helped her get settled again. He must have come from the hospital, his suit was rumpled and his tie pulled askew.

"I'm sorry," he said, hesitantly.

"I've spent a lot of time making you hate me," she said carefully, deliberately.

"And laughing about it." He looked into her eyes, though Jules couldn't say what he might be looking for, and he brushed the hair back from her face with his fingertips, right at her temple where she'd noticed the grays, which meant he noticed the grays.

This was the wrong time and also the right time. She almost drowned last night. What better way to celebrate surviving? He was careful with her, more careful than he'd been even before he hated her. Neither of them undressed completely; they didn't know how much time they would have, and it wasn't like that time in the games room. They were hurried, but he took care, and when she cried out it surprised both of them and he covered her mouth with his, sustained the same rhythm until she did it again, and again, and then he stiffened and groaned. Then he arranged her clothes and dropped a kiss on her forehead, surprising her again, before he went into her bathroom and washed up. He'd never kissed her like that before. Maybe he talked to her more after that, maybe not; Jules fell asleep again.

Chapter Twenty Seven

She woke, shocked and disoriented, when the covers were ripped off of her. She leaned on her hurt arm to sit up, fell back, and looked up into Hector's angry face, sweaty and lunch-drunk, by the smell of it. "Wake up, you little slut," he growled.

"Hector what the hell?" She choked out, entirely unprepared for this.

"We're going to talk about your behavior and how it affects your mother."

"Oh are we?" She sat up again, more carefully, but he didn't move away from the bed so she could stand.

"Yes, we are. You aren't going to fuck this up for me. You can't keep doing things like this, do you even consider what it does to your mother?"

"I can't consider how every single thing I do might affect my mother, no, what is wrong with you? Do you consider that?"

"Of course I do. I've dedicated my life to Gladys." Oh like that isn't creepy, Jules thought, but he kept going. "So you're going to have some new rules. I know you haven't had many rules but do try and pay attention. You can't fuck everything that moves. You can't fuck around in the ocean in the middle of the night and get us dragged out to the hospital. Not unless you're going to do the decent thing and finish the job."

"What did you just say?" Jules was never afraid of Hector before. She thought probably he killed her dad, now she definitely thought he killed her dad, and she definitely felt like she had to get away from the estate, but that was just the idea of fearing him. This was the reality of fearing him. She was now afraid. "How do you think Mom would feel if I told her you said that to me?"

"She'd think you were lying. She'd think it was your trauma making you act out and say outrageous things. And she'd be sad and angry that you were trying to turn her against me. She would feel as though she had some hard decisions to make." He was probably right, the smug bastard. She had to be very careful.

"I just don't really know what you hope to accomplish here," she said slowly. There was water on her bedside table, did John leave that there for her?

"I'm just pointing out an option. Either you should be more careful or you should just go ahead and take yourself out of the equation. Do you ever think about it, how much better things might be without you? How many people you've messed up that would be fine if they didn't have to worry about you anymore?"

"Get the fuck out of here," she said, struggling to stand up, push past him. Where was Ashley? Where was Yorick? No, it was better that the dog wasn't here. If he attacked Hector he'd be put down and it would be her fault. "No, I never think about killing myself get the fuck away from me." If she had the gun she'd put it right into the fleshy part of his underjaw and pull the trigger.

"After everything that's happened, that surprises me. Especially after last night. Because that was definitely your fault."

She finally pushed past him and stood unsteadily between the beds. She wasn't going to cede the room to him, it was her goddamn room. "It was not my fault," she said.

"Una never did anything like that before in her life, it couldn't possibly have been her decision."

"That's the thing about people, Hector, they'll always surprise you." She drank the water, then wondered if Hector put it there and it was poisoned and cough-choked on the final gulps and then just couldn't stop coughing.

Gladys appeared as if summoned, and Jules was rarely so happy to see her. "Oh good you're awake," she said, breezing in. "Are you alright?"

"She's fine, she swallowed some water wrong," Hector said dismissively, and through her tears, from coughing and from anger, Jules saw Gladys pause just slightly. "You're back from you're meeting, I didn't—"

"I think that's quite enough, Hector, I'll see you for dinner."

"Of course," he said, strolling out as though it was his idea, as though he was not incensed at the interruption. Though maybe Jules could trust him to not hurt her mother. Maybe. Dedicated his life to Gladys, heaven help them.

"You must try to stay calm, dear," Gladys said, rubbing her back as the coughing subsided. "You had quite the scare last night, it isn't good for you to be. Agitated. You need your rest."

"You're probably right," Jules said, after a moment of internal struggle, whether to try and immediately blow open Hector's duplicity or not. But no, he was right. Gladys would never, ever, believe that he told Jules to kill herself.

"Are you hungry? Do you need anything?"

"I should probably be hungry," she said.

"Hey I just got called in, so I'm gonna—oh hi Mrs. Duncan." Ashley paused in the doorway.

"Called in? To *work*? Nonsense, you are my guest and just went through a trauma. They can't possibly expect you to pour drink and let strangers ogle you after that."

"Probably they don't really care? I mean, at least one of the bars I work at has an okay owner but, mileage varies."

"It's still nonsense. Put me on the phone with them."

Ashley and Jules exchanged a glance and then Ashes shrugged and got out her phone. "I mean, welcome to capitalism, but okay." She got the guy on the phone, and then Gladys swooped in and walked out to the hall. "I'm gonna get fired," she said.

"Or Gladys is gonna buy the bar," Jules said, laughing a little.

"Can you just imagine? I want to see her in a place like that, just once."

"Sometimes dreams do come true." Now that she was up, and talking, and had her life threatened at least once, Jules thought maybe she'd get dressed, walk around the estate a little with Yorick and maybe Ashley by the looks of it. Maybe she'd get hungry, that would make Gladys happy.

"Okay that's settled." Gladys returned, handed Ashley her phone.

"Mom, what did you do?" Jules asked, horrified in an amused sort of way.

"I gave them the name of somebody else they can call in for the next few nights, while Ashley still maintains her position with them at no fault to her record."

"Okay, cool. Thanks Mrs. Duncan!"

"Juliet, I thought you were going to rest," Gladys said, turning her attention back to her daughter.

"I was but I'm too awake now. I kind of want to wander around the estate for a while, maybe go to the orchard. And I'm sure Yorick is eating a crate somewhere about now, so I'll rescue him."

"Just be careful," Gladys said, as though any amount of care could handle the unexpected regard of the universe.

"I will," Jules said, as though it was possible for her to keep that kind of a promise.

"The orchard?" Ashley asked after Gladys was gone.

"I keep feeling driven back there I can't help it," she said. "And it's where I found this cross." She took the necklace off and handed it over. It was some small miracle she didn't lose it in the ocean.

"You found it? When?"

"Last time I was here." She pulled off her nightgown, pulled on a dress. "In a locked box grown into the roots of a tree. With a bottle of apple seeds and a tiny little gun."

"A gun?" Jules held her hand out for the necklace again and Ashley held onto it for a second, staring at her.

"Just a little one, yeah. I don't know if it even works. It was kind of gunked up but not a lot?"

"Where is it?"

"My purse, so, in my bedroom at the apartment."

"Juliet Duncan you have been carrying a tiny gun around in your purse? That may or may not work?"

"Well when you say it like that..." Ashley didn't smile though, just gave her the necklace back.

"This is serious, Jules, they actually arrest people for that. Or, people get hurt trying to shoot a gun like that and it explodes in their hand."

"Yeah, I know." But she needed this. She needed Ashley to tell her no, no gun. The gun wasn't the way. "I'll figure out what to do with it." She actually brushed her hair; it seemed to be growing again so quickly, some of it almost to her shoulders. She was going to have to go to a stylist to turn this into something workable. After. After everything. It felt like a resolution was impossible, and also looming.

"Thank you."

"What are friends for."

It was beautiful out, a perfect summer day. Humid, but that was beach life. Only a few pulled-cotton clouds in the blue blue sky, and Jules loved it and hated it at the same time. She could hear her dad asking if she wanted to go fishing, asking if she wanted to go get ice cream, asking her to come to the orchard. But did she really hear him? Like before? She needed to go to the orchard, like she was a broken compass and it was the only thing she knew to be true North. Yorick wasn't kenneled after all, and found them immediately, falling into step with Jules.

In the orchard Jules headed straight for the bench with some idea of conning Ashley into doing some quick and dirty spellwork while they were there, who cared if it was broad daylight. Who cared if she'd just told her mom she'd be careful, how many times had she lied to her mother before, and how many more times was she going to lie to her mom?

The bench wasn't there.

She walked right up to where it would be, and then past, still distracted by where they might center the circle, and how. She stopped, backed up. Looked at the blank sandy spot in the grass where it ought to have been. Looked around as though somebody might be playing a trick on her.

"What's wrong?" Ashley asked, but then she looked. "Oh."

"Where is it?" Jules asked. "They waited this long to take it out?" But she knew. She knew. After she saw Hector out here, staring at it. Staring at the bloodstain. He couldn't take the reminder, right there for everybody to see. He didn't want to see it again, now that he was the man of the house, the lord of the manor. He'd claimed his prize and anything else was just the details. Including his best friend's blood. Including his best friend's daughter. She didn't need to hear his smug fucking voice telling her that they got rid of it. Smashed it to bits with a sledgehammer, threw it in the ocean, all of the above, none of the above.

"Jules, I'm sorry," Ashes said, like she knew it wasn't the right words and knew that there weren't right words.

Though if ever Jules expected her father's ghost to start roaring at her anew, now was the time, and there was nothing. No prickling of the hairs on the back of her neck, no itching of her witch's knot tattoo to let her know something supernatural was stirring around her, no ringing in her ears, no sparkles in her vision. Nothing. She looked at Ashley and just felt blank. A radio station but no broadcast.

"This is really wrong," she said, like it made any kind of sense but Ashley seemed to get it.

"I wasn't out here before but something is off," she said. "Is it more than just the bench being gone?"

"I don't know." Jules walked further, walked through all the stunted and twisted apple trees, but couldn't see anything else wrong. She even stopped at the tree with the box in it, and it looked the way she left it. All the other benches, and statues, were where they should be. None of the trees were touched. Nothing was different except that her father's bench, like her father, was gone. "It looks like just the bench," she said finally, grudgingly. The bench and the intentionality of its removal, maybe those combined were the problem. Or maybe just everything was the problem, every last goddamn thing.

"Why don't we go back inside," Ashley said after a while. "Have some more milkshakes, with or without Bailey's. Have something ridiculous to eat."

"Okay." Yorick whined as they went, and she put her hand on his head. He understood so much, and so little, and she understood so much, and so little, and there was no way to fill the gaps.

Ashley's phone rang as they got inside, and she looked at the screen and made a face. "It's my mom, I need to—"

"Go ahead, go to the game room or something. If I don't find you, I'm probably in my room."

"Okay. Hey Mom!" She disappeared down the hall. Ashley spent enough time at the estate over the years that she was comfortable enough there. The staff left her alone, like it was a perfectly normal place to have constant teen girl sleepovers at. Which, for Jules, it was.

And for Una, it was, though really she was just included in Jules and Ashley's sleepovers some of the time. She didn't have any of her own.

Her stomach twisted when she thought of Una, and she just went to her room. If she needed anything, she could figure it out from there. Call the staff. Have Ashley do it. Or maybe John would come back. Her door wasn't quite closed, but she didn't remember closing or locking it, so whatever. But there was a charge in the air, and, like the orchard, she stood and tried to figure out what seemed different. What seemed off. There was a phone on her dresser, and she thought for a moment that maybe John told her mother, and Gladys got her a new phone. But no. It was her dad's phone.

Chapter Twenty Eight

She had to go back to the apartment. The estate was never the seat of her magical power, was not where she'd done her first scraps of spellwork, was not where she and Ashley learned together. She picked up her dad's phone, scared it would vanish or explode or ring. She pressed a button to wake up the screen and it was fully charged, though wouldn't be for long; there were about a billion notifications filling the screen. He was like that, never really checking anything, but not turning any of those things off either. She should give his phone to the police; whoever had it took it from the orchard when he was killed. Before John got to her. She could see Hector, in her mind's eye, standing beneath the weeping willow and waiting for Julian to lurch and slump like JFK. Waiting for her to collapse like a cut-string puppet.

She would not give the phone to the police.

Everything she needed was at the apartment: salt, chalk, the turntable, the records. She put the t-shirt she used the first time into her purse, wrapped around the phone, though she let go of it with effort. Anything else? No. She'd use the apple seeds. Yorick mournfully watched her pace the room, agitated. He'd found a tennis ball somewhere but it had wetly rolled off to the side. He couldn't come with her. He'd stop her. She couldn't leave him, it would be too suspicious. Oh god damn it.

"Let's go for a ride, buddy," she said the way she used to. When she drove herself around. She rummaged in her bedside table and found her spare car keys, spare apartment keys. Ashley would still be on the phone with her mother, Janie always had stories, and Jules walked briskly to the garage. She would not sneak in her own home, but it was tempting. Somehow, she saw nobody but staff, though was very aware of the cameras. There were always eyes watching, on the estate. Off the estate too; she paused mid-step, remembering Una say that security sometimes watches her. They didn't the night she and Una went to the beach. Was that just last night? So many missteps, so much wasted time.

She didn't see her car at first but, peeking under drop cloths, found it finally. It looked okay; tires filled. She didn't know what you looked for when a car hadn't been driven in months. Yorick hopped in the front seat and she made him get out, get in back. She didn't have his harness, didn't have the time. The car started right away, and she backed out smoothly. This was fine. She didn't remember to put shoes on. Whatever. She slid sunglasses on and drove serenely to the gate at the bridge.

"Miss Duncan?" The security guy wasn't able to hide his surprise. "I wasn't aware that you—"

"I finally got the doctor's clearance, can you believe it took so long?" she asked with her most winning smile.

"Good to see you up and about again, ma'am," he said, smiling back reflexively, still sounding a little unsure. Open the fucking gate, Jules thought, and he seemed to shake himself off a little bit. "Have a good day!"

"Thank you, you too!" she said, and drove off the island.

It was so strange and so utterly familiar, being behind the wheel again. Shifting. Clutch and gas and brake. Left arm and elbow protesting, keeping things straight mostly by hooking her thumb on the left side of the steering wheel and letting it hang. The stop and go of early afternoon traffic. Too many commercials on the radio but she couldn't settle on a station, on a song on her CD player, anything on the satellite, and she just periodically punched a button and changed it, her head buzzing, her thoughts agitated but not coalescing into words, sentences, plans. It was like every movie when a bomb goes off, there was a tremendous bang, then silence with the pop-squeal of ringing ears taking over. She was going to the apartment. She was going to call her father.

Yorick settled on the back seat and groaned. She should've put the top down, she put all the windows down instead, breathing in the hot salt air. There were clouds building up over the ocean, it was going to storm like hell in a little while, the kind of storm that would blacken the midsummer day and electrify everything. Good. She could make that work for her. She wasn't sure how, but so much of this was figuring it out on your own. Self-discovery, tapping into the chords of the universe. Trying to protect yourself while trying to extend your reach further and further. Seeing just how much you needed to protect yourself while stretching a little more.

The first cold fat raindrops started to fall when Jules parked in front of the apartment. Her absence was probably noted by now. Maybe even that her car was missing. Would Gladys come looking for her or send a lackey? Send Ashley? She might not have much time.

The apartment was as she and Una left it. The rosary still on the kitchen table. The ghosts still in the corners, vibrating with agitation, filling up on the weather. Puck came dancing to meet them and then stood on his hind legs and puffed up. As Yorick sniffed around the base of all the walls, his hackles up, Puck went up one of the bookcases to his vantage point by the molding. Jules went and got her chalk, her salt. Like last time, she laid out the circle carefully, shoving the coffee table out of the way, rolling back the rug, with his t-shirt in the middle, his phone. The shirt still smelled like the aftershave she got him every father's day, barely. She was afraid to breathe it in too deeply, like she might waste it. Like she might just use him all up.

She let her fingers walk through the crate of albums like automatic writing and picked out Pink Floyd's Wish You Were Here, so perfect but she didn't have it at the estate the first time. She felt like the man who was on fire as she dropped the needle onto the record. Yorick stared at her, his head low, unmoving, the whites of his eyes showing just a little. "Go lie down," she said, and her voice seemed distant. He didn't move.

She lit the candles she'd brought. Lit a stick of incense and breathed it in as thunder boomed out over the ocean. You were supposed to count, when lightning flashed, and she did until thunder rolled but couldn't remember what it was supposed to mean. Miles, somehow. She got to twenty the first time. Twelve the next. Nine. Eyes unfocused, swaying on the edge of the salt circle, music playing, feeling like a conduit for some kind of cosmic energy that she didn't really have a name for. The tips of her fingers and toes tingled and all the ghosts fled and it felt like the top of her head was open, like some thrilling crescendo had been reached...and nothing. The phone did not ring. Her father's ghost did not present himself in the circle. She called, and nobody answered.

She let her concentration drop, walked around the apartment shaking her hands out, wincing at the pain in her left, doing it anyway. She went out onto the fire escape and the rain plastered her hair to her face immediately. She had to try again. Maybe she missed something. She went back inside and dusted everything away, laid the circle again, Yorick groaning, bumping his nose against the backs of her legs as she walked, the witch's knot on the inside of her wrist itching, burning. She ran out of sea salt, had to go to the kitchen for the white plastic shaker from one of those disposable picnic salt and pepper shaker sets. Shaking it out took too long and she haphazardly sawed the top off open with a steak knife, coating her fingers with the little grains, the candle flames flaring up when she shed salt into them with her passing. The record was still playing, that wasn't a worry.

Jules closed her eyes, did some deep breathing to try to calm herself. She missed something, it was okay, she'd try again. On impulse, she got the jar of apple seeds from the orchard and scattered them in the circle. Added the gun. It seemed to make such a thud when she set it gently down, like it weighed a hundred times more than it did. Like she'd never be able to pick it up again, it was so heavy. She walked around the circle once, twice, as thunder boomed and lightning flashed at almost the same time and she cut herself just little bits, like she had before, and the house shook and still her dad's phone didn't ring, she didn't feel her dad, the crackle of the universe's answer sparking in her veins, firing her synapses, her dad wasn't there anymore. He'd already used himself up, getting her out of the ocean. Saving her and saving Una. She couldn't talk to him anymore, couldn't tell him that she was going to go for Hector, couldn't ask how to do it right so that it would satisfy him, soothe him. He was gone. He was gone.

She stumbled away from the circle, blinded by tears. Stumbled into the kitchen, Yorick padding after her, trying to mouth at her hands and she held her hands up away from him, shouted something wordless that made him stop and shrink back and she felt bad but she couldn't fix it. Her head pounded with all the power she was trying to bring to bear, veins in her eyes throbbing, vision spotting. She was going to go outside again, stand in the rain again to recharge, but kicked the recycling bin, made it rattle. She looked down reflexively; the wine bottle, when was that from? It was broken, the neck intact, the body a puzzle that would never be put back together.

She looked at it for too long, head tilted one way, then the other, like she was looking at a solution to her problem. It dawned on her that she was; she could fix her Hector problem with that. The house shook around her, the storm right over the roof, as she plucked the bottleneck from the bin, the glass so dark green it was almost black. It felt like she was in the ocean again, currents of magic closing around her like fingers on a giant unseen hand, and she thought that if Jenner could summon something big and ugly for no reason other than to talk, she could summon something big and ugly to end her father's murderer. He was gone and nothing she could do would bring him back, but she could at least honor him with the vengeance he desired.

She went back to the living room, unwinding the bandages from her left arm, flexing her hand as she went. Her wrist was on fire and she looked to see if the tattoo was actually glowing. It wasn't, but why tattoo yourself with a protective warning if you weren't going to listen to it? She'd made so many mistakes. She shed all her bracelets, clattering, to the floor. She almost paused, almost stopped, then looked at the t-shirt and phone and burning-down candles, and right before the record ended she drew the jagged glass up the inside of her left arm from wrist to elbow, like opening a package, like undoing a zipper. She'd already brought all this power to bear, the universe would take notice.

She knew she didn't have much time and dropped to her hands and knees, scribbling hasty runes on the circle she already had, slapping down a big pentagram like Jenner had spray painted, using the entire palm of her right hand. The left swiftly losing feeling, weariness rapidly overtaking her, Yorick barking, jumping on her, barking barking big and deep and she called and something answered, out there in the margins, in the spaces between, something turned and gave her its regard and she reached for a breath that wasn't there and instead grabbed hold of the memory of her father's voice roaring IT WAS HECTOR as she slumped face first into all the salt and blood and chalk and all the attendant ghosts reached down with their pale hands to take her.

Chapter Twenty Nine

She woke up, which confused her. On the apartment floor, with Yorick frantically licking her face and the smell of spent candles and burned electronics and fresh tomato plants in the air. She tried to move, didn't move, thought harder about it and tried again, but hands pushed her shoulders down.

"Don't," Ashes said from somewhere nearby, voice raspy with tears.

"I thought you were smarter than this," another voice said, and it took her some time to shuffle through the people she knew in her head. Not Gladys, not Una, not the school nurse. MaryAnne. She pried her eyes open and stared into their teacher's stern face. Former teacher. Hell, maybe MaryAnne just used them the way Jenner used them, to try and get something done before moving forward with her own education and she felt the tiniest spark of anger at that possibility. The urge to explain herself. MaryAnne always smelled like tomato plants.

"I needed," she said, but the thought petered out. She felt husked out, spent. All of her emotions were in a glass box, just out of reach. Did it work? Would some unknowable force put out Hector's light? How long would she have to wait? What else would she have to pay? She lifted her arm, blood-smeared, whole again somehow. Not unmarked; mostly just a pale line, but her witch's knot was split, broken. Maybe she'd already paid, and paid again, and paid again. She'd lost track of her page in the ledger. She was rich, but not this kind of rich.

"You needed to stop is what you needed but you just pushed and pushed. Every goddamn witch in New Jersey felt what you just did. Maybe the tristate area."

"Didn't." She closed her eyes again. The floor wasn't so bad. Yorick calmed his licking then stopped, laid down next to her with his head on her belly. Somebody was going to have to clean up all the blood. She should clean up all the blood. Or did it crumble away like the chalk normally did? How did MaryAnne save her? Why? She couldn't tell if she was relieved, or if she felt robbed. She knew that she shouldn't ask if it worked. She knew that it worked.

"What the hell is going on here?" MaryAnne pressed, and when Jules didn't answer, Ashley told her, haltingly. Her lighter flicked and clove scent filled the air, soothing, numbing. "Jenner," Maryanne said when Ashley got that far. "He is such a fucking asshole."

"You know him?" Jules asked.

"Of course I do. Goddamn edgelord." Cool fingers on Jules' wrist, taking her pulse. That was happening a lot lately, it seemed. "Have you seen your friend since?"

"It was just last night," Ashley said, and Jules frowned, wanting to argue. It seemed like a million years ago. It was just last night. "She's in the hospital for observation, to make sure she doesn't get aspiration pneumonia or something. But John said she seems okay. With it. I wonder if what happened broke Jenner's hold."

"It might have." A long silence, the two of them smoking. Jules wanted to ask for a drag but kept her peace for once. "And you brought her into the fold?"

"We were trying," Ashley said. "And Jenner made her forget, over and over."

"Yeah he's an asshole, and he works hard. It's a surprise but not a surprise. I'll see what we can do."

"We?" Jules asked with a stuttering laugh. "You left us with no way to contact you."

"Well and your phone blew up so how was I going to?"

"We needed you before that. And Ashley's phone didn't blow up, she's not that kind of girl."

"Thanks Jules."

"Girls." If MaryAnne had a shortcoming, it was an intolerance for Jules' bullshit. Or maybe that was one of her strengths. It depended on Jules' mood. It depended on her aim. "Juliet I need you to tell me what you did."

"What my father asked me to do," she said, with a smile that was more like a baring of teeth. But really, did he ask that? When did he ask that? Of course he did; there was no other point in telling her it was Hector if he didn't want her to do something. No other point in blowing up her phone when Gladys married Hector, if he didn't want her to do something. And then he rescued her instead. She closed her eyes again, and tears spilled down her cheeks and dripped into her ears.

"Ashley, can you just make sense of this for me?"

"Well I told you everything," she said slowly. She lit another cigarette, stuck it between Jules' lips.

Jules listened to MaryAnne stand, walk around the room. The neck of the wine bottle rolled across the uneven wooden floor and came to a gently ringing stop against something. A bookcase maybe. "Whose phone is this?"

"My dad's."

More walking, just slow and measured steps. Every once in a while, the floor still shook from the storm, and the rain on the roof sounded like somebody was dumping bag after bag of ice onto it. "These are the kind of runes Jenner uses. Did he teach you?"

"No. But we were there for—"

"Bless us, but you always were a quick study." Jules didn't think that statement required a reply and sat up with her back against the couch to smoke her cigarette. Her hands were shaking; that was probably to be expected. I am Lazarus, come from the dead. She looked at Ashley, who was very thin-lipped and pale, Puck scrunched around her neck with hanks of her hair wrapped in his little paws, face pressed against her neck. The floor was a bloody, salty mess. The chalk was gone. It worked, she thought, too tired to be triumphant. It worked. MaryAnne stood with her hands on her hips, looking down at the wreckage. "I'm going to try again. Juliet, tell me what this was."

"I tried to call my dad and it didn't work this time," she said.

"But it did before."

"Yeah." MaryAnne waited and Jules dragged on her cigarette and her glue-y thoughts came around to the notion that maybe she should expand more on that. "Ashley told you. He told me that Hector killed him."

"And you took this to mean that—"

"I should kill Hector." Ashley bit her lip and MaryAnne was still quiet. "It's not like I could call the police and say excuse me, my father's ghost said that Hector killed him. Yeah, the same guy that you just cleared so he married my mom."

"I suppose not." Jules had never seen MaryAnne this kind of angry, and it fascinated her, in a detached way. "And when it didn't work?"

"I tried again. And it didn't work." How much time had passed? Was it done already? Her mother couldn't call her. No, she could, the apartment had a landline.

"And then?" MaryAnne prompted, from right in front of her.

"I called something else." Was it the same something else that Jenner called? It would've had her scent. Would Jenner know that she called it? Let him come. She wouldn't have to shoot Hector now. She could shoot Jenner. She almost smiled.

"I don't think I can fix this," MaryAnne said, frustrated, resigned.

Jules looked up at her, baffled, and Ashley reached over and pulled the burning-up cigarette from her fingers, dropped it into the ashtray. "What do you mean, fix this?"

"Stop whatever you set into motion."

"I don't want you to do that," Jules said. "Why would I want you to stop it? You see what I did to get it."

"I think you probably don't know what you really did."

"Oh fuck you MaryAnne. You were *gone*. You've been gone forever! What was I supposed to do?"

"I don't really know, but doing up a circle to summon something in a language you didn't know to avenge your father's death wasn't on my list of possibilities. You had no idea what you were dealing with! How could you be so *stupid*?"

"Don't talk to me like that."

"Well somebody needs to! Did you consider what else might happen? Did you think only Hector would be in its path?"

"What?" Of course she'd only been thinking of Hector. But she didn't know what that unknowable thing would do to Hector, or how. Oh shit. The world was pulling into tighter focus, and the thunder rumbled more distantly, like laughter.

"No of course you didn't."

"What do you mean? Do you think Gladys..." She struggled to her feet, the world see-sawing around her.

"I don't know, is my point. And you *really* don't know, is my other point."

"We need to —"

"We? You haven't done enough?"

"You just said *you* can't fix it," Jules spat, grabbing onto Yorick before she fell over. "That means it's still my responsibility."

"Jules, you need to take it easy," Ashley said, coming over. "You almost just." Her voice broke. "You need to relax. Take it easy."

"I can't relax. I both don't know what I've done and also am maybe the only one who can fix what I've done. Does that sound about right, MaryAnne?"

"Maybe not the only one in the world but the only one in proximity. Though there's a point at which you just have to let things run their course."

"Clearly, I'm not at that point."

"You might make things worse."

"I might have already made things worse."

"I'm not talking about for you, personally. The world exists beyond you and your family and your estate."

"I know that." They stared at each other, Jules wavering on her feet, MaryAnne with her arms crossed. Jules had never known MaryAnne to change her mind about anything. "Help me or get out of my way," she said finally, and turned to go to her room. The Bible from the orchard was there, a bunch of her rosaries, maybe other things she could use. She had no idea. Her dress was soaked in blood, though, and step one was changing out of that. She'd already used this blood once, using it again was unlikely to work. The next step would be packing things up. She used all the salt. She could find more salt at the estate.

Her knees buckled partway across the room, and Ashley came to support her. "I can't drive your car, Jules," she said.

"What about the bug?"

"It didn't start last night. I walked to work, and then didn't take care of it today with...everything."

"Fuck." She was so tired. So much of her hurt that she wasn't sure of what didn't hurt. Her throat was fixed, somehow. She peeled off her dress and left it in a bloody pile on the floor, pulled the first one that came to hand over her head. Ashley was staring at her.

"What?"

"You've been cutting?"

"Jesus, Ashes, not now okay? Please not now? What are we going to do, call an Uber?" How many more people was she willing to pull into her sphere of influence? How many more people's lives was she going to risk? "Wait how did you and MaryAnne get here?"

"I am absolutely not driving you," MaryAnne said from the next room.

"Weird for you to come all this way and then not even tag along to watch how it plays out," Jules said. "Couldn't you maybe have a little more sympathy? Or schadenfreude?"

MaryAnne came to her doorway. "I'm sorry I was gone," she said, her tone softer. "I'm sorry about your father. I know how hard that is."

"Thank you." She leaned against her bed a moment, used it to get to the bedside table. Touching the little Bible had a grounding effect, made her head stop spinning. She put it in her dress pocket. She tried to take the edge off her tone. "We could really use your help."

MaryAnne was quiet for a long time, as Jules haphazardly shoved tarot cards, a bunch of beach glass she'd collected, chalk, and holy water into a bag. She brushed past her into the other room and swept up a handful of apple seeds. Picked up the gun. Was she crying? She was so fucking tired of crying. She was so fucking tired of all of this. "I don't know if my help will be enough," MaryAnne said finally. "Forces like that aren't in my wheelhouse."

"Three is better than two," Ashley pointed out.

"It is." Even though MaryAnne was wavering, Jules couldn't find anything else to say to convince her. She'd already said everything, or Ashley had already explained everything, and she couldn't conceive of how no was a reasonable answer.

The apartment doorknob rattled, and they all turned as John let himself in. He saw Jules, looked relieved, and then irritated, and then noticed Ashley and MaryAnne. Yorick ran to him as if to say oh finally, somebody sane who can help us. "Am I interrupting something?"

Chapter Thirty

"What are you doing here?" Jules asked.

"Your mother had me get you a phone," he said, holding up a Verizon bag. "And then you'd left the estate and I didn't think you should be alone." He looked at Ashley, looked at MaryAnne. "Can I talk to you? In private?"

"Sure." She put the gun and the bag on the coffee table together, hoped the gun wouldn't go off. It probably didn't work anyway. It probably wasn't even useful as a talisman for her. She felt no closer and no more distant from it than she did before she put it in the circle. She didn't know anything about it, had nobody to ask, and had already rigged a workaround to the Hector problem. Which she might need to undo. She didn't have the fucking time for John. MaryAnne and Ashley stood unmoving in the living room. She led him into her room, frowned because somehow she forgot she didn't have a door, led him to the bathroom and closed that door. The light pouring through the window was slate gray, and it was raining hard enough that she couldn't see the street. "What is it?"

"Who is that?"

"MaryAnne. Ashley and I have known her for a few years. She was away."

He nodded, then looked at her more closely, reached out and touched her face. "Is that...blood? Juliet why are you covered in blood?"

"No I—" She spent so much time never telling John anything, the idea of just telling him everything was so new and crazy that it just might work. "I tried to kill myself."

"Last night? On the jetty?"

"Shh, stop yelling. No, no. Tonight. Just a little while ago." She held out her arm, and he squinted at it, reached over and turned on the vanity light. He looked at the line through her tattoo, lightly traced the scar up to her elbow, her skin crackling with dried blood.

"This is new," he said. He wasn't asking; he knew what her arms looked like recently enough that she couldn't have healed from an injury in a normal amount of time. "But how? How is it like this?"

"You're going to think I'm bullshitting you and I don't blame you one bit but. Magic. It was magic. Ashley and me have been practicing magic, and MaryAnne out there is the one who taught us in the first place."

He frowned, staring at the scar, then peered into her face. "Okay I'll bite. Why'd you try to kill yourself?"

"Maybe I framed it wrong. I knew killing myself was a possible outcome, let's say. I was. I wanted more power, to fix a problem. But as it turns out, that was probably a bad fucking idea, I know you're really surprised. And we need to try to fix the problem that I created while trying to fix the problem that I had all along."

"I know you think you're making sense but you're not."

She took a deep breath, and closed her eyes, and she told him. It was all fresh in her mind, it just happened. It was fresh in her poor battered mind, she just listened to Ashley tell MaryAnne. She didn't hide anything, not the gun, not the sneaking around, not how she almost shot Hector that afternoon. For once in their lives, he didn't interrupt her, and when she was done, she opened her eyes. He had a resigned look on his face, and she couldn't tell at first if he was going to coddle her like a crazy person and then go have Gladys have her committed, or if he believed her. Then he reached past her, got a washcloth off the shelves behind her, ran hot water over it.

"John?"

"Let's get you cleaned up. You're not going out in public like that."

"You believe me?"

"Yeah. Yeah, I think I do."

"Why?" It seemed impossible to believe him.

"Because for once in your life, it seemed like you weren't lying." He wiped her face, kissing close, and as she was about to kiss him he said "Turn around."

"What?"

"I have something for you." She did, and he lowered some kind of necklace around her neck, fastened it. She tried to look down, but the chain was just slightly too short, pushed over to look in the mirror. It was the shark tooth she found in the water the day she almost shot Hector, silver delicately encasing the top of it, hung on a silver chain.

"I didn't know what I did with it."

"You handed it to me, and you were really out of it, so I stuck it in my shirt pocket. And then Shirley said that I should be on the lookout for a gift from you and I decided to take a chance."

"I lied to her to get bullets. I said I was having cufflinks made for you." She turned back to him and kissed him firmly. "I love it, thank you."

"You're welcome." He put the washcloth in the sink. "That's probably the best we're going to get."

"It's fine."

"Do you have any idea how—"

"Nope, I'm gonna wing it, just like everything else I do." He nodded, looking unsurprised.

"And what can I do?"

"I guess drive me to the estate. Or me and Ashley." She chewed her bottom lip. "We could go pick up Una."

"Una is in the hospital."

"If she's okay, she won't want to be in the hospital. And she'll want to help." Jules left the bathroom, went back into the living room, John trailing behind. "MaryAnne, can you be persuaded to evacuate my mother, if we all go to the estate? Is that letting me clean up my own mess enough for you?"

"If you think your mother would come with me..." MaryAnne said dubiously.

"I think I could convince her, given the time. Which is what we don't have. Can we all go or what?" Yorick went to the door immediately, turned and looked at the group of them, whined pointedly. "Oh buddy..." Jules said.

"Bring him," MaryAnne said. "Normally, with conditions like these, I'd say absolutely not. But bring him."

"Okay."

And they went down the stairs in the rain-dark house, carrying less than when they came, like John, or carrying what they weren't sure would help, like Jules and Ashley. MaryAnne remained a dubious, if wavering, cipher. It went against her ethics to turn her back on them, Jules thought. But she was probably telling the truth when she said she didn't really know what they would be able to do. But Jules couldn't just let things run their course, not without being sure Gladys was okay. Mr. Poling, for John and Una's sake. They did have an evacuation protocol, if the water rose too far; they had to do it for Hurricane Sandy, and maybe they were already doing it now.

In the car, Yorick panting loudly in the back, Jules turned on her new phone and tried to call her mother It half rang once, and then the super loud doo-doo-doo "we're sorry, your call cannot be completed at this time" pierced her skull. She figured the lady who recorded that message must have done so fifty years ago, back when there were still party lines and some phone numbers had words in them. Why pay somebody to do a new one? She hoped that lady was okay. Had lived a good life. Maybe free of the joy but cost and heartache of magic. Not that magic was her entire problem, but right now, it was a significant problem.

She made John give her his free hand and wrapped a rosary around his wrist for protection. Then she drew a witch's knot on the back of it with a sharpie that she found in the car's cup holder. "What do you think any of that will do?" he asked dryly. Trying not to seem too curious, she thought.

"Protect you, I hope," she said.

"Do you?"

"Yeah, I do. Don't be an asshole." He laughed, enough of a rarity that she was glad. The drive to the hospital was short, and took them right out of the rain. The sky was still dark, roiling, but there was blue sky visible further west. All of the trees, all of the grass, was furiously green, like somebody upset the color balance on the Instagram filter for the cosmos.

"What room is she in?" Jules asked when John pulled down into a spot in one of the side lots.

"She's in the old part, in 312."

"Okay, we'll be out soon."

"You're not just going to..."

"Magic, John. Magic." Of course, she'd never magicked anybody out of a hospital before, but there was a first time for anything. And her first time at bad decision-making was so many years ago she'd lost count.

Every time Jules was in a hospital, she thought about how much she'd like to roller skate through the shiny shiny halls. Not that she'd ever roller skated very much, or rollerbladed, or hoverboarded, or any of it. It was just what the floors seemed to invite, unimpeded, forbidden gliding. She thought that about school hallways too, and indeed had once skateboarded down the main hall at their private school. When the hall monitor finally chased her down, ready to bring down detention, or suspension, or even some good old red-faced, forehead vein yelling, he looked into the face of Juliet Duncan at the bottom of a short stairway (that last bit didn't go as smoothly as she'd intended), knees bleeding, and assumed it would cost him his job. The skateboard owner got his property back, though, and the floors were rewaxed without comment.

But that's what Jules thought about as she walked through the hospital halls. Gliding. Unimpeded. Nobody stopping her even as she dripped a trail of water like breadcrumbs. And she got to Una's room without anybody even looking up. Una was awake, in one of the few private rooms, cycling idly through television channels. Probably Mr. Poling was going to bring her a book later. Or maybe they were going to discharge her later, or tomorrow; they didn't like keeping people in the hospital for very long at all anymore.

"Hey," Jules said softly, and Una's big blue eyes turned to her, a big sweet smile lit up her face.

"Juliet!" she said.

"Shh." Jules opened the hospital closet; there were clothes there, bless Gladys, she probably brought them. "Here, get dressed. John's waiting outside."

"Am I being discharged? Dad said he'd be back for that tomorrow morning."

"We're kind of. Playing hooky."

"Oh, I don't know."

Jules sat on the edge of her bed and grabbed her hand. "I know it's weird, and actually it's probably pretty awful of me to come here like this, and ask you this, but I need your help. I need you to be number three for me and Ashley."

"Juliet, I don't know what you're talking about," Una said, but then she stopped, brow furrowed. She looked down at her hands, at her tattoos. "I do know what you're talking about," she said slowly. "You tried to tell me. And then it got all cloudy."

"I know. And I'm so goddamn sorry about that." Una's eyes filled with tears, and Jules scooched closer and hugged her. "I'm sorry, I didn't want it to be like this."

"It's okay. It's not your fault, you saved me," Una murmured into her neck.

"My dad saved us," Jules said.

Una drew back, amazed. "What?"

"He pulled us out of the water. And I dragged you out of the waves. And then he was gone." Gone, gone, gone, she thought, her own eyes stinging with tears, swallowing hard and blinking them away furiously.

"Let me get dressed. You can explain on the way."

"Do you need help?"

"I feel fine, actually. I was a little mad that they even kept me this long, but you know Dad…"

They held hands and walked out the way Jules came in. The floor was still wet where she'd walked, and when she looked back, it dried with their passage. At one of the nurse's stations, it seemed like a nurse was going to call out to them, but then an announcement came over the intercom and he went to deal with that.

Jules let Una get in the front seat and got in the back with Yorick, who licked both of them as best he could reach before Jules made him lie down again. "How'd it go?" John asked.

"Like I said," Jules said. "I just had to convince her."

"You just had to tell me you needed me," Una said. "So John knows?"

"Yes, John knows," he said.

Chapter Thirty One

They drove back into the storm. The world around them was hardly visible for the sheets of rain, though the thunder was getting louder. They were getting closer to the thunder as they neared the estate. The storm wasn't moving anymore. If this wasn't such a dire fucking situation, she'd be in sort of proud awe of what she'd done. Harnessed something to a thunderstorm to kill her stepdad, that was some epic spellwork right there. Not something she'd ever be able to brag about. If they lived through this. She'd already died, or almost died, once today. Once last year. Once last night. It was impossible to panic when she'd sampled the inevitable over and over again. Hello darkness, my old friend.

John swore and swerved around a fallen tree, and for a brief heart-stopping moment the car just continued to slew in that direction, kicking up a white plume of water like a speedboat. He handled it, though, got them straight again, got them moving again.

"Wow!" Una said brightly, and Jules practically cackled with laughter. This was all so ridiculous. She didn't even know who she wanted to save at this point. Gladys, yes. Una, but dragging her back into the storm seemed like the exact opposite of that. Dragging everybody into this seemed like a great way to get everybody killed.

"Almost there," John said, even though nobody asked. The GPS display in the dashboard was just a square of gray static with an image of the car on it, like they were traveling through another world and would just pop out at their destination.

Waves were coming up the street as they drove toward the estate bridge. Little rippling ones, not completely covering the road, but they were there, where water had so rarely risen. Not even during full moon tides. Only during the worst hurricanes. What would the news call this storm, Jules wondered? She didn't have the weather vocabulary to even bullshit something.

Water slapped at the estate bridge, but it wasn't covered yet. The security gate was up, the guard house empty, and John threw the car in park and got out to go look. The logs, Jules thought, hoping everybody was gone and that they could just leave. She'd figure out Hector another time, after the storm passed.

"Mrs. Duncan gave the order to evacuate," John said, coming back with his suit plastered to him. "And it looks like all personnel did."

"Just personnel?"

"It doesn't say that Mrs. Duncan or Hector left, no." John did not turn to look at her, he just pulled forward.

Oh shit she still thinks I'm here, Jules thought. The car was barely stopped in front of the front steps before Jules was out and running to the door, MaryAnne's car was there too, parked and empty. Yorick trotting along with her. Thunder cracked when she flung the door open and screamed "MOM!" but she listened anyway, like Gladys would have some kind of mom sense and answer her. More than once in her life, it'd seemed like Gladys had some kind of mom sense. More than once in her life, though, it'd also seemed like Gladys was a stranger.

Jules ran through the halls the way she hadn't run since she was a kid, balling her fists, leaning into it, her bag slapping her leg. John called after her but didn't sound urgent enough for her to stop. Gladys's office was empty, the master suite was empty, thunder rolled and all of the estate lost power at once, with a noise like a cartoon factory shutting down. She stopped, breathing hard, Yorick panting hard, and listened. John and Una, calling "Mrs. Duncan! Mrs. Duncan?" But nobody answering. Then she thought back to this morning, three million years ago, when she told her mother that she was going to the orchard, and she ran again.

She found John first and gasped "Outside" and left him to interpret that, and follow her, or not. There was a pain up under her ribs and she leaned into that too. Pain had fueled her so much lately. Since she woke up in a world where her dad wasn't. She slipped more than once on the path to the orchard, fell once, scraping the heels of her hands, and her knees, just like when she skateboarded that single time in her life. Skin zinging, lightning crawling overhead, the heavy rain was like a hand on her back telling her to quit, to stay down. But there was a hand under her arm, and John helped her up. Una looked like she was trying to wrestle with an umbrella, but it was squashing down on her head with the weight of water, and as they continued, she dropped it.

They found another discarded umbrella, further along, a large black one. Gladys, maybe. Hector, maybe. The water was risen almost to the path, puddled in the grass, broken off apple tree limbs, everything smelling like salt and sweet fury. And there, where her father's bench had been, Gladys stood, Ashley obviously pleading with her, MaryAnne standing a little off. No Hector, where was Hector. At least it was raining too hard for anybody to shoot anybody, Jules thought. Hoped.

The waves surged eagerly, cold and lace-edged, and where they did not belong. Or was this estate what didn't belong, jutting out here into the water, on land that wasn't land two hundred years prior? She was almost to Gladys before her mother saw her, and she was unprepared for the sudden, fierce embrace, the weirdly pitched yowl of thunder directly overhead. Maybe they'd be struck by lightning and never have to worry about anything again, Jules thought wildly, but they weren't the tallest thing here. The apple trees were. But that only counted if it was normal lightning.

Jules looked up, and it seemed like the sky opened and she saw a looming face there, like when the mountain came to life in the original Fantasia. She disentangled herself from Gladys and reached for Ashley, flapping her hand frantically, and Ashley took it. She grabbed John with her other hand and they didn't have time, they had to be the circle themselves, with Gladys in the middle, as the water rose around them and pounded down on them. Then Yorick, in the circle with Gladys, turned and snarled loudly enough that Jules felt it in her chest and in her belly, his lips wrinkled all the way back from gleaming white teeth and pink gums. Then came Hector's voice as he returned from further in the orchard. Gladys must have sent him to keep looking while Ashley talked to her. He was bent against the storm and Jules just hated him, hated him on sight, hated him for everything he'd done and everything she'd done because of him. She'd made those choices, but she wouldn't have. She could've just had her life the way it was supposed to be, instead of this.

A wave surged almost to their collective knees, and Jules only stayed up because of John, salt stinging in her knees, her palms slick and gritty. Hector stumbled to one knee, got up, saw them. It got darker, which didn't seem possible, and Hector looked up. He saw the face, Jules was sure of it, she saw him recoil, put his hands up. Saw the fear in his pale face when the lightning flashed. Hector never expected to get caught, but here and now, he seemed to know exactly what he was being punished for.

Gladys still didn't understand, though. She saw Hector and pushed against Jules. "Why are we standing here? We need to evacuate! Hector!"

"There isn't time, Mom," Jules said, and she wasn't sure Gladys heard her. Hector saw her face, though, and edged closer, arranging himself in an approximation of repentance. God knew what he thought of his weird stepdaughter, and what she and her friends were doing, but he had a coward's sense of what might save him.

"Juliet, what are you doing?" he asked. "Juliet, this is dangerous."

Una twisted to look at him, and looked at Jules when she shook her head. MaryAnne looked at her with resignation. She didn't want this. Now they all just had to weather it.

"Juliet why aren't you answering him?" Gladys was very still suddenly, making herself heard with effort.

"He killed Dad," Jules said. She'd thought about saying it any number of ways, thought about saying it to Gladys any number of times, and this was none of those scenarios. But it was the one they had. It didn't matter if he pulled the trigger himself or just paid to pull the trigger and watched the result. Gave Jules her dad's phone back in the hopes she would remove herself from the equation. It almost worked.

"I don't understand," Gladys said, the storm grasping at her voice, pulling it into thin threads.

"I'm sorry," Jules said, and Ashley and John squeezed her hands at the same time.

"Juliet you can't leave me out here like this," Hector shouted, as the water rose to their knees but stopped, straining pushing and pulling, rose to his knees and then past his knees and kept rising. *"Juliet I am begging you."*

Jules was gasping now, the thunder her heartbeat, the lightning her intentions. It lanced through the closest tree, spidered across the whitecaps, and she thought that if there was land here anymore, maybe somebody could dig the fulgurites out of the sand. Maybe they could be used for something. Protection from storms. She laughed as the darkness stooped down from the sky, covering everything outside of their circle, pressing against their backs like static, like the amusement park rides that spun and stuck you to the wall, and there was a noise like the world was breaking, like the estate was tearing apart and still she hung on, and the circle was unbroken, Gladys safe and shielded inside, Hector's pleading turned to a wordless scream, cut short.

And then the waves took them all.

Chapter Thirty Two

Ashley once told Jules that she had swimming lessons at the Asbury Park YMCA when she was 3 or 4 or 5, and when everybody got together at the edge of the pool, the instructor asked who'd been swimming before. Ashes, maybe thinking of her backyard pool that was maybe two feet deep and filled with a hose, said she had, absolutely. The instructor let her get off the side and into the water, where she sank immediately. Ashley's mom fished her out, and the instructor, before Ashes could react or start crying, smiled big and said "Did you visit the turtles?"

Jules could only think of that now, in the angry waters, the inlet normally so calm. Visiting the turtles. Except it felt more like they were visiting the sharks, frenzied, panicked, up and down confused again and again the second she thought she had it straight. Was it just last night that she almost drowned? Jules couldn't hope her dad could rescue her again. Jules hoped her dad could rescue her again, but she couldn't formulate thoughts, intentions, there was only the water, the salt.

Something bumped her and she grabbed for it, hoping it was something to float with, hoping it was somebody she wanted to live. She connected with a slick body, and her scrabbling fingers found purchase on Yorick's wide leather collar, and she saw the whites of his eyes as he glanced at her and started to paddle. She felt calmer immediately, now that she had contact, and she sidestroked along with him and tried to look for others. Tried to think, at all. Was what she called still a danger to them, or was its obligation discharged with

251

Hector? Was a boat likely to just mow them down without seeing them? A Coast Guard boat maybe, for added irony.

She was surprised, that she wanted to live.

She outlived Hector, so technically she won. But she had to keep going, not just let go now. Of course she'd swum from the estate to land before, for fun. Swam across the inlet, or one time, more than a little tipsy, swam out to the bridge. She tried not to worry about anything, just thinking about stroke after stroke. Her breathing. The water. She tried that now. Breathing. Swimming. Breathing. The water. She couldn't feel her left hand, wrist, arm, and couldn't worry about that now.

The rain might have stopped, she couldn't tell, but the sky was still solid pencil-lead colored, like somebody just scribbled on a fresh rough white piece of paper with a brand new pencil, sharpening it to a dagger every time it dulled down and scribbling anew.

Where *was* everybody? How was it possible for her to be alone?

Maybe she'd died after all and would be left endlessly swimming. This was her purgatory, for what she'd visited upon Hector and the world. The thought that she'd dragged Yorick into it with her made her eyes burn, made her choke back a sob. Did she get Una killed after all? Ashes?

No wonder she used her dad up, she waited too long, she fucked it all up.

She should be at land by now. Or the marina. Or a bridge. Something. Yorick didn't seem to be getting tired, but she was. Maybe she only thought she was swimming, and she was dying. Maybe she was still on the apartment floor, and this was her purgatory. Swimming. The story ended with her still swimming.

Jules heard a boat. She could feel it in her body too, raw-edged nerve that she'd turned into. She turned her head, tried to see. Couldn't tell where it was coming from. Yorick changed course, though. Maybe it would be strangers, people who didn't know who she was, and she could feign amnesia and start a new life somewhere else. Use magic to make people forget her, and to get by, drifting through university libraries, ferreting out all the books that were bound in human skin, because they had to be grimoires or something, nobody was binding Emily Dickinson's work like that. Shakespeare.

But no, no, that was too much like Jenner for comfort. She was getting too far into her head, she needed to keep her wits about her, keep going. Yorick kept swimming. She was never going to be able to make him understand how important he was. How good he was. There weren't enough french fries in the world. Enough tennis balls and grossass raw meaty bones.

The boat got closer, got closer, cut its engines. For a wild minute she thought no, I have to save myself or it won't count, but doing that got her exactly to this place to begin with. She could finally see, and it was one of the estate boats. It was Mr. Poling. It was John.

Yorick swam to the deck thing on the back of the boat, where there was a little ladder, and she had to let go of Yorick to slap a hand at it. She slipped off, went under again. A hand grabbed her wrist, though, and John pulled her up. His jacket was torn, his tie askew, and his shirt looked bloody and she couldn't tell if he was hurt. Yorick scrabbled onto the decking, gathered himself, jumped up and got mostly over the railing before ungainfully flopping the rest of the way in.

"Miss Duncan, are you hurt?" Mr. Poling asked, and Jules just wanted to laugh wildly. If ever there was a time he could just use her fucking name, it was now.

"I don't know." John was pulling his necktie the rest of the way off.

"Sit down," John said, his voice raw edged, doing something with her left arm, practically in her armpit. She looked down at herself;

her arm, where MaryAnne had healed it, was open again, wrist to elbow. That had to mean Maryanne was—

"Another boat picked up your friend Ashley," Mr. Poling said, still mild, still calm. Did he not know Ashley's last name? Did he not think she was a Miss _____? Jules couldn't remember noticing before.

"Fuck." She crumpled into one of the molded fiberglass seats, looked out at the water without really seeing it. Yorick slumped onto her feet with a groan, and she put her other hand on his neck, then his ear, just for something to hold onto. She was so tired. Just husked out, used up. She didn't feel anything, maybe she was dying for good this time, but without any accompanying dramatics. No more magic, no more wishes, no more worries. The radio crackled and she couldn't hear it, and with effort she brought her right hand up to her throat, shark's tooth still there, and pricked her thumb on the point of it, dragging her gluey focus to that bright spot of pain. "Is it Gladys?" she asked, or tried to ask.

"Mrs. Duncan is okay," John said, and she believed him. She didn't think he would ever lie to make her feel better, and she let go, even as Yorick's nails scraped on the bottom of the boat and he scrabbled to his feet and barked in her face, even as she heard sirens nearing. She would wake up or she wouldn't. Maybe it would be less surprising this time.

Chapter Thirty Three
(or, epilogue?)

They could never go back, of course. After the storm, the estate island was a handful of sand running through black rock fingers. The roof of the house was gone, the foundation was split, the bulkhead ruptured. It was miraculous, the papers said, all that destruction, all that violence of the waves, and only one life lost. Even the Duncan Dobermans all survived. Gladys, twice-widowed, built a new estate on property out past Freehold. Far past where the ocean would reach in any of their lifetimes. She nagged Jules less about coming home. They had Sunday dinners and did not talk about Julian Duncan, or about Hector. They talked about hyperloops and whether Gladys should get horses after all this time, and whether Jules wanted to go to grad school. They did not talk about the storm.

So much of her time felt as though it was borrowed. Twice-drowned, thrice cheater of death, caller of storms, if she was given to a litany of ridiculous titles, if their culture was, they were building up.

Ashley and Una and Jules gathered on the beach, and they lit a small bonfire, even though it was illegal and they would have to work fast. And what were the police going to do, arrest Juliet Duncan? She'd pay the fine.

They traced their symbols with driftwood and passed a tiny bottle of whiskey, enough for a swallow each, and then they joined hands around the fire, which made Jules think of s'mores rather than magic, though maybe s'mores were magic, and turned their faces to the moon and stars. Yorick boofed deeply, but quietly. Nothing bad or scary happening, everything was intentional and calm.

That familiar thrum of big magic, from the crown of her head to the tip of her toes, was more of a high to Jules than anything else ever was. And when the universe took notice, and the wheel of stars slowed, they put their censure on Jenner for what he had done. Let him come for them if he would, they were ready for that, for him, forever after.

They put the fire out and spread the embers, dumped a bucket of water on it all for good measure. Ashley offered Jules a cigarette, and they smoked and looked at the waves. Una coughed pointedly, delicately, somewhere behind them, and Yorick shouldered into Jules' leg.

Maybe it was possible to have a future, Jules thought. Maybe it was possible to be happy.

There was only one way to find out.

Acknowledgements

E xit Ghost is the combination (or maybe culmination) of a lot of things: my grief for my dad, my love of Shakespeare, my love of the Jersey Shore, and a longer story about the types of witches that I've been writing about for years. Writing is by its very nature solitary, and also not, and I have just so many people who lift me up whenever I need it.

For Jim, my husband, my love, it means so much to me that you're so proud of me that I'm published

To Tori, thank you for always supporting my publishing dreams, self and otherwise. Your patience and input is so valuable to me, I don't know what I'd do without you.

To Jazzi, for helping me with emotional balance, and for always being able to answer me when I'm not sure if anything is [tense/scary/sad] enough.

Thank you to Premee for being my enthusiastic co-cap'n on this writerly voyage, for your encouragement and your commiserations, and your love of Yorick even as I for some reason couldn't settle on what breed he should be. Yes, Great Dane would've been funnier, but Doberman was more correct.

Thank you to Lennon, for reading and catching my typos and for being so supportive of my writing.

Thank you to my patrons, Brian White and Sheryl Hutcherson, I'm so glad that you signed up and stuck with me.

Jennifer R. Donohue grew up at the Jersey Shore and now lives in central New York with her husband and their Doberman. She works at her local public library where she also facilitates a writing workshop. Her work has appeared in *Apex Magazine, Escape Pod, Fusion Fragment,* and elsewhere. Her Run With the Hunted novella series is available in paperback and on most digital platforms. She tweets @AuthorizedMusin and you can subscribe to her Patreon for a new short story every month: https://www.patreon.com/Jennifer-RDonohue

Other Works by Jennifer R. Donohue:

Witchy short stories:
"Sugar and Spice," Sockdolager, Summer 2016 & Overcast 99
"The Pearl That Were His Eyes," Andromeda Spaceways 75
"Be Careful What You Wish For," Patreon
"Licorice Whip Thunderbolt," Patreon
"Serpent's Tooth," Patreon, Daikaijuzine 12
"Inheritance," Patreon
"Into the Dark" Fantasy Magazine 86

The Drowned Heir

Run With the Hunted (series)
Run With the Hunted
Run With the Hunted 2: Ctrl Alt Delete
Run With the Hunted 3: Standard Operating Procedure
Run With the Hunted 4: VIP
Run With the Hunted 5: Insert Coin to Play

CPSIA information can be obtained
at www.ICGtesting.com
Printed in the USA
LVHW022257060323
741079LV00003B/104